A Line in the Sand

TERI WILSON

sourcebooks
casablanca

For Charm

Copyright © 2022 by Teri Wilson
Cover and internal design © 2022 by Sourcebooks
Cover illustration by Monika Roe/Shannon Associates

Sourcebooks and the colophon are registered trademarks of Sourcebooks.

The characters and events portrayed in this book are fictitious or
are used fictitiously. Any similarity to real persons, living or dead,
is purely coincidental and not intended by the author.

All brand names and product names used in this book are trademarks,
registered trademarks, or trade names of their respective holders.
Sourcebooks is not associated with any product or vendor in this book.

Published by Sourcebooks Casablanca, an imprint of Sourcebooks
P.O. Box 4410, Naperville, Illinois 60567-4410
(630) 961-3900
sourcebooks.com

Cataloging-in-Publication Data is on file with the Library of Congress.

Printed and bound in Canada.
MBP 10 9 8 7 6 5 4 3 2 1

Chapter 1

ON ANY GIVEN WEEKDAY evening, the dog beach on the small barrier island known as Turtle Beach, North Carolina, was typically occupied by two Dalmatians, six or more octogenarians, and any number of canines of dubious origin.

Plus one mermaid.

Make no mistake, Molly Prince, the mermaid in question, was every bit as human as the aforementioned octogenarians. Mermaiding was simply Molly's day job, but sometimes she wore her costume home instead of changing out of her emerald-green sequined fishtail and clamshell bustier. For modesty's sake, the bustier was attached to a flesh-colored body stocking adorned with a sprinkling of rhinestone starfish and draped with no fewer than six strings of pearls. Getting out of the thing was no easy task.

Molly would get to that once she and Ursula, her Cavalier King Charles spaniel puppy, got to the quaint oceanfront cottage they called home. Ursula was a recent addition to Molly's life and due to the puppy's extreme separation anxiety, she rarely left Molly's sequin-clad side. The little chestnut-and-white spaniel was also prone to bursts of the zoomies, hence their regular stops at the dog beach after work.

"Look at that little dog go." Ethel Banks, resident of Turtle Beach Senior Center and one of Molly's favorite octogenarians, peered over her purple-framed bifocals and grinned as Ursula charged at a flock of sandpiper birds chasing waves along the shoreline.

Three aluminum walkers were lined up in front of the smooth wooden bench where Ethel sat alongside Opal Lewinsky and Mavis Hubbard—or, as everyone in town called their little trio, the OG Charlie's Angels. Nibbles, a teacup Chihuahua, sat shivering in the basket of the walker belonging to Mavis.

"Ursula really loves other animals," Molly said. "You should have seen her today at the aquarium. She sat right in front of the shark tank, totally rapt."

Opal snorted. "Like Mavis and her new boyfriend Larry every night when *Jeopardy!* is on."

Molly bit back a smile. Was it weird that her senior citizen friends seemed to have more active social lives than she did?

Mavis muttered something in response—laced with snark, no doubt—but whatever it was went into one of Molly's ears and right out of the other one. Her attention had snagged on a man wading knee-deep through the waves, just beyond the shallows where Ursula pawed at the tiny silver fish that always skittered through the foamy water.

"Do any of you know who that guy is?" Molly felt herself frown.

The dog beach was too close to the crest—local speak for the southernmost tip of the island—to be safe for swimming far from the shore. The surf close to the crest was rougher and the riptides stronger, due to warm water from the bay spilling into the salty depths of the open sea. Swimming past the sandbar wasn't allowed, for humans and dogs alike.

Opal, Mavis, and Ethel narrowed their gazes in the stranger's direction and then shrugged in unison.

"Where's his dog?" Molly did a quick inventory of the canines enjoying their freedom on their small designated strip of sand. She'd been here enough times to know precisely who each dog belonged to.

"All the pups here are accounted for," Ethel said. Clover the corgi woofed in agreement at her feet.

Weird. What was he doing at the dog beach, dogless?

"He's staring into the water like he lost something." Opal pressed a hand to her heart as a wave rocked into the man's chest. "He really shouldn't be so far out there."

Mavis shook her head. "Definitely not."

Ursula romped back toward them and spun in excited circles around Molly's mermaid tail.

Oh, yeah…the costume.

Super. Molly was going to have to go out there and warn the stranger about the riptide while she looked like Daryl Hannah straight off the set of *Splash* in 1984. Not ideal, but she didn't have much of a choice. Molly certainly didn't want the guy to drown, and she was currently the only person in sight who was fully ambulatory. The dog beach was dotted with more walkers and electric scooters than actual canines. Where were the Dalmatian owners? They always helped bring the median age at the dog beach down by a decade. Or three.

"He's drifting farther out," Ethel said. "Molly, maybe we should do something."

"I'm on it." Molly took a deep breath and headed toward the shoreline in urgent-yet-tiny footsteps, since her fishtail was almost as confining as it was glittery. The costume was never a problem on the turquoise vintage Vespa she used to get around the island. Of course, she didn't normally have to rescue swimmers on the way home from work.

Ursula romped after Molly, just like she always did.

"Don't worry. We're just going to stand right at the edge of the water and yell at that guy to come back to the shallows. We'll be on the couch in front of the *Great British Baking Show* before you know it," Molly said, not altogether sure if she was talking to her dog or herself. Possibly both.

But just as they moved from the sugary sand of the dunes onto the damp shore, the tide rushed in. The man bobbed up and down in the water, and he finally looked up as he seemed to realize how far he'd wandered offshore. A wave smacked him right in the face.

Oh no.

Molly's stomach tumbled. "Hey, are you okay?"

Ursula paced at the water's edge, leaving a trail of frantic, tiny paw prints in her wake.

Molly waited a beat for the man to resurface, but all she could see was sunlight glinting off something shiny floating in the water. She shaded her eyes with her hand. *Eyeglasses.* Not a good sign at all, considering they were missing the head that they belonged to.

"Wait here!" she said to Ursula. "I'm going in."

Hoyt Hooper, the senior center's bingo caller, rolled to a stop nearby in his mechanical scooter. His pug, Hops, sat in the scooter's basket, dressed in a Hawaiian shirt that matched the one

Hooper was wearing, down to the last hibiscus. "That man's got to be in trouble. I'm calling 911."

Molly nodded. "Good idea."

But would they get to the dog beach in time to help him? Doubtful.

She glanced at the red Igloo cooler strapped to Hoyt's scooter with a bungee cord. "Hoyt, remember that safety demo the fire department gave at the library last year?"

He nodded. "Yeah, why?"

"I'm going to need your cooler." According to the fire department, a fiberglass cooler could be used as a flotation device in an emergency situation. And this was definitely beginning to feel like an emergency.

"Does this mean you're going in after that guy?" Hoyt grabbed the Igloo and handed it to her.

Molly dumped out the contents—three frosty cans of root beer and a pile of ice. "I sure am."

Ursula's tail wagged as she licked the spilled ice cubes.

"I'll watch your pup. Be careful, Molly," Hoyt said as he climbed off his scooter. "Please."

"It's going to be fine," she said, not quite sure whether she was talking to Hoyt, Ursula, or herself.

Molly waddled as fast as she could into the water while Hoyt scooped Ursula into his arms and the other seniors made their way toward the scene with their walkers leaving winding trails behind them in the sand. The dogs gathered round, barking at the ocean while their ears flapped in the salty breeze. Molly suddenly felt like she was in a very bizarre episode of *Baywatch*.

It occurred to her that she didn't even know if her costume was waterproof. She'd never actually gotten it wet before. Some mermaid she was.

She held her breath, dove into the waves and breaststroked her way with one arm to the place where the man had disappeared, clutching the cooler tightly with the other. The water this close to shore was murky, filled with tumbling seashells and stirred-up sand. Molly's eyes burned, and her chest ached. A wave splashed into her face, and she couldn't see a thing. Then she blinked a few times and spotted him.

The man's arms flailed at the waves. He gasped for air. Molly could feel the riptide pulling at her ridiculous fishtail, threatening to drag her out to sea. She clutched the cooler as tightly as she could.

No way. She was *not* going to die like this—costumed, while the greater senior citizen and dog populations of Turtle Beach looked on. Absolutely not. She flat-out refused.

"Grab my hand," she yelled above the roar of the waves and sea spray.

The panicked man's head jerked in her direction. Their eyes met, and his gaze filled with a combination of wonder and relief. Molly's heart thumped hard—adrenaline, no doubt. Still, there was just something about those soulful eyes that made Molly's head spin.

She only hoped it wasn't because they were about to drown together. Drowning was nowhere on Molly's to-do list, and the stranger was far too cute to get lost at sea. She simply couldn't picture him with a Tom Hanks *Cast Away* beard, crying over a volleyball with a face.

Why on earth were these crazy thoughts flitting through her head? Was she drowning *right now*?

She reached for the man as hard as she could, kicked her mermaid tail against the current and yelled at the top of her lungs. "Wilson!"

———

The first, and last, time that Max Miller had eaten a raw oyster, his first impression had been that it tasted like he'd just licked the ocean floor. Salty...wet...

And gritty. So *very* gritty. Max had not been a fan, nor had he been inclined to repeat the experience. Besides, oyster reefs were currently the most endangered marine habitat on the entire planet. Best to leave the poor, non-delicious things right where they belonged.

At the moment, though, Max was having some sort of gustatory flashback, because that highly memorable oyster taste was permeating his senses again—in his mouth, his nose, the back of his throat. Even his eyeballs, glued shut with sand and salt and any and all manner of fish excrement (sometimes being a marine biologist afforded a person with more knowledge than was preferable in moments such as this one), seemed to taste the oyster.

But when at last Max managed to pry his eyes open, there wasn't an oyster in sight. Just a mermaid, gazing down at him with worried eyes the color of a stormy sea while her lush, blonde mermaid hair whipped around her face. Max closed his eyes again. Mermaids weren't real. Maybe he was dreaming, or maybe he'd died. He certainly didn't feel particularly alive at the moment.

Salty bile rose up the back of his throat. He gagged and sputtered until someone—the imaginary mermaid, probably—rolled him onto his side and he coughed up what seemed like a gallon of seawater. An upturned Igloo cooler sat about a foot from his head for some odd reason.

Max groaned into the sand, and then a wet, warm tongue swiped the side of his face. Someone was attempting mouth-to-mouth resuscitation, but they were doing a terrible job of it.

"I'm fine," he said.

Max was *not* fine. His gut churned with equal parts nausea and humiliation. This was the first day of his new life in Turtle Beach, North Carolina. He'd hoped to slip seamlessly into the sleepy little town by the sea, not land with such a splash—pun definitely not intended. Max wasn't a punny person in the slightest. An ex-girlfriend had once told him that he had a PhD in place of a sense of humor.

"Ursula, *no*," the mermaid said.

Max squinted at her through sand-crusted eyes, but all he saw was an extreme close-up of a face that was distinctly canine in nature, as opposed to mythical sea creature-esque. The dog, a tiny white-and-chestnut-colored spaniel, licked Max's face again in direct opposition to the mermaid's command.

Max turned his head. Three elderly women gripping aluminum walkers loomed over him. A dog the size of a squirrel sat trembling in the basket of one of the walkers. The block lettering on its identification tag spelled out the word NIBBLES.

Where on earth am I?

Max had known that a small island like Turtle Beach would

be different from Baltimore, but his Uncle Henry had in no way prepared him for how truly quirky it apparently was.

Mermaids? Little toy spaniels named Ursula? And why so many dogs? An enormous poodle with pink bows on its ears poked at Max with a narrow snout. He felt like Alice, falling down a very deep and uncommonly sandy rabbit hole.

Ursula came toward him again, pink tongue lolling out of the side of her tiny mouth. Max sat up in order to avoid another attempt of mouth-to-mouth. He coughed a few times, rubbed his eyes, and when he opened them, he found the mermaid staring down at him. Not a hallucination after all. And here he thought she'd just been an imaginary by-product of his near-death experience.

"You're from out of town, aren't you?" The mermaid jammed her hands on her iridescent, scaly hips.

The scales weren't real, obviously. They appeared to be satin, covered in copious amounts of sequins. Now that Max had gotten a proper look at the woman, he realized that she was in costume, of course. Still, how odd.

"Yes." Max nodded. "Just arrived today."

He didn't have the energy to say more. It took every last shred of energy to form words and pull himself to his feet.

"You're really not supposed to swim this close to the crest. The riptide is too strong beyond the shallows," she said.

Strands of long, wet hair clung to her face. Max had the absurd notion to peel it away from her eyes and kiss her full on the lips, right there in front of the growing collection of dogs and retirees surrounding them.

He angled his head toward her, searching her gaze. "You saved me."

It was a statement, not a question. She'd been the one who'd just pulled Max from the water. In his panic, he'd thought he'd imagined a mermaid coming to his rescue. She'd been real, though. Go figure.

"Indeed she did," one of the senior citizens said. She wore purple glasses and an identical expression to the corgi panting at her feet.

"It was the most romantic thing I've ever seen," the woman beside her—the Chihuahua enthusiast—gushed.

The mermaid rolled her eyes, and her porcelain face went seashell pink. She shoved his glasses at him. "It wasn't romantic in the slightest."

Disappointment settled in Max's gut, along with what felt like a liter of salt water. He wasn't thinking clearly at all. Had he hit his head on something in the ocean?

He slid his glasses in place. The lenses were hopelessly smudged so he removed them and tucked them into the pocket of his sodden dress shirt. As he did, a small fish leapt out and flopped onto the sand.

Max glanced down at it. The tiny critter was a *Membras martinica*, more commonly known as a rough silverside. He picked it up by the tail and tossed it back into the surf before returning his attention to the mermaid.

"You called me Wilson." Max felt his lips twitch into a grin. *Cast Away.* He loved that movie. "The name's Max, actually."

The mermaid eyed him with concern and crossed her arms.

She started to shiver like Nibbles. "And you're okay, right? Do I need to call 911 or anything?"

"I'm fine," Max repeated. He'd already made enough of a spectacle of himself. The last thing he needed was to add sirens to the mix. He cleared his throat. "Are you okay, though? You look…" *Beautiful.* "Cold."

"I'm just peachy." She gave him a grim smile and wrapped her arms tighter around her torso, which was decorated with a sparkling assortment of strategically placed starfish, shells, and pearls.

Max did his best to look elsewhere.

The little spaniel yipped and came toward him with a full body wiggle. Max bent to scoop the dog into his arms. The tiny thing couldn't have weighed more than six or seven pounds, but he could barely lift her. He felt himself sway a little on his feet. Almost drowning was exhausting.

He nodded at the mermaid. "I get it now. Her name is Ursula— from *The Little Mermaid*, right? Your name isn't Ariel, is it?"

"It's Molly," Nibbles's owner said before Molly herself could chime in.

Molly the mermaid. Cute. "Well, it's nice to meet you, Molly. Thanks for the rescue."

Molly plucked Ursula from his grasp and hugged the puppy to her chest. "You're welcome. But really, swimming isn't allowed at the dog beach. The current is too strong out here."

This was a dog beach. Well, that certainly explained a few things. "Noted. Although for the record, I wasn't going for a swim. I saw something in the water—a *caretta caretta*."

"A whatta whatta?" one of the older women asked.

"He means a sea turtle," Molly said. "Specifically, a logger-head."

Max arched a brow.

Molly lifted her chin and tucked a damp strand of hair behind her ear. Highlights the color of pink cotton candy were mixed in with her mass of blonde waves. Tiny droplets of seawater starred her eyelashes. "That's right, I know the scientific name for a loggerhead sea turtle. I'm not a cartoon character. Don't let the costume fool you."

"I wouldn't dream of it," Max said. After all, she'd very probably saved his life.

"There are loads of loggerheads at this beach. Try not to chase any more of them out to sea. Deal?"

Max nodded. "Deal."

Loads of loggerheads? Now she *really* had his attention. He wanted to know more, but before he could utter another word, she scooted past him in the sort of quick, tiny steps that a mermaid tail necessitated. Ursula planted her little head on Molly's shoulder and watched him as the little pup's mistress carried her away.

Max stared after them until they became glittering silhouettes against the molten light of the setting sun. Then a throat cleared nearby and he turned to find every set of eyes on the dog beach, both human and canine alike, watching him with keen interest.

"Welcome to Turtle Beach." The woman with the purple glasses flashed him a wink.

She aimed her walker toward the dunes, and the rest of the retirees followed. A white-haired man and a pug in matching

Hawaiian shirts zipped past on a motorized scooter. The man waved, while the pug seemed to smile at Max with his goofy pug face.

Max just shook his head. He and his uncle were going to have a nice, long chat—sooner rather than later. Uncle Henry had some explaining to do.

Welcome to Turtle Beach, indeed.

Chapter 2

IT WASN'T JUST THE nuttiness of the dog beach encounter and Max's near-drowning that had him rattled. Being back in Turtle Beach after so many years away somehow felt both familiar and surreal at the same time.

He climbed the steps of his uncle's beach cottage—now *Max's* oceanfront home—on shaky legs and plopped down onto a deck chair with a sigh. So far, the island was exactly the way he remembered it, from the rickety Salty Dog pier where Max had spent hours upon hours as a teenager fishing in the moonlight (catch and release, obviously) to the old-timey roller rink above the post office. Back when Max had summered on Turtle Beach, the floor of the small roller rink had been like a vinyl record album, worn with grooves from generations of summer skaters. How the place was still standing was a mystery he couldn't begin to fathom.

Nostalgia had washed over him like a tidal wave the moment he'd crossed the bridge from the mainland and seen the familiar boardwalk and the park by the bay, lit with twinkle lights. The Turtle Beach library, the bookshop that doubled as a coffee bar, the ice cream parlor where as a kid he'd consumed his body weight in chocolate malts were all still there. Aside from fresh paint jobs, the mom-and-pop local businesses looked exactly the same, as did Turtle Beach's modest downtown area on Seashell Drive. Max could hardly believe his eyes.

Where were the improvements his uncle had mentioned? In their phone calls over the past few months, Uncle Henry had made it sound as if Turtle Beach had been on the verge of becoming the next Outer Banks or Myrtle Beach. He'd known his uncle had been exaggerating, but the last thing Max had expected was to find the island looking like it had been lovingly preserved in a time capsule for the past twelve years.

Everything was going to be fine, though. Max hadn't given up a perfectly good job, home, and life in Baltimore because he thought he'd be moving to a booming beach metropolis. This was about more than that. It was about something he hadn't given much thought to in quite a while—family.

And the turtles, obviously.

Max could make a meaningful difference here. He hoped so, anyway. His uncle had assured him that he could.

He also told you that Turtle Beach had a Starbucks now. And a Krispy Kreme.

Right. So far, there wasn't a cup of Pike Place roast or a glazed donut in sight. The only visible difference between the modern-day version of Turtle Beach and the one Max remembered was the booming canine population. Why so many dogs? They even had their own private beach.

That was definitely new. As was the mermaid.

Max yawned. With the move and the drive down from the D.C. area in a rental car, he'd barely slept a wink in the past twenty-four hours. Everything that had just happened at the beach seemed like a fever dream—one he didn't care to repeat anytime soon. Or ever, for that matter. What Max needed most was sleep. He'd deal with his uncle, his mess of moving boxes, and the aquarium in the morning.

A sliver of moon hung high in the twilight sky, bathing the ocean with silvery light. Stars were already visible, glittering like diamonds against soft velvet. Max stood and leaned against the deck's railing, taking it all in.

How had he stayed away from the Carolina coast for so long? And why?

The fact that he had no substantive answers to those questions made his gut churn. After college and graduate school, he'd just gotten so caught up in his career that one year turned into two, two into three, and so on. But this was where it had all started—right here on this tiny, precious island. And just like sea turtles always returned to their birthplace to lay their eggs, Max had found his way back to where he belonged.

Did he belong, though? The jury was still out on that. Nearly drowning before he'd unpacked a single moving box or set eyes on his uncle didn't seem like a good sign.

Max sighed and raked a hand through his hair, salty and damp from his impromptu swim. It was too late for regrets. The deed was done. Surely things would seem more normal in the morning. What he needed most right now was a hot shower and a good night's sleep.

He turned to open the sliding glass door and step inside the weathered beach house, but just as he grabbed hold of the door handle, his gaze snagged on a flash of white in his periphery. Max squinted in the semi-darkness and realized it was a dog. Not just any dog—*the* dog.

"Ursula?" Max said.

The little spaniel's tail waved back and forth. She was standing on the deck of the beach cottage situated right next door, watching Max through the white lattice trim of his neighbor's deck.

It had to be the same dog, right? What were the odds of an island the size of Turtle Beach having two of those fancy toy-sized spaniels?

Max snorted. As dog-crazy as this place was, there was no telling. He walked toward the railing, hoping to get a better look, but the little dog turned away and trotted through the open French doors of the other beach cottage and disappeared.

Max told himself he didn't care one way or another if he lived next door to Ursula, but that night he dreamt he was underwater again. Sea foam and kelp danced around him as he tried to follow a bale of sea turtles, their flippers moving through the eerie darkness like graceful angels' wings. Beside him, just beyond his reach, was a mermaid. Her long hair danced in the water, obscuring her face. Max couldn't tell whether or not she was *the* mermaid. *His* mermaid. She seemed to grow fainter and fainter the closer he got to her, until he finally woke up in a cold sweat.

Max chugged a cup of black coffee from his uncle's ancient percolator and tried to shake off the dream. He was losing it. For starters, sea turtles rarely if ever swam in groups. And mermaids were definitely not real, recent events notwithstanding.

He threw on a pair of khakis and a light blue oxford shirt,

grabbed the keys to his uncle's Jeep, and headed down the steps of the deck toward the gravel driveway, more than ready for a face-to-face with Henry. The automobile was old enough to be considered vintage, with a stick shift that required serious elbow grease. After stalling out a few times as he backed out onto the street, Max snuck a glance at the cottage next door and saw the Cavalier King Charles pup watching him from an upstairs window. Max wrestled the Jeep into first gear and looked away.

Mere minutes later, he knocked on the door of Uncle Henry's new residence at the Turtle Beach Senior Center. Henry's room was located just off the main lobby, where Max had passed a group of retirees who'd seemed to be gathering for some sort of exercise class. The shivering Chihuahua from the dog beach was nestled inside the basket of one of their walkers. Why did Max feel like he was being stalked by random canines?

"Max!" Uncle Henry looked him up and down as he swung the door open. He was exactly how Max remembered him— powder-white hair, eyes full of laughter, and a face weathered from a lifetime of island living.

The only thing missing was the scent of Captain Black cherry pipe tobacco. Henry had given up smoking a while back, but the sweet, aromatic scent had burrowed into the pine wood paneling of the beach cottage years ago. The absence of it here in Henry's new home was startling to Max.

As was the sight of a turquoise yoga mat rolled up and tucked beneath his uncle's arm.

"You made it. Good. Good." Henry nodded. "I'm glad you

stopped by, but I'm afraid I don't have time to visit. Class starts in just a few minutes."

Uncle Henry stepped into the hallway, shut the door behind him, and began hustling toward the lobby.

Max blinked. *What the…*

"Wait." He chased after his uncle. "Where are you going?"

"Yoga," Henry said without missing a beat.

"Yoga." Max felt himself frown. "You do *yoga* now?"

"Five days a week. It's very refreshing," Henry said, as if a reclusive eighty-year-old scientist suddenly taking up group yoga classes was the most normal thing in the world.

"That's…um, great, actually." So much to unpack here, but first things first. "Look, we need to talk."

Henry glanced at him, but kept walking. "You got into the house okay, didn't you? The key was right where I left it?"

Max nodded. "Underneath the conch shell on the upper deck of the porch, the same place where you always hid it when I was a kid. Ace security. It's a good thing this island isn't exactly a hotbed of criminal activity. Getting into the house wasn't a problem at all."

"Good," Henry said as they rounded the corner into the foyer.

Max looked around at the room where he'd played bingo every Tuesday night of the summer visits when he was a kid. Now it was filled with rows of colorful yoga mats stretched from one wall to the other. A black-and-white spotted Dalmatian trotted from mat to mat, greeting the elderly yogis with a wagging tail, because of course.

Max sighed. "Uncle Henry, what exactly is going on here?"

Henry unspooled his yoga mat and flapped it onto the tile floor with a *thwack*. "I told you already—yoga."

"Good morning, everyone. Are we ready to get started?" The instructor, a woman who looked much closer to Max's age than Henry's, stood at the front of the room in leggings covered in a pink cupcake print. The Dalmatian romped in circles around her as she glanced around the class. Her gaze settled on Max and she paused. "Oh good, we have a guest."

Max shook his head. "No, I'm just here visiting my—"

"The more the merrier. Extra mats are over there." She pointed to a stack of yoga mats beside what looked like an official parking area for ambulatory devices. "Let's begin with pretzel pose."

Pretzel pose? Was that Sanskrit? Max wholeheartedly doubted it.

"Uncle Henry, I…"

"You heard her." Henry shrugged. "If you're staying, go get a mat. A little yoga would probably do you some good."

He could *not* be serious.

Oh, but he was. Uncle Henry sat down and proceeded to close his eyes and take deep breaths while Max stood there trying to process what was happening.

"Fine," he finally said, planting his hands on his knees and bending over to whisper-scream at his uncle. "But I'll be back tonight right after the aquarium closes, and we're going to talk."

Uncle Henry popped one eye open. "Sorry, no can do. Tonight is trivia night here at the senior center."

"Seriously?" Max arched a brow. "And I suppose you're busy tomorrow, too. What's on Tuesday's agenda? Pilates? Book club?"

"Don't be silly. Tomorrow night is bingo. You should know

that." Henry frowned at him in a very non-Zen, non-yoga-ish sort of way.

Max sighed. He knew all about bingo night. Anyone who'd ever set foot on Turtle Beach did. It had simply slipped his mind for a second, what with the near-drowning and his uncle's total transformation into a different person.

"Hi, there. I'm Violet." The yoga instructor and her Dalmatian were suddenly standing right beside Max. Now that he got a look at the dog up close, Max realized her collar had tiny cupcakes printed all over it, just like Violet's leggings. "It looks like you're staying, so here."

She shoved a yoga mat at him, and Max had no choice but to take it.

"Okay, then," he muttered as he kicked off his shoes.

If this was the only way he was going to get some actual face time with his uncle, then so be it. Max situated the mat beside Henry's and plopped down into a pretzel shape.

"You lied," Max said under his breath, just loud enough for his uncle to hear him.

"About what?"

"Okay, everyone. Let's transition into rearview mirror pose," Violet called from the head of the class.

Rearview mirror? What kind of nutty yoga class was this?

The seniors all twisted to look over their right shoulder, so Max did the same. He took advantage of the posture to glare at his uncle.

"About *everything*," Max hissed. "There's no Starbucks, and there's no Krispy Kreme."

"Sure there are…just over the bridge in Wilmington." Henry cleared his throat and swiveled his gaze to peer over the opposite shoulder.

Max did the same. Maybe yoga wasn't a half bad idea. He was beginning to feel like his head might explode. "Wilmington is almost an hour away, Uncle Henry. You told me the island had changed. You made it sound like—"

"Like what?" Henry said, at last meeting Max's gaze head-on. "Like someplace important enough for you to visit?"

Ouch.

Max swallowed. He knew better than to issue a denial when his behavior over the past twelve years spoke for itself.

Then Violet's teacher voice rang out, mercifully breaking the tense silence that had just fallen between Max and his uncle. "Looking good, everyone. Let's move into secretly-checking-your-phone pose."

Henry and the other seniors all brought their hands into prayer-like positions and shifted their gazes downward. Max had to hand it to Violet. As bizarre as these pose names were, they were spot-on.

"I'm here, okay? And I'm not going anywhere," Max said quietly. It wasn't as if he had a choice. He'd tendered his resignation. Someone else was already sitting behind his desk at the National Aquarium—and more to the point, there was a new name etched on the aquarium director's door, and it wasn't Max's. That ship had sailed. Where else would he go? "You may as well tell me the rest. Is there anything else I should know?"

Violet called out another pose—downward facing Dalmatian. Henry shifted forward and shot Max an upside-down glance.

"There might be one little thing," he said.

Max pressed his hands into his mat, lifted his hips, and took a deep breath. *Whatever it is, you can handle it. It can't be that bad.* "And what might that be?"

"It's the aquarium," Henry said.

Max's heart pounded hard in his chest.

Not the aquarium. Anything *but the aquarium.*

"Henry, I love overpriced coffee and donuts as much as the next person, but the false promises of big city conveniences like Starbucks and Krispy Kreme aren't what convinced me to leave my life in Baltimore and start over here. You founded the Turtle Beach Aquarium nearly a decade ago and have served as the director since its inception. When you told me you were ready to step down, you *insisted* I was the only person who could step into your shoes."

Max had been reeling from being passed over for the promotion at the National Aquarium, and his uncle's offer had felt like fate stepping in to set everything right.

Why not take over Uncle Henry's job? There was something poetic about coming back to the island, back to the beach where he'd learned to love everything about marine life. Like a loggerhead finding its way home. *Caretta caretta.*

But Max wasn't a turtle, and as a scientist he knew better than to anthropomorphize. He should have, anyway.

"So, what about the aquarium?" Max craned his neck and studied his uncle's upside-down face.

Henry didn't even pretend to look Max in the eye. Something was wrong. Something big.

"The aquarium is about to go broke."

Chapter 3

"Is it true?" Caroline Martin, owner of Turtle Books, slid a Milky Way frozen latte across the counter toward Molly and raised her eyebrows. "Did you really save a man from drowning at the dog beach yesterday?"

Molly took a big, cold sip through her lime-green jumbo-sized reusable straw. *Ahh.* Caffeine, chocolate, and caramel. Was there a better way to start the day? No, definitely not.

She eyed Molly over the top of her latte while she dropped onto a barstool with Ursula in her lap. "How on earth do you know about that?"

Caroline laughed. "Are you forgetting where you live? There are no secrets in Turtle Beach. I know you know this."

How could she not? Both Molly and Caroline had grown up on the island and had been best friends since their days at Turtle Beach Elementary School. They knew how intimate their small coastal town could be as much as any of the other longtime locals did.

"Griff told me, actually. He was out checking the fire hydrants at the senior center yesterday, and the Charlie's Angels told him all about it." Caroline arched a brow. "In detail. You know nothing significant happens in Turtle Beach without Opal, Mavis, and Ethel somehow being involved."

Fabulous. There probably wasn't a soul on the island who hadn't heard all about it by now.

"I don't know why you're looking at me like something scandalous happened," Molly said. Caroline's brother Griff was pretty level-headed. He wasn't the type to embellish. The Charlie's Angels…not so much, bless their meddlesome hearts. "I saw a guy who seemed like he was in trouble, and I dragged him out of the water. It was no big deal, really."

Ursula craned her skinny puppy neck and tried to lick the condensation off the outside of Molly's latte, but Molly nudged it out of reach.

"No big deal?" Caroline smirked. "So he wasn't as insanely hot as the Charlie's Angels say he was? And you didn't scream out 'Wilson' like you'd been trapped on a desert island for years and he was the only thing keeping your will to live intact?"

Molly's cheeks went warm. She slurped another gulp of her Milky Way frozen latte, ice cream headache be damned.

"Aha! So it *is* true!" Caroline's entire face lit up. "Tell me everything."

"There's honestly nothing to tell," Molly said.

So she'd dragged a man ashore…a man with the bone structure of a Greek god, who also had a shockingly proficient working knowledge of sea turtles, which happened to be Molly's second-favorite animal—her first favorite being Cavalier King Charles spaniels. Obviously. And yes, maybe she'd gotten just a little caught up in the moment and pulled a Tom Hanks.

But Tom got along just fine after Wilson drifted off into the sunset, and Molly would too.

She sat up a little straighter on her barstool. "He was definitely a tourist."

"That again?" Caroline rolled her eyes. "You do realize that if you eliminate tourists from the prospective dating pool pretty much all that's left around here are senior citizens."

"Doesn't matter. I'm not dating anymore, remember? I have a dog now." Molly rested a hand on Ursula's dainty back. The puppy blinked up at her with huge, melting eyes. No man had ever looked at Molly with such complete and utter devotion. The very suggestion was laughable.

"The two aren't mutually exclusive, you know. Plenty of dog owners date." Caroline reached to give Ursula a scratch behind one of her copper ears.

"Well, this one doesn't. My life is perfectly full at the moment. The last thing Ursula and I need is a man." Molly stabbed aggressively at her latte with her straw.

"Even a man who just washed ashore and magically landed at your feet?" Caroline said.

"Max didn't wash ashore. I dragged him there, which just proves my point." Molly didn't want or need a Wilson. She'd always hated volleyball, both literally and now metaphorically. "He's basically dead weight."

Dead weight with an impossibly square jawline and the bluest eyes Molly had ever seen, but dead weight nonetheless.

"Wow," Caroline said.

Ursula swiveled her cute little head as she glanced from Molly to Caroline and back again. Thank goodness dogs couldn't talk. Molly had a feeling Ursula would have had a lot to say on the subject at hand, given the way she'd seemingly tried to give Max mouth-to-mouth.

"Can we talk about something else now?" Molly polished off her latte and glanced at the time on her phone. She needed to get to work. "Are you going to bingo tonight?"

Ursula spun in a circle and barked, like she always did whenever she heard the word bingo. Everyone on the island loved bingo night, but no one loved it quite as much as Molly's puppy did.

Caroline laughed. "Where else would I be on a Tuesday night? You are too, right? Opal would send out a search party if we no-showed."

"We'll see you tonight, then." Molly slid off of her barstool and tucked Ursula under one arm. "I've got to get to work. Thanks for the coffee."

Caroline tilted her head. "Is it weird that I have an overwhelming urge to scream 'Wilson' as you depart?"

"Don't you dare."

———

Max didn't make it through the rest of yoga.

He tried. He really did. He moved through a series of poses with ridiculous monikers and did his best to keep up with Uncle Henry and the room full of surprisingly limber octogenarians and nonagenarians. But Max bailed during final relaxation at the end of class, and not just because Violet called it "murder victim pose," although, truth be told, it freaked him out a little bit.

Max had bigger things to worry about than lying spread eagle on the floor and pretending that he'd just been the victim of a serial killer—most notably, the bomb Henry had just dropped about the aquarium.

His uncle had refused to elaborate, probably because his announcement caused Max to fall out of his downward facing Dalmatian and land squarely on his face. His glasses, which had already taken a thorough beating the day before, were now bent and sat crooked on his face. Again, Max couldn't have cared less. He just wanted to get to the aquarium and figure out what sort of disaster he'd unknowingly signed on for.

"Where are you going?" Henry asked from his spot on the floor as Max scrambled to his feet.

"To work," he said flatly.

"I'll save you a seat tonight at bingo." Henry closed his eyes and resumed playing dead.

Max stared down at him and contemplated killing him for real.

Nope, that wouldn't solve anything. Besides, part of the reason Max had moved to Turtle Beach was to repair their relationship. Doing so was apparently going to be far more complicated than he'd anticipated, but he couldn't give up on it already.

Still, the very last thing on Max's mind was bingo.

He made his way through the maze of "murder victims" and stalked toward the exit with Violet's Dalmatian hot on his heels. Just as he pushed the door open, the dog latched onto the hem of his khakis and tried to drag him back inside the building.

"You've got to be kidding me," Max said to the dog.

She wagged her tail and yanked, as if Max was nothing but

a stuffed dog toy. The dogs in this town were seriously out of control. If the aquarium was as bad off as Henry made it sound, perhaps Max could get a job as an animal control officer.

He told himself things weren't that dire...yet.

Max somehow managed to jerk his leg free, leaving behind a chunk of khaki fabric in the Dalmatian's mouth in the process. The dog romped back to the head of the room, tossing her prize in the air and playing catch with it.

Max buckled himself into the front seat of his Jeep and pulled away from the senior center in a few jerky movements, happy to leave that particular brand of wacky in the rearview.

The Turtle Beach Aquarium and Sea Turtle Hospital was located on the sound side of the island, past the bridge, at the opposite end of town. Back when Max had spent his summers in Turtle Beach, the north end of the island had been mostly uninhabited. A monster hurricane in the late eighties had wiped out the row of oceanfront homes at the north end and caused so much beach erosion that rebuilding wasn't an option.

Nature was a miraculous thing, though, as Max knew all too well. The shore at the north end had repaired itself naturally over time. Now, the area that Max remembered as an untouched strip of sugary sand boasted three rows of tall, slender beach cottages built on pilings. They were painted in Easter egg hues with white lattice trim to match the other homes on the island and surrounded by lush coastal vegetation to protect the area from further storm damage. Beach grass, sea oats, and live oak trees, weathered and curved into twisted shapes by the salty wind, also provided a safe haven for birds and mammals. Max couldn't wait to take a closer look. It was the perfect setting for an aquarium that specialized in sea life native to the Carolina coast.

The aquarium itself sat at the edge of the glassy calm waters of the bay, a stark contrast to the massive steel and glass building where Max had worked in Baltimore. The National Aquarium hosted more than a million visitors per year and was one of Maryland's biggest tourist attractions. It could have eaten the modest building Max was currently looking at for breakfast.

Max didn't care about appearances, though. In fact, he rather liked the colorful mural that wrapped around all sides of the Turtle Beach Aquarium. It featured sea turtles swimming against a vibrant blue background. Colorful bits of coral, orange-and-white clown fish, and pink and turquoise sea anemones lined the bottom of the mural, and the top of the brick wall was awash with sunny yellow light.

Max's breath bottled up in his chest when his gaze moved from the painted turtles to the sign above the double glass doors at the aquarium's entrance. TURTLE BEACH AQUARIUM AND SEA TURTLE HOSPITAL. That latter part was pure Henry. He'd taught Max everything he knew about his beloved sea turtles, and he'd devoted his life to protecting them against extinction. Now it was up to Max to carry on his uncle's legacy.

If he could somehow get the aquarium back into the black.

Max stepped out of the Jeep, grabbed the cardboard box of his personal office effects out of the backseat, and slammed the door with a tad too much force. Of course he could get the aquarium on the straight and narrow. He'd do whatever it took. First things first, though. He needed to see for himself just how big a mess he'd inherited.

The temptation to linger in the big garage-style complex that held individual open-air tanks for the injured turtles was great. Max went from tank to tank, checking on the five turtles currently in residence—four loggerheads and one Kemp's Ridley—and then took a quick pass through the aquarium area. The building's interior was every bit as colorful as the exterior, with interactive games for kids, a touch pool, a shark tank, a seahorse exhibit, and a series of special glow-in-the-dark jellyfish tanks. At the center of everything sat an enormous clamshell with a small bench-seat, draped with fishnet and glittery pink starfish.

Max angled his head and studied it. If he didn't know better, he would have thought it looked like some sort of throne.

Weird.

Max glanced around, and his gaze snagged on a driftwood sign with the aquarium's hours. They were scheduled to open in forty-five minutes. He tightened his grip on his cardboard box and headed toward the aquarium director's office.

Everything about the small space reminded him of his uncle. Henry was everywhere, from the sweet cherry aroma to the sea turtle figurines covering every available surface. Crayon drawings of turtles, turtle nests, and tiny hatchlings making their way from the dunes to the shore were tacked on the wall behind the desk, along with notes left from aquarium visitors in children's handwriting.

Max set his box down on the desk and reached for one of the drawings. The paper was yellowed, and there was something

undeniably familiar about the drawing—a mother turtle returning to sea after laying her eggs, leaving a telltale trail behind her in
the sand. Then Max took a closer look, and he saw his own initials
scrawled in the bottom right-hand corner of the paper.

MM.

No wonder the drawing of the turtle looked familiar. Max
had drawn it himself the very first summer he'd come to visit
Turtle Beach. On the day of Max's arrival, Henry had taken
him out walking late at night with a pair of small shovels and a
bucket. They'd methodically filled in any holes that had been left
behind by kids who liked to dig at the shore or tourists making
sand castles. Holes were dangerous for nesting turtles who came
ashore in the moonlight on summer nights to lay their eggs.
Henry explained this to Max as they meandered half a mile in
either direction of Henry's cottage, filling in holes and patting
down sand.

Just as they arrived back at the beach house, they'd heard a
rhythmic swishing sound high up on the dune. Henry had placed
his big palm on the center of Max's tiny chest, stopping him in
his tracks.

"Turtle," his uncle had whispered.

Then they'd crouched down behind the sea grass and watched
the big mama turtle make her nest. Henry had called her "the
grand lady" and spoke of her with such reverence that Max had
known without a doubt he was witnessing something magical.
The next morning, he'd drawn the turtle's picture with crayons
Henry kept in an old metal Folgers tin.

And his uncle had kept the drawing all these years.

The paper shook in Max's trembling hand. He took a ragged inhale and pinned it back in its place with a rusty thumbtack.

This, he thought, gaze lingering on the old drawing. *This is just the reminder I needed. This is why I'm here.* This *is why I have to fix whatever has gone wrong.*

Max sat down in his uncle's squeaky leather chair, turned on the outdated desktop computer, and dug through the drawers until he found a stack of ledgers, a checkbook, and accounting documents for the past three years.

Dread settled in his gut as he pored over them. Things were not good. He was going to have to make some budget cuts, and he was going to have to do it fast. They were at the height of tourist season, so ticket sales would be at peak for the next two months. But without a plan, the aquarium wouldn't make it through the winter.

"Wilson?"

Max dragged his gaze away from the mess of numbers in front of him and looked up to find Molly the mermaid standing in the doorway of the office, dressed head-to-toe in her full mermaid regalia.

"Max." She shook her head, and blonde waves spilled down her back. Max couldn't be sure, but he thought he spied pink glitter in her hair. "I meant Max, not Wilson. Sorry, you caught me off guard. You're um…well…you're the last person I expected to see here."

"No offense taken. I could say the same," he said, and then he rose from his chair like it was the 1950s and he was at a country club cotillion or something.

Why did he feel so unsettled around this woman?

"I work here," she said, brow furrowing. "Isn't that obvious?"

Molly waved a hand, indicating her fish tail, the pearls draped around her neck, and her clamshell bustier. Max felt like there was suddenly no place safe to look, so he dropped his gaze to the floor. That's when he noticed Ursula, sitting politely at Molly's feet, dressed in a bright-red lobster costume. Plush claws stuck out from her tiny shoulders and a hat with wobbly antennae eyes sat at a jaunty angle on the spaniel's head.

"So you're Henry's nephew…our new director?" Molly asked, dragging his attention away from Ursula's get-up.

"Yes." Max hiked a thumb in the direction of the lobby. "I'm guessing you're the reason for Poseidon's throne out there?"

"Actually, we call it the mermaid grotto." Molly gave him a lopsided smile. "But, yes."

Warmth flooded Max's chest. She had a lovely smile. He hadn't had much of a chance to see it on the beach while he'd been retching up salt water and sand.

The woman had saved his life, which was going to make what came next all the more awkward.

"Mermaid grotto." Max shook his head. "Cute, but…"

"But?" Molly's pretty smile froze in place.

"But why does the aquarium need a mermaid? It's scientifically insignificant." Max crossed his arms and cut his gaze toward Ursula. "And while we're on the subject of marine authenticity, why is your dog here?"

Max didn't want to be the bad guy, but come on. Nothing about this scenario made sense.

Molly's eyebrows drew together and she was suddenly looking at him as if *he* was the crazy one. Perhaps he should have shown up for his first day on the job dressed as Captain Jack Sparrow.

"You mean my lobster," she said flatly.

Ursula woofed.

Max's temples throbbed. Going over the numbers had been enough to give him a raging migraine, and now here he was, arguing about semantics with a mermaid and her Cavalier King Charles spaniel.

He gritted his teeth. "No, I mean your dog."

Ursula wagged her tail, clearly pleased to be the center of attention. She darted toward Max, but Molly scurried after her in quick mermaid-sized steps and scooped the lobster into her arms.

The puppy, *not the lobster.* Max massaged his temples and prayed there was a bottle of ibuprofen rattling around somewhere in Uncle Henry's desk.

"What do you have against dogs?" Molly said, looking him up and down. If he'd been an actual volleyball, the expression on her face would have deflated him in an instant.

"Nothing. I'm just trying to figure out why there's one in my aquarium." He felt himself frown. "It's like they're taking over the town."

"Maybe because people love dogs." Molly lifted her chin. "But in this particular instance, it's an emotional support animal type of situation."

Max glanced at Ursula and back at Molly. They made an awfully cute pair, despite having zero basis in science. Or reality as a whole. "This puppy is your emotional support animal?"

"Not exactly. More the opposite, really." Molly cleared her throat. "I'm her emotional support human."

Max closed his eyes and sighed. *Emotional support human?* It was the last straw. Nothing on this island made a lick of sense.

Molly kept on talking, seemingly oblivious to Max's existential crisis. "She has separation anxiety. Your uncle suggested I start bringing her to work with me, and it's worked out great. The tourists just love her, especially the kids."

Max opened his eyes. This entire conversation would have been so much easier if the puppy weren't so damned adorable, not to mention the mermaid. "But this is an aquarium. Tourists come here to see marine life, not dogs."

"That's why she's dressed as a lobster." Molly tapped one of Ursula's antennae with the tip of her finger. It bobbed in front of Ursula's face and she snapped at it with her tiny teeth.

Max sank into his chair and forced himself to focus on the papers spread all over the desk—and the stack of bills waiting to be paid. So. Many. Bills. "I'm sorry, Molly. But things are about to change. My uncle has a heart of gold and he's built an amazing thing here, but as is, it's just not sustainable."

Molly moved closer. *Swish swish swish* went her mermaid tail. "What are you saying?"

"I'm saying that without drastic cutbacks, the aquarium isn't going to survive." Max looked up and pointed at Ursula with one of the mechanical pencils his uncle had always loved so much. "I'm also saying that an aquarium is no place for a dog."

"I see." Storm clouds gathered in Molly's eyes, and she glared at him. "Anything else I should know?"

"Yes, actually." Max stood again and crossed his arms. *Just do it. Rip off the Band-Aid.* "An aquarium is also no place for a mermaid."

"Wait...you're serious?" Molly's face fell. Ursula blinked her absurdly big puppy eyes.

Max reminded himself he was a scientist, and he'd been put in charge of an aquarium, not a Disney-themed doggy day care. "Mermaids are mythical creatures. They're not real. It makes no sense to have a mermaid display when we can barely afford fish food. I'm sorry, but..."

"But what?" Molly's bottom lip began to quiver, and Max almost wished she'd gone ahead and let him drown the day before.

"You're fired."

Chapter 4

"*Fired.* Like, fired for real? Can he even do that?" Caroline passed another frozen Milky Way latte across the counter to Molly—her third since she'd come bursting through the door of Turtle Books after her disastrous encounter with Max at the aquarium.

Her stomach churned, and not because of all the coffee, caramel, and chocolate. Well, not completely, anyway.

Molly slurped at the straw in her drink. At this rate, she wouldn't be able to fit into her mermaid costume by morning. But what difference did it make? She was officially unemployed. At least she'd had the forethought to change into regular clothes before storming out of the aquarium. Although her red cap-sleeved T-shirt and high-waisted nautical shorts were a little too marine-themed for her liking at the moment. "I'm pretty sure he can. He's the director of the aquarium now—the top dog."

Molly glanced down at Ursula sleeping soundly in her lap and corrected herself. "Never mind. We can't call him that since he hates dogs."

Caroline gasped. "He *hates dogs?*"

The bells on the door to the bookstore jingled and Violet March walked inside the shop with a pink cardboard box in her arms and her Dalmatian, Sprinkles, trotting at the end of a pink leash decorated with tiny cupcakes.

Violet glanced back and forth between Caroline and Molly. "Someone on this island hates dogs?"

Caroline looked at Molly, prompting her to either explain or change the subject.

Molly gnawed on her straw. She was still trying to wrap her head around her firing. Maybe spreading rumors about Max wasn't the wisest idea. After all, he could change his mind, couldn't he? Venting to Caroline when the only customers presently in the shop were browsing the bookshelves clear on the other side of the room and no one else was within earshot was one thing, but involving Violet was another matter entirely.

Not that Turtle Beach's resident cupcake baker slash yoga teacher was a gossip or anything. Violet was a sweetheart. It was just that news had a tendency to travel like wildfire on their tiny island.

"Wait a minute." Violet sat down on the barstool beside Molly and deposited the box of cupcakes on the counter while Sprinkles sniffed at Ursula with her quivering heart-shaped nose. "I bet I know who you two are talking about—Henry Miller's nephew. Am I right?"

A smile tugged at Molly's lips for the first time since she'd been unceremoniously expelled from the mermaid grotto. "How did you guess?"

Violet shrugged. "He was at yoga with Henry at the senior center this morning and kept giving Sprinkles the side-eye."

Sprinkles's tail thumped against the legs of Violet's barstool at the sound of her name. Caroline reached for the jar beside the cash register where she kept homemade cheese biscuits for her canine customers. She offered a large one to Sprinkles, and the Dalmatian stretched onto the floor to gnaw on it. Ursula sat up at attention, and Caroline slipped her a smaller biscuit—Ursula's third. Molly's puppy was matching her, treat for treat.

"Max was at yoga?" Molly let out a most unladylike snort. "I can't see him doing anything quite that ethereal."

"He wasn't very into it. I basically had to force him to participate, and he left midway through murder victim pose because he couldn't keep still." Violet's gaze dropped to Molly's latte and she aimed a hopeful grin at Caroline. "Can I get one of those to go? You're the last of my cupcake deliveries this morning. I'm having lunch with Sam at the firehouse on the way home, and I can take my dad a coffee while I'm in the area. You know how much he loves Milky Way lattes."

"Of course. It's on the house—anything for the chief of police." Caroline reached into her vintage red-and-white refrigerator for a bottle of chocolate syrup.

Molly shook her head. "I still can't believe Max was at yoga right before he fired me."

"He hates dogs *and* he fired you?" Violet pulled a face. "Is he trying to become the super-villain of Turtle Beach?"

Caroline pointed at Molly with the chocolate syrup. "He could have been swept out to sea yesterday, if not for you. How dare he fire you."

"Seriously. That's just exceedingly rude." Violet shook her head. "I got a play-by-play of the rescue from the Charlie's Angels.

If saving your boss's life doesn't guarantee job security, then I don't know what will."

"The aquarium is struggling financially. I suspected as much, but I had no idea it was this bad." Molly dropped her head on the counter. She could now add an ice cream headache to her list of current problems.

Caroline flicked the blender to the on position, poured the latte for Violet's dad, and secured the top of the cup with a to-go lid. "Does he have any idea how much you do for the aquarium?"

"Our conversation wasn't exactly a two-way street," Molly said. "What am I going to do? There's not exactly a huge demand for out-of-work mermaids, especially on an island this small. I have dog treats to buy and rent to pay."

Granted, the rent went to her parents since she was their unofficial permanent tenant in what was formerly the family summer home. But now that Molly thought about it, the unofficial part of that arrangement meant that her mom and dad could change their minds at any time.

They could *evict* her.

"I have to find another job." Molly reached for her latte again. Her hand shook so hard she could no longer aim the straw at her mouth with any sort of accuracy, so she slammed the drink back down on the counter. Ursula gave a little start. "Like, today."

"It's going to be okay, Molls." Caroline shot her a sympathetic glance.

"My parents can't find out I've been fired, especially my dad. You know he always has a lot to say about my life choices, especially since my breakup with The Tourist." Molly pulled a face.

"Really, though, he never understood why I came back here after I graduated from Vanderbilt. After five years, you'd think he would have gotten used to the idea."

While Molly had been away at school in Tennessee, her mother and father had made their move to Pennsylvania. Her dad, a lifelong academic, gave up his job at the university in nearby Wilmington and signed on to be the head of the history department at a fancy private college in Philadelphia. Her mother had outfitted their new guest house for Molly as a surprise graduation gift. Mom and Dad had just assumed she'd move back home, even though "home" was in a strange place. Dad couldn't understand why Molly hadn't wanted to come earn her PhD at his college or start teaching in a classroom like her mother. Instead, she'd taken her shiny new education degree back to their summer home in Turtle Beach and signed on for mermaid duty at the brand-new aquarium. Every summer, he made a case for her to quit, but this year, the pressure had been relentless. If Dad knew she'd been fired, she'd never hear the end of it.

"You could always help out here while you try to find something else." Caroline waved her arms to encompass the entirety of the bookshop. "You know how crazy the store gets during the summer, especially in the late afternoons once the tourists are finished soaking up the sun for the day."

"You know I love you, but that sounds like a pity offer," Molly said.

Although at this point, she couldn't afford to turn down anyone's pity. Literally.

"Caroline's right." Violet slid her gaze over to Molly. "You do so much for the aquarium. Max needs a stern talking to. He probably has no idea."

Zero. He had no clue whatsoever.

Molly twirled the straw in her drink. Ursula watched it go round and round. "If the aquarium is really in serious trouble, I'm not sure I want to kick him while he's down."

Who was she kidding, though? The thought of kicking Max Miller while he was down wasn't without merit. Besides, if anyone was down right now, it was Molly. Not that it was a contest, but if it were, she would totally win.

Caroline crossed her arms. "Did Max bother asking you about any of those fundraising ideas you've been working on?"

No, actually. He hadn't.

Molly shook her head.

"Did he get any input from you at all, or did he just fire you on the spot?" Violet asked.

Molly blew out a breath. "Definitely the latter, and he sort of fired Ursula too."

How had he so succinctly put it?

An aquarium is no place for a dog.

Tourists loved Ursula's little lobster costume. And bonus: she didn't frighten the children like the sharks in the shark tank did.

"That settles it—he's a monster," Caroline said and slipped Ursula another bite of cheese biscuit.

"Maybe you should simply fight back," Violet said, as if waging war on an infuriating scientist was a viable possibility.

Come to think of it, though, Violet had done just that against the island's fire marshal recently and things had definitely turned out in her favor. As in, she and Sam Nash, the fire marshal in question, were currently involved in a whirlwind summer romance. The Charlie's Angels had already started one of those gambling grids for their pending engagement.

Not that Molly wanted to marry Wilson…er, Max. Honestly, why did she keep calling him that? It had to stop, even in her head.

"Fight back?" Caroline's gaze narrowed.

No. Fighting back was the last thing Molly needed to do. Even if she managed to get un-fired, Max clearly wasn't going anywhere. He was the new director of the aquarium. She couldn't work for him. Not after today, even if the sight of him fully dressed and soaking wet yesterday evening had made her feel all fluttery inside.

Again, this morning, he'd looked so adorably charming sitting at his uncle's desk with his glasses all askew and his hair rumpled, as if he'd recently rolled quite handsomely out of bed. He had a whole absentminded professor thing going on that made Molly swoon. Last night when she'd climbed into bed with Ursula snuggled by her side and closed her eyes, she kept hearing Max's voice in her head.

Caretta caretta.

She had a soft spot for men who appreciated sea turtles. It was a most unfortunate occupational hazard, especially now.

Molly was taking a much-needed break from dating, though. Maybe even permanently, given what had happened last summer. Also the man had *fired* her less than twenty-four hours after she'd saved his life.

"What exactly are you suggesting?" Molly heard herself say. Maybe she wasn't so opposed to fighting back, after all.

—◦◦◦—

Even after the fateful yoga class with his Uncle Henry, Max fully expected firing a mermaid and a puppy to be the low point of his day. Oh, how wrong that assumption turned out to be.

Within minutes of Molly's departure, the aquarium erupted into chaos. The veterinary school intern who was supposed to work the morning shift in the turtle hospital called in sick. One of the PVC pipes that filtered water into the largest loggerhead sick bay burst. Seconds later, Max was wading through ankle-deep water, while at the same time trying to haul a three-hundred-fifty-pound sea turtle out of the broken tank and into another one—with very little assistance. To top things off, a five-year-old visiting the aquarium with his kindergarten class tried to sneak a live starfish from the touch pool into one of the pockets of his cargo shorts.

Any of those various catastrophes would have been bad enough, but they were all made exponentially worse by the reaction of whatever aquarium staff happened to be nearby at the time of occurrence.

"Where's Molly? She'd know just how to handle this."

Max had heard the sentiment so many times that the words were now on permanent repeat in his head, like one of the vintage vinyl records from the roller rink above the post office. He got it now. He'd messed up big time.

Max had no excuse, other than the fact that he'd been

overwhelmed by the sudden responsibility of saving the aquarium, his job, his uncle's legacy, and the island's endangered sea turtle population, all in one fell swoop. The turtles, he'd been prepared for. Everything else? Not so much.

He'd acted on impulse—something that Max never did—and now he was paying the price.

Never? Not quite. The truth was that Max had been flying by the seat of his pants since the day he'd found out he hadn't been selected as the new director of the National Aquarium.

He'd been so certain the job was his. Something inside of him had apparently snapped once the announcement was made, especially given the board of directors' reasoning. They thought Max had no concept of work–life balance. They worried he'd burn himself out. Since when had that become a bad thing from an employer's point of view? Not the burnout, obviously, but the work ethic. Max couldn't make sense of it, even now. In the span of three weeks, he'd quit his job, sold his condo, and moved to the island without ever having set eyes on the aquarium that he was now solely responsible for.

Maybe Max was having some sort of midlife crisis, although he hated to put such a dismissive label on it. All he knew was that he'd suddenly started thinking with his heart instead of his head, and consequently, he'd managed to turn his life into a total train wreck in record time. He never wanted to hear the phrase "work–life balance" ever again.

Max hauled a wet vac from the storage closet into the garage-style space that served as the sea turtle hospital. It smelled like fish and wet concrete.

Oh, how the mighty had fallen.

He flipped the power switch, but nothing happened. Because of course it didn't. Par for the course.

"That old thing is tricky." Nate, one of the vet school interns, nodded at the wet vac. "You have to jiggle the on-switch at least four times before you try to power it up."

Max wiggled the power switch back and forth and tried again. Nothing.

"At least four times," Nate said. "That was only three."

Max gave him a tight smile. "So the machine knows how to count?"

Nate frowned. "Dude, it's a vacuum."

"Sorry." Max raked a hand through his hair. He needed to get a grip. The kid was only trying to help. "Four times. Got it."

He tried again, and this time, the wet vac roared to life. Max felt like whooping for joy. At last, something had gone right.

He grinned at Nate as he went to work vacuuming up the standing water that had collected on the ground in between the turtles' individual pools. "How did you discover that trick?"

"I didn't. Molly figured it out. She's been here since the aquarium started, apparently. She knows everything about this place." Nate's gaze darted in the direction of the lobby. "Where is she, anyway? I haven't seen her today. Or her cute little puppy."

"I fired her," Max said.

Nate's eyes widened. "Dude."

Max nodded. "The dog, too."

"*Dude.*" Nate shook his head. "Not cool."

The wet vac stuttered to a stop, as if even the machinery around here was so appalled by Max's behavior that it refused to cooperate.

Would this day ever end?

"What are you going to do?" Nate tipped his head toward the wet vac.

"*We*—" Max gestured back and forth between them. "—are going to find some towels and clean up this mess. And then I'm going to find our mermaid and get her back."

"The dog too?" Nate asked.

"We'll see."

Max still wasn't sold on the puppy. He was officially back to his old, logical self. And logic still dictated that a dog had no place in an aquarium. Max also wasn't buying into the fact that Molly was Ursula's emotional support human. But admittedly, he wasn't exactly in a position to argue.

Nate strode to a utility shelf on the far side of the room, flip-flops slapping against the damp floor as he went. He gathered a stack of towels and went to work sopping up water without further commentary on Max's canine hiring practices. Somehow his silence on the matter made Max feel even worse.

The aquarium closed its doors at four o'clock. Max made it through the rest of the afternoon without any further major disasters, not counting the fact that they were still teetering on the brink of financial collapse, or that Nate was the only member of the staff who seemed to be speaking to him after word got out that he'd fired Molly and Ursula.

Everything would be better tomorrow. All he needed to do

was calmly and rationally explain to Molly that he'd made an error in judgment and ask her to return to work.

Luckily, since this was a Tuesday in Turtle Beach, he knew just where to find her.

Chapter 5

THE SENIOR CENTER ALREADY appeared to be a hive of activity by the time Max chugged to a stop in the Jeep. Flags emblazoned with the word BINGO flapped in the breeze at each corner of the building. The parking lot was packed, and tourists poured into the senior center's lobby, their faces pink and hair salty from a day at the beach. A silver Airstream trailer topped with a huge spinning cupcake sat in the parking lot, and a line snaked from the order window all the way to the gravel sidewalk that ran alongside Seashell Drive.

"That's new," Max said as he shifted the Jeep into park.

"What's new?" Nate said, surveying the bingo night landscape.

The intern had stayed past closing, helping Max with a juvenile Kemp's Ridley that had been brought in by a fisherman who'd found the sea turtle tangled in his net. Fortunately, the little guy had minimal injuries and was in his new tank happily munching on squid when Max headed out for bingo. Nate had been going too, of course, and when Max realized the intern intended to skateboard from one end of the island to the other, he'd offered him a ride.

"The cupcake truck." Max directed his gaze toward the Airstream.

"Sweetness on Wheels is always here on bingo nights. Violet makes special themed cupcakes every week. It's a whole thing. She sells them out here before bingo starts and then runs the concession stand inside for the rest of the night," Nate said.

Max's stomach grumbled. He'd been so busy putting out fires all day that he hadn't eaten a thing. A cupcake didn't sound half bad. "Let's get some. My treat."

"Oh. Wow." Nate grinned. "Thanks."

The kid didn't have to look so surprised. Max did possess some redeeming qualities.

You fire one mermaid and suddenly you're a super-villain.

He slammed the door of the Jeep and headed toward the Airstream. Nate jammed his hands in his pockets and walked alongside.

Back in Baltimore, Max had never cultivated friendships at work. It was generally considered unprofessional, and the scientists and interns never mixed outside the aquarium. Island life was different, though. Max knew this. At least that's what he told himself when, again, his old analytical self was hinting otherwise.

Professionalism and methodology aside, Max could use a friend. His life in Turtle Beach had gotten off to a rocky start.

He and Nate fell in line behind the crowd of beachgoers and senior citizens. Either Max was imagining things, or a few hostile stares were aimed his way. Happy chatter and conversation seemed to grind to a halt.

Max shifted his weight from one foot to the other. Beside him, Nate cleared his throat and took a nearly imperceptible sidestep, putting a sliver of space between them.

Again, Max told himself he was simply being overly conscious of everything going on around him. It wasn't as if the entire island had suddenly banded together and decided he was a terrible person.

But then he and Nate reached the front of the line, and Max got a glimpse of the cupcake menu. There was the usual assortment of vanilla, chocolate, and red velvet, albeit with frivolous names like Vanilla Bean Dream, Hot Fudge Tuesday, and Ravishing Red Velvet. The specials of the day, however, had a place of honor on a chalkboard sign placed right beside the order window. Max grew still as he read the names of the flavors.

Mermaid Marshmallow Cream and Sidekick Snickerdoodle.

For a fleeting moment, he let himself believe it was only a coincidence. But then he caught a glimpse of the snickerdoodle cupcake. Ursula's cute little copper-and-white face was frosted onto the top of it, from her fluffy ears to her black jellybean nose.

No doubt about it. He was being trolled...in sugar and frosting.

"Can I help you?"

Max tore his gaze away from Ursula's frosted face to lock eyes with the woman manning the cupcake truck. It was Violet, the yoga teacher from this morning. She arched a brow and shot Max a smile that appeared to be decidedly less Zen than the soothing air she'd exuded at yoga class.

"I'll take a Sidekick Snickerdoodle, please," Nate said.

Max glared at Nate. *Seriously?*

Nate shrugged. "What? I like cinnamon and sugar."

Violet handed Nate one of the Ursula-decorated cupcakes

along with a pink and white polka dot napkin before turning her attention back to Max. "And you?"

"Vanilla, please," he said through gritted teeth. His hunger was the only thing keeping him from walking away cupcake-less.

Also the smell of warm cake was making his mouth water. Screw his pride. He'd choke down a cupcake, along with a side of humble pie.

"Sorry." Violet shook her head. "We no longer have vanilla available."

"Okay." Max took another glance at the menu. "Carrot cake sounds good. I'll have that."

"So sorry," Violet said in a tone that indicated she wasn't sorry in the slightest.

Max regarded her through narrowed eyes. "Chocolate."

"Again, my apologies." Violet crossed her arms.

Behind her, Max could see at least a dozen chocolate cupcakes lined up in a row like neat little soldiers.

"Dude," Nate said.

It was astounding how versatile that single annoying word could be.

Max felt a muscle in his jaw twitch. "In that case, I'll have a Mermaid Marshmallow Cream."

Violet beamed at him. "Excellent choice."

She handed him a cupcake piled ludicrously high with glittery sprinkles and gaudy rainbow-colored frosting that had been fashioned into a fishtail.

"Thanks," Max said.

As he walked away from the cupcake truck, he heard the kid

in line behind him order a red velvet and a chocolate. Violet answered him with a chirpy *coming right up.*

A lesser man might have given up on his mission, turned tail, and shut himself up inside his beach house for the rest of the night. But Max was no chicken. He wasn't about to let a cupcake scare him away.

Or maybe he was just desperate.

—∿—

"Here he comes." Molly squared her shoulders, tightened her grip on Ursula's leash, and did her best to ignore the sudden *thump thump thump* of her heart as Max walked toward the senior center lobby.

He had a mermaid cupcake in his hand and a scowl on his face, a combination which inexplicably made her feel more attracted to him than ever. Ugh. Something was *seriously* wrong with her.

Ethel Banks peered over the top of her purple bifocals as Max grew closer. "Goodness gracious, that man is even more good-looking dry than he is wet."

Mavis nodded. "That jawline. And that boyish swagger. He's like a modern-day Cary Grant."

Molly wasn't so sure. Max's swagger didn't seem boyish in the slightest. In fact, it oozed irritation—possibly even aggression.

Opal redirected her walker so that she could look Molly directly in the eye. "Are you sure you want to alienate him, dear?"

"I'm not trying to alienate him," Molly countered. "I'm simply trying to get my job back."

Was she, though? Was she really?

Molly's gaze flitted toward Ursula straining at her leash and dressed in her goofy little lobster costume. Okay, perhaps her efforts to let Max Miller know exactly how beloved she and Ursula were by the community at large had gone a tad overboard. Mavis's Chihuahua was nestled in her walker basket, dressed as a lobster in solidarity. Technically, it was a shrimp costume, but that was the best Molly could do for a teacup-sized dog on such short notice. She'd driven all the way across the bridge to Wilmington in search of shellfish attire for the island's canine population. She'd managed to score lobster costumes for Violet's Dalmatian Sprinkles, as well as Sprinkles's better-behaved counterpart, Cinder, the Dalmatian who belonged to Violet's fireman boyfriend, Sam Nash. Clover the corgi was also decked out in a red felt "shell" with wonky antennae, as were Hoyt Hooper Jr.'s aging Golden Retriever and the fluffy gray Persian feline companion to Mavis's boyfriend Larry Sims.

Definitely overboard. Molly's cheeks went impossibly hot. *Too late now. Just go with it.*

The automatic doors swished open, and Max walked into the lobby with Nate Harper, one of the sea turtle hospital interns. Molly had been so focused on Max and his swoony swagger that she hadn't noticed Nate's presence until just then.

Molly adored Nate. Everyone did. He was the human equivalent of a St. Bernard puppy, with shaggy hair, deep-set brown eyes, and a tendency to trip over his own feet. A total sweetheart.

Still, it stung a little to see him hanging out after hours with her archenemy. Molly was beginning to feel better and better about all the four-legged lobsters currently weaving their way among the bingo tables.

"Good evening, gentlemen," Opal said, grinning from Max to Nate and back again while Ursula strained at her leash in an effort to get to Max.

The Cavalier threw herself at Max's feet and batted at his shins with her tiny paws, clearly oblivious that this was the man who'd fired the both of them just hours before. Or maybe she knew, and she'd decided to forgive and forget. Either way, it was beyond mortifying.

Molly tugged gently at the puppy's leash and tried to reel her back in.

"Welcome to bingo." Mavis peeled a sheet from her pad of bingo card pages and handed one to Nate.

Ethel offered him his choice of ink daubers from the box in her walker basket. Nate took a blue one.

The Charlie's Angels made up the official welcoming committee for bingo night. No one on the island had the opportunity to yell bingo without first getting past Opal, Ethel, and Mavis.

"Thank you." Nate scooted past the women and lingered, waiting for Max to gather his bingo-playing accoutrements and join him at one of the tables.

Max, however, seemed momentarily paralyzed. He stood rooted to the spot, staring at Nibbles in his tiny shrimp costume. Then his gaze moved slowly to Skippy the Persian, nestled beside Nibbles in Mavis's walker basket. The set of Max's jaw seemed to turn to granite as he took in the cat's lobster claws while Skippy rolled onto her back and batted at her left antenna.

Sprinkles the Dalmatian suddenly leapt into view, red lobster claws flying anywhere and everywhere, and made a grab for the mermaid cupcake in Max's hand. It was gone before he could move a muscle.

Opal's eyes went wide. Mavis clasped a hand over her mouth, and Ethel shook with silent laughter. Even Max's uncle, who was sitting at one of the tables right up front, let out a snort of amusement. The timing of Sprinkles's antics had always been impeccable.

Max Miller, hater of dogs, terminator of mermaids, turned toward Molly. An angry muscle flexed in his jaw. The effort to keep his head from exploding must have been monumental. "Can we have a word?"

Here it was. He was going to cave and beg her to come back to the aquarium. Molly knew it.

She was tempted to make him do it right here and now, in front of the Charlie's Angels, Nate, and the bingo-loving public at large. But that definitely seemed like overkill. Molly had made her point. Max had probably suffered enough.

"Absolutely." She shot him a triumphant smile. "Shall we?"

She waved toward the far end of the lobby where a set of French double doors led to a deck overlooking the bay.

Max gave her a terse nod.

Everyone in the room, both human and canine alike, watched as Molly and Max walked toward the back porch. Ursula trotted between them at the end of her leash, antennae waving. She kept glancing up at Max with a wide doggy smile on her face. The stars in her eyes reminded Molly of the way she'd felt last summer when she'd dated The Tourist. Poor naive thing.

The sky was ablaze with a late summer sunset, so molten that it looked like the clouds were spilling liquid gold straight into the bay. A row of pelicans glided above the smooth sea, dipping the tips of their wings into the water. It would have been a lovely evening for a romantic stroll along the beach…with someone other than Wilson.

Obviously.

Even so, Molly's pulse kicked up a notch when Max's blue eyes found hers. *It's just nerves. That's all.* She swallowed hard and waited for the begging to commence.

He studied her for a beat without saying a word—just long enough for Molly to begin to wonder if perhaps she'd miscalculated. Maybe he wasn't going to ask her to come back to work after all.

Impossible. Turtle Beach was a small island, and Molly already knew plenty about how Max's first day as the director of the aquarium had gone. It had been an unmitigated disaster, even before he'd seen the public display of support for her and Ursula.

Max needed her. She knew it, and now he knew it too.

"I'm sorry about this morning," he finally said. "It wasn't personal. I need you to know that."

To Molly's horror, she felt her bottom lip start to quiver. *It sure felt personal to me.* She wanted to say the words out loud, just as she wanted to explain to Max how much she loved the aquarium, how much she'd given up to come back to the island she adored and to build a life here.

But she couldn't. If she did, the tears she'd been holding back all day might finally spill over, and that couldn't happen. Crying was *not* part of the plan.

Max looked down at Ursula, who'd just collapsed belly-up at his feet in a desperate bid for affection. "Also, I don't hate dogs."

"You just think they don't belong in an aquarium. Or at bingo." Molly gave him her best attempt at a saccharine smile. "Or at yoga."

Max's lips curved into a smug grin. Wait, why was he smiling?

"Been checking up on me, have you?" he asked.

Yes.

Molly licked her lips. They tasted like salty sea air and longing. "Don't flatter yourself. It's a tiny island. Word gets around."

"So I noticed." He took a step closer and every nerve ending in Molly's body seemed to go on high alert.

For a second, it was just the two of them again, clasping hands in the ocean. Nothing else mattered. Then Max's gaze cut to one of the lobby windows overlooking the deck, where a group of senior citizens and dogs dressed as lobsters were spying on their conversation.

A tidal wave of embarrassment washed over Molly. She crossed her arms, a barrier.

Focus.

"If you wanted to send me a message, you could have talked to me instead of doing it with cupcakes and costumed dogs," Max said. The muscle in his jaw ticked again. "Plus the one cat."

Molly blinked. He might actually have just made a valid point.

Except where was all this willingness to chat when he'd up and fired her?

"You weren't so eager to talk earlier this morning," she countered.

"We're here now." He shrugged one muscular shoulder. "Let's talk."

Molly relaxed a little. Good, they were getting things back on track. "Sounds great. I'm ready."

He nodded. "Me too."

Their eyes locked again. The water in the bay swished gently against the shore. Seagrass swayed. The sound side of the island was so different from the beachfront, so calm. Soothing. Molly felt her defenses slipping slowly away.

How had things gotten so crazy between her and Max, anyway? It was silly, really.

Ursula, clearly fed up with not being the center of attention, pawed at Max's shins. He bent down to scoop the puppy into his arms, and Molly melted just a little bit inside. Maybe he wasn't such a dog hater after all.

"I forgive you," she said.

Ursula licked the side of Max's neck, and Molly stared at the place where her pink tongue made contact with his skin. Was she *jealous* of her dog?

"For what?" Max said.

Molly snapped out of her nonsensical trance. When she looked back up at Max's face, he was frowning again. Deep lines creased his forehead.

"For firing me, obviously. And for the deeply unflattering things you said about dogs and mermaids. That's what we were getting at, right? Your apology?" She laughed.

Max, pointedly, did not. "I was waiting for *you* to apologize to *me*."

"Me?" Molly gaped at him. "What on earth do I have to apologize for?"

"Apparently I'm only allowed to order a single flavor of cupcake." Max's jaw visibly clenched. "Not that it matters since a Dalmatian with lobster claws stole it right out of my hand."

Right. That.

"In my defense, I had nothing to do with Sprinkles stealing your cupcake. She's just like that sometimes. Ask anyone." Molly waved a hand toward the window. Bingo must have started, because their audience had dispersed.

Still, when she caught a glimpse of the Charlie's Angels at a table overlooking the bay, each of the older women seemed to be absently stamping the table's bare surface with their sponge-tipped daubers instead of their bingo sheets as they stole glances outside.

"I can't ask anyone, seeing as you've turned the entire town against me in a matter of hours." Max threw up his free hand. His other one was already occupied, snuggling a blissful Ursula against his chest.

So much for loyalty.

"Let me get this straight—you *didn't* come here tonight to offer me my job back?" Molly asked.

Go ahead. Try to deny it. They both knew he had zero intention of playing bingo.

"On the contrary, that's exactly why I came here." The corner of Max's mouth curved into a grin. Finally.

"I accept," Molly said.

But at the exact same moment the words left her mouth, Max said, "I've since changed my mind."

"Wait. *What?*" Molly's face burned with humiliation.

"Clearly, working together would be a mistake." Max's tone was a little too cocky for Molly's liking.

She couldn't believe she'd been so willing to forgive and forget. The man was impossible. He'd fired her puppy, for goodness' sake.

She snatched Ursula away from him.

"A *big* mistake," Molly blurted.

Max's blue eyes hardened, glittering like beach glass. "Huge."

Molly was aggressively annoyed and more than a little hurt, although she couldn't imagine why. She'd rather blend Milky Way lattes at Turtle Books for the rest of her life than agree to work for Max Miller.

Not that he'd asked.

"For the record, I stand by my earlier statement. Mermaids are scientifically insignificant, and emotional support humans aren't a thing," he said, driving the final nail into the coffin of their nonexistent working relationship.

Molly felt her bottom lip begin to quiver. She bit down hard on it to get it to stop. She absolutely *refused* to appear vulnerable in front of this horrible man. "And what exactly would you know about being human?"

Chapter 6

MAX DIDN'T STICK AROUND for bingo, even though he knew he probably should have. What better way to prove his "humanity" to the good people of Turtle Beach?

He couldn't, though. He just didn't have it in him. Today had been a *day*, and tomorrow's forecast wasn't looking any better. Now that Molly wasn't coming back, he was going to have to figure some things out. A lot of things. Too many to count, if today had been any indication. So instead of pretending he in any way belonged at a table with a bingo card in front of him and a mermaid cupcake in his hand, Max had bid goodbye to his Uncle Henry—who'd managed to guilt Max into promising to attend yoga in the morning—and then he'd left the senior center for the serenity of the back deck of Henry's beach cottage.

Except it wasn't Henry's beach house anymore, it was Max's. Like it or not, he was officially part of a town that had just collectively attempted to force his hand to rehire a mermaid and her dog.

Max plopped into a deck chair and stared out at the moonlit sea. Foamy waves tumbled against the shore and retreated back again in the timeless push and pull of the tides. Max sort of felt like he was being dragged along for the ride.

Idiot.

He shouldn't have dug in. He should have simply stuck to his plan, admitted he'd jumped the gun, and asked her to come back. But he hadn't anticipated the cupcakes or the costumed dogs or the feeling that he'd suddenly been cast in the role of town villain. He was a *scientist.* He ran a hospital for turtles. He'd spent the afternoon hand-feeding squid to an endangered animal. How could he possibly be the villain in this scenario?

When Molly had announced that he was forgiven before he'd uttered a word of apology, he'd lost it, plain and simple. No way. *No possible way* was he going to grovel after she'd launched an all-out, cutesy offensive against him. Not now, and not ever.

Max didn't do cute. Science itself was the antithesis of frivolity. There was nothing wrong with being logical and focusing on things that mattered. It didn't make him a robot. Or nonhuman. Working together would have been a disaster of epic proportions, that's all there was to it. He'd probably just done them both a favor.

Although somehow he suspected that Molly wouldn't see it that way.

He pushed out of the Adirondack chair he'd been sitting in and took the deck stairs two at a time as he headed toward the open-air storage area beneath the house. Like all the other homes on Turtle Beach, the cottage was built on pilings. Beach houses used the ground level for storing sun chairs, fishing poles, bicycles, and other summer paraphernalia. The space was piled with things new and old, but Max found what he was looking for right away. The old buckets and shovels were precisely where Henry always kept them, tucked beneath the hammock that stretched between two of the rough-hewn columns that held up the house.

Max's throat closed when he saw his childhood bucket, still sitting beside Henry's larger one, faded from decades of sun and sea air. He wasn't sure why it caught him off guard. The interior of the beach cottage looked exactly the same as when Max had last visited, years ago. Nothing about the pine paneling or rows of seashells lined up on the windowsill got under Max's skin like seeing his old bucket did, though. It was almost like Henry had left it there all this time, just waiting for Max to come back...to come *home*.

Max reached for it. Henry's larger bucket would have been more convenient, but old habits died hard. Bucket in hand, he grabbed one of the long-handled shovels that were propped against the wall, slung it over his shoulder and headed toward the beach.

The shore was dotted with holes, just like it always was during tourist season, although fewer than if it had still been high summer. Max filled his bucket with sand skimmed evenly from the berm. Then he moved methodically from one hole to the next, filling them and patting down the loose sand with the back of the shovel. There was something comforting about the ritual. Timeless. Max's shirt whipped in the wind and his glasses fogged over with damp sea air. Ghost crabs skittered sideways in his path, and he remembered flashlight beams moving over the sand on warm summer nights when he was a kid. While friends back home had been shut inside playing video games, Max had been on Turtle Beach, chasing crabs and hoping for a sea turtle sighting. Life had been so much easier back then. So pure.

Which made his current predicament all the more baffling. He should have known better than to mess with a mermaid, though. Folklore was full of cautionary tales about doing so.

Since when do you pay attention to folklore?

Since never, which was precisely the point.

He patted down one last hole, then turned around, took two steps, and stumbled into a shallow dip in the sand.

How was that possible? He was on the same stretch of beach that he'd just covered.

Max inspected the hole as best he could in the dark. It was on the small side, but definitely too big to be the work of a crab. He peered into the darkness as he used his shovel to spread sand into an even layer. Once, when Max had been about fourteen years old, he'd spotted a sea otter on Turtle Beach. At first glance, he'd mistaken it for a cat, scampering straight toward him early one morning from the direction of the pier. Then the animal had veered off course toward the water. Max had gasped out loud when he'd spied the telltale hump on the otter's back. It had been his one and only otter sighting on the island. *Enhydra lutris.*

Max glanced overhead. The moon was high in the sky, but it was still too early for otters to be out foraging. He must have missed the hole somehow on his first pass. The beach was quiet, save for the gentle rush of the surf. Max got the feeling he was the only person out walking in the dark.

Probably because the rest of the island was still playing bingo. Max couldn't be sure. He'd lost track of the time since his escape from the senior center.

Either way, he needed to get home. Tomorrow he'd have to break the news to Nate that the aquarium would remain mermaid-free. Good times.

But as soon as Max took a few more steps, his gaze landed on another shallow hole. And another…and *another*.

What the—?

"Ursula?" someone called.

Not just someone. *Her.* Max's favorite mermaid—a sentiment that didn't necessarily mean anything, considering that Molly was the only mermaid he'd ever met.

Max groaned. He'd forgotten about the puppy from the balcony next door. Apparently, the tiny spaniel was indeed Ursula, which meant that Molly was Max's neighbor. What were the odds, even on an island this small?

Max stood there, frozen in the moonlight, hoping against hope that Molly and her little dog would head back home and he wouldn't be forced to deal with this new, wholly inconvenient twist in his and Molly's nonexistent relationship until morning. But then Ursula suddenly burst toward him from the shadows in a flurry of sand and floppy puppy ears.

The sweet Cavalier wiggled at his feet as she made cute little whimpering sounds.

Max's ever-logical heartstrings gave a definite tug. He had no choice but to drop the shovel and pick up the puppy. It would have been rude not to, as if confirming that he was, in fact, a dog hater. Which he wasn't, all evidence to the contrary. Max was already treading on thin enough ice where the island's canine population was concerned, so he scooped the puppy into his arms. Ursula immediately planted her paws on his chest and commenced to lick his face.

"There you are, Ursula. I…"

Max shifted Ursula to the crook of his elbow and waved at Molly. "Hi, there."

"You." Molly crossed her arms. "Again."

Her hair flew in a furious halo around her face, and her bottle-green eyes glittered like jewels from a sunken treasure chest.

Max's mouth tugged into a reluctant grin. "Howdy, neighbor."

―⁓―

"You're kidding. He lives *right next door*?" Caroline stared open-mouthed at Molly as steamed milk overflowed from the mug she was holding beneath the frother on the fancy espresso machine at Turtle Books the following morning.

"Ouch." Caroline jumped back and reached for a dish towel.

"Sorry." Molly winced. "I should know better than to drop a bomb on you like that when you're operating dangerous equipment."

Caroline waved a hand. "It's not that dangerous. And as soon as you get a little practice in, I won't be the one manning this bad boy. You will."

Right. Because Molly worked here now, thanks to a certain overly pragmatic scientist who'd caught her completely off guard last night on the beach. Not to mention Molly's initial firing and the way her cutesy revenge plan had spiraled so quickly out of control.

If her personal life had been one of the island's notoriously competitive fire department versus police department softball games, the score would be dreadful. Max Miller: 3, Molly Prince: 0.

Molly eyed the espresso machine. How complicated could it possibly be?

"Don't look so freaked out. Think of it as a glorified Keurig," Caroline said without quite meeting Molly's gaze. Molly's Keurig was a single-serve wonder with one giant gray button, so basic that a toddler could operate it. Somehow she doubted the comparison was in any way accurate. "Besides, coffee can wait. I want to hear more about your new neighbor."

Ugh. Caroline suddenly had the same giddy smile on her face that the Charlie's Angels always got whenever the subject of Molly's nemesis came up.

"There's nothing else to say, really. He's moved into Henry's old beach cottage." Molly tied her new frilly Turtle Books apron around her waist. She missed her ropes of pearls and sequined fishtail far more than she wanted to admit.

Plus, Ursula looked decidedly naked without her lobster costume. Molly was just grateful that Caroline had agreed to let the puppy come to work with her—a decision that wasn't altogether popular with Sebastian the bookshop cat. The spotted Bengal was currently sulking atop a bookshelf in the children's section, just out of reach of Ursula's dainty paws.

"You truly had no idea?" Caroline asked as she handed a freshly made latte to a tourist whose face bore a sunburn so pink that Molly could see the exact shape of the sunglasses he must have worn the day before.

Caroline noticed the sunburn and winced. "The gift shop next door has some cream for that burn. Best on the island."

"Thanks." The tourist smiled, white teeth glowing against his crimson face. He left the bookshop, latte in hand, and headed in the direction of the gift shop.

Molly turned toward Caroline. "I had no idea whatsoever. Nothing seemed different over there. Max is apparently also driving Henry's Jeep now. In any case, it's like he's taking over his uncle's entire life."

Molly sighed. She didn't want to talk about Max anymore, especially since Caroline's level of indignation where he was concerned seemed to have taken a serious hit after she'd seen the man face-to-face at bingo night.

She tried to steer the conversation in a different direction. "You're really going out of your way to help the sunburned tourists these days, huh?"

"It's called customer service," Caroline said. "And it's your job too now."

"Goody," Molly said flatly.

She'd interacted with tourists all the time at the aquarium, obviously. But that had been different. Most of the visitors were families with small children. Of course there'd been the occasional creeper who'd seemed a little over-interested in her clamshell bustier, but at least those types were easily identifiable. Unlike, say, beachgoers who disguised themselves as single and charming, when in fact they were two-timing jerks who had fiancées back home in the big city.

"You just have to be nice to the tourists, not date them." Caroline gave Molly a playful swat with her dish towel.

Molly shot her a look.

"Oh, that's right. You're still determined to be the world's first spinster mermaid. You know I love you, but I really think you should reassess. Max seems…"

"Evil?" Molly prompted.

"Hot," Caroline said, eyebrows waggling. "Seriously, Molls. How did you fail to mention his sexy professor vibe?"

Molly rolled her eyes, even as her heart beat hard at the memory of Max's perfect forearms, just visible beneath the rolled-up sleeves of his crisp blue oxford shirt. Who wore an actual *dress shirt* at the beach? "Please. You sound like the Charlie's Angels."

"Speak of the devil," Caroline said. "Or should I say devils?"

She tipped her head in the direction of the glass door to the bookshop, and Molly followed her gaze. Opal, Mavis, and Ethel were headed straight toward Turtle Books, their walkers plunking in unison against the wood surface of the boardwalk.

Molly rushed to hold the door open for the older women as they filed inside, still dressed in all manner of neon spandex from their morning yoga class at the senior center.

"Thank you, dear," Opal said, pausing to pat Molly's cheek.

"Anytime. This is a nice surprise." Molly grinned. "I didn't expect you three to pop in today."

"Well, the activity bus was heading this way to take some of the residents to doctor appointments across the bridge, so we thought we'd hitch a ride and come support you at your first day on the job." Mavis parked her walker at the counter. As usual, Nibbles the Chihuahua sat in a shivering heap in the walker basket, nose twitching at the smell of freshly brewed coffee in the air.

Ethel nodded. "We didn't want to miss your ballistic debut."

Molly and Caroline exchanged a bemused glance.

"*Barista*, not ballistic," Opal corrected, enunciating each syllable with exaggerated care. "She's making coffee, not blowing her top."

"I don't know," Mavis muttered under her breath. "She seemed awfully annoyed last night at bingo."

Molly's face went warm. "What can I get you ladies this fine morning?"

Of course she'd been annoyed. For all intents and purposes, Max had *re*-fired her. Anyone would be miffed, having been fired twice in a single day.

Molly refused to take the bait and get into another conversation about her grumpy neighbor.

Neighbor. Gah! Molly died a little bit inside every time she remembered that she and Max now shared the same pristine stretch of sand and sea.

"Whatever you'd like to make is fine." Opal winked. Bless her and her flexibility, yoga-esque and otherwise.

Ethel and Mavis rattled off their orders, both complicated flavored lattes that Molly had enjoyed many times but had zero clue how to make. She poured Opal a plain, basic drip coffee and began wrestling with the espresso machine while Caroline rang up a few book and newspaper sales.

"This is delicious, dear," Ethel said, pulling a face as she sipped her drink.

Delicious, my foot. Molly gave her older friends a weak smile. "I'm still learning."

"You'll get the hang of things in no time." Mavis nudged her barely touched latte away from her with a push of her bony pointer finger.

On the other side of the bookshop, Sebastian hissed. A stack of children's picture books fell from a shelf and narrowly missed conking Ursula on the head. The puppy yelped, ran toward Molly, and pawed at her shins to be picked up.

Molly tried to resist, but Ursula was relentless, so she caved. Maybe she could start carrying Ursula around in one of those slings across her chest so she could work hands-free. That was normal, wasn't it?

None of this is normal. You belong at the aquarium.

Molly wondered how Rocky, the oldest turtle in the sea turtle hospital, was doing, or if Silver, the pregnant seahorse, had given birth yet. She missed the animals even more than she missed her clamshells.

"Are you okay, dear? You seem sort of—" Opal looked Molly up and down. "—bland."

"It's the apron." Ethel picked up her latte, took a sip, and blanched.

"She's right." Mavis nodded. "It's far less flattering than your mermaid costume."

"Hey." Caroline looked down at her own apron, bottom lip turning down into a pout.

"Don't be silly. Everything is fine. *I'm* fine." Molly forced a smile. "Just peachy."

She had a job, albeit one she was terrible at and that would barely cover the cost of the rent she paid to her parents. She had her perfect cottage, although its serene ambiance was now ruined by the grump next door. And she had parents who loved her so much that they would probably try to physically wrestle her away from Turtle Beach once they found out that she was now fully wasting her education degree.

Okay, perhaps she wasn't completely fine, after all. But at least she had Ursula, the most loyal creature to ever set paw on the planet.

She snuggled the puppy closer. Then Molly remembered how Ursula had launched herself at Max last night the moment she'd seen him, and she almost felt like crying.

"Well, if it's any consolation, Max was at yoga again this morning, and he looked as tense as ever," Mavis said.

"I have absolutely no interest in Max's recreational activities." Unless he fell out of his downward dog and landed on his smug face. Now that, Molly might find worthy of her time and attention.

"Did you hear?" Caroline grinned at the Charlie's Angels. "Max moved into Henry's beach house."

Opal's eyes lit up. "Oh, good. Maybe you two can form some sort of truce."

Seriously?

Molly couldn't help feeling a bit wounded. "Whose side are all of you on, exactly?"

"Yours," they said in unison.

An awkward silence followed.

Opal was the first to break it. "We're just wondering if sides are really necessary. If the aquarium is really struggling, Max needs you. And he's the only member of Henry's family who's ever come to the island. It's good that Max is here. Surely there's a way for you two to work together."

Molly bit her lip as Max's self-righteous words whirled through her thoughts.

Clearly working together would be a mistake.

"Never going to happen," Molly said, smiling to keep the tears at bay. She should have let the man drown when she'd had the chance. "Let's move on to other things, shall we? Does anyone have fun plans for this weekend?"

Molly intended the question purely as a conversational detour, so she was caught off guard when all four of her friends responded with puzzled glances.

"We all do." Opal pointed at her. "And so do you."

Molly blinked.

"Don't feel bad if you've forgotten, dear. We all have senior moments from time to time." Ethel shot Molly a sympathetic smile. "Although you're starting a bit young."

"SandFest is this weekend," Caroline said. "Did it truly slip your mind?"

It had. Molly had been so distracted by recent traumatic events that she'd forgotten all about the island's biggest party of the year. The annual sand sculpture competition, known simply as SandFest, was always a sight to behold, from the kids' sand-castle contest to the main event's intricate, larger-than-life sand creations.

SandFest had been Molly's favorite weekend of the year since its inception eight years ago. The event always kicked off early

Saturday morning with a pancake breakfast at the Salty Dog pier. Even the dog beach got in on the action with a special competition for children.

By Friday afternoon, traffic would be backed up from the bridge all the way to Wilmington, over an hour away. People traveled for miles to attend SandFest.

Molly went still, and the happy little zing that had coursed through her when she'd realized SandFest was just days away settled in the pit of her stomach like a lead weight.

People come from miles away...

They did indeed. And to Molly's great horror, those people always included her mom and dad.

Chapter 7

THINGS AT THE AQUARIUM mildly improved on Max's second day, but he'd take what he could get.

He even pretended to laugh along when some of the staff started referring to him as The Merminator, a ridiculous mash-up of the words *mermaid* and *terminator*. As nicknames went, Max didn't exactly love it. It certainly didn't make electricity skitter over his skin the way it did when Molly called him Wilson.

But there were worse things than being known as The Merminator, like potentially being known as the guy who'd driven the aquarium and sea turtle hospital into bankruptcy. Max definitely didn't want to be that guy. Ever.

So he did his best to ignore the way his jaw clenched every time someone called him The Merminator and told himself he had more important things to worry about than his unflattering reputation—such as keeping the aquarium afloat. And trying to find out what exactly the sea turtle hospital was doing to protect local nesting grounds. And SandFest, whatever the heck that might be.

"SandFest," Nate repeated for the third time, gazing at Max from behind his floppy blond curtain of surfer hair. "You know."

Max shook his head. "No. I don't know. That's why I'm asking you to explain it to me."

Max and Nate were standing in the far-left corner of the aquarium's main lobby, known as the Seahorse Dude Ranch. The walls were painted turquoise and featured a mural of bright orange seahorses wearing cowboy hats on their spiky heads and spurs on their whirly-curled tails. Never mind the fact that the largest tank in the Seahorse Dude Ranch actually held sea dragons, not seahorses. *Phycodurus eques* as opposed to *Hippocampus*. Not the same. Max was beginning to lose track of the scientific inaccuracies that surrounded him on a daily basis.

At the moment, he was more concerned with the pregnant seahorse in the dude ranch's showcase tank than he was with the area's overly whimsical decor. Silver's brood pouch was swollen to the extent that it looked like the poor animal had swallowed a Ping-Pong ball. The blessed event was imminent. And Silver was looking a bit lackluster, slowly bobbing up and down in the tank.

Seahorses and sea dragons were the only species in which the males got pregnant and gave birth. Once Silver's babies were born, he wouldn't eat for a few hours, but after the new dad had gotten some rest, he might see the newborns as a snack. Nature was a miraculous—and sometimes cruel—thing.

"Don't forget that we need to remove Silver from the tank as soon as we see tiny seahorses floating around in here. Got it?" Max said. He'd spent the majority of the past hour giving the intern a lesson that could have been called *What to Expect When Your Seahorse Is Expecting.*

Nate nodded. "Yes, sir."

"You don't have to call me 'sir,'" Max said, although perhaps it was preferable to *dude*.

Nate's gaze flitted briefly to the Windsor knot in Max's tie. "Um, okay."

Max was going to have to start dressing more like a local. And he would, as soon as he had time to go shopping for flip-flops and board shorts.

"Now, back to SandFest," Max prompted.

"Oh, right." Nate raked a hand through his sun-bleached hair. "It's a huge deal. Everything starts with a big pancake breakfast at the pier on Saturday morning and then there are sand sculpture contests for the rest of the weekend. The island is going to be packed."

"A whole new wave of tourists really flock to Turtle Beach to watch people build sand castles?"

"Dude." Nate laughed. They were back to *dude* now, Windsor knot aside. "It's not just castles. We're talking a really big scale. As in bigger than that Jeep you've been driving."

Again, Max tore his gaze away from the expectant seahorse. "Wow."

Nate nodded. "People get really into it. There's prize money and everything."

Now he had Max's full attention. "How much money?"

"Ten grand for first place, then smaller amounts for second and third," Nate said.

"*Ten thousand dollars?*" For building a glorified sandcastle?

It wasn't enough money to solve all of the aquarium's problems, but it would keep the doors open for a few more months. Ten grand could buy Max some time…and possibly his sanity.

"How do we enter?" he heard himself say.

"You mean you and me?" Nate suddenly looked like a kid on Christmas morning.

"Actually, I meant the aquarium."

Nate's face fell slightly.

"We're already entered. The aquarium competes every year," he said. *Way to bury the lede, Nate.* "The Turtle Team always takes charge of the aquarium's SandFest entry."

"What's the Turtle Team?" Sometimes Max felt like everyone in Turtle Beach was speaking a foreign language—a reminder that no matter how many summers he'd spent on the island, he was still an outsider.

It would help matters if Uncle Henry would simply fill Max in on the inner workings of the aquarium, but so far, Max's uncle had yet to make time in his busy social life for anything remotely resembling business. Meanwhile, Max kept jumping through hoops involving murder victim pose and bingo, hoping Uncle Henry would eventually acquiesce.

Nate shrugged one shoulder. "It's the team of volunteers who support the turtle hospital."

Max instantly felt borderline drunk with happiness. "We have *volunteers*?"

Things were finally looking up. Now all he needed was for said volunteers to be unusually adept at sandcastle architecture. If so, Max might be able to start sleeping at night.

"We do." Nate glanced at the smart watch strapped to his

wrist. "They should be here in half an hour or less for the Turtle Team's biweekly meeting. I forgot all about it. Molly was always in charge of the volunteers."

Of course she was.

But for once, the mention of Turtle Beach's overachieving mermaid didn't faze him. He had volunteers. He had a plan.

And for the first time since Max had made the questionable choice of leaving his careful, orderly world behind, he had the most precious thing of all—a faint glimmer of hope.

—⁓—

Max's hope took a serious hit half an hour later when he headed toward the conference room to meet the Turtle Team. He wasn't sure what—or, more specifically, whom—he'd expected, but the sight that greeted him as he rounded the hallway corner stopped him in his tracks.

Walkers…

Walkers *everywhere*.

Mobility devices were parked outside the conference room in a jumble of aluminum legs, metal wicker baskets, and those fuzzy dissected tennis balls that were supposed to make walkers easier to slide along the floor. Max crossed his arms and regarded the gridlock. The narrow aquarium hallway looked like a parking lot for an AARP convention.

It's fine, he told himself. Max loved that the senior citizens of Turtle Beach were such an active part of the community. Max might be many things, Merminator included, but he was *not* ageist. Sea turtles often lived to see their one hundredth birthdays, a fact that Max had gleefully committed to memory when he'd been a little boy. He'd started doing yoga every morning with the eighty-plus crowd, for crying out loud. Max loved older people.

He just wasn't so sure they had what it took to build an award-winning sand sculpture that would dwarf Henry's vintage Jeep Wrangler.

Relax. Max took a deep breath. *They can't all be elderly.*

But oh, yes. Yes, they could. Max strode into the conference room and sure enough, he found a dozen or so of the bingo-loving yogis from the senior center sitting around the table dressed in blue and green tie-dye T-shirts with the words Turtle Team emblazoned across their chests. The three women who'd had front row seats to Max's near-drowning at the dog beach—Opal, Mavis, and Ethel—occupied the chairs closest to the head of the table. Because of course they did.

"Ladies." Max nodded in recognition.

"Good morning, Max." Opal Lewinsky stood and handed him something that looked like a chocolate milkshake and smelled like Starbucks on steroids. He noticed she was still wearing her neon yoga clothes beneath her Turtle Team T-shirt. "Ethel, Mavis, and I brought you a treat from Turtle Books to celebrate your first meeting with the Turtle Team."

"Thank you." Max took the drink.

The women stared at him expectantly until he took a sip. It tasted like a candy bar that had been dunked in coffee.

"Mmm." Max took another pull from the purple, oversized straw. "Delicious."

"It's a Milky Way frozen latte," Ethel said.

"From Turtle Books," Opal repeated. "It's a cute little book-store and coffee shop on the boardwalk."

Mavis nodded. "You should stop by sometime."

"Soon." Opal grinned.

Max narrowed his gaze at the three of them. Why did he have a feeling the Turtle Team queens were up to something? "Perhaps I will."

"Good." Opal beamed at him and sat back down.

"Shall we move on to business now?" Max said.

Everyone nodded.

"Great." Max took his seat at the head of the table. He resisted the temptation to dive straight into SandFest business. He needed to get a general idea of what the group did first. "Why don't you tell me what the Turtle Team is all about?"

The seniors all glanced at each other until Opal, who was apparently the unofficial Turtle Team captain, spoke up again. "We support the aquarium and the sea turtle hospital. We also help preserve the island's shoreline as a nesting ground for endangered sea turtles."

Max nodded. So far so good. "What exactly does that entail?" A man who Max recognized as the bingo caller from the night before leaned forward with his elbows planted on the conference table. "During the summer, we take turns walking the beach early in the morning, looking for turtle tracks in the sand."

A sound plan, considering that female turtles typically came ashore in the wee hours of the morning on summer nights to lay their eggs. Monitoring the beach for evidence of turtle activity was key for all sea turtle preservation programs.

"What do you do when you locate a nesting spot?" Max asked.

"We mark it with stakes and neon tape so beachgoers know not to disturb the nest," Mavis said.

"Good, good." Max nodded. He'd been down to the beach for the past three days in a row and he hadn't seen any marked nests, though. "Excellent work. About how much of the island do you think you covered during the summer months?"

The bingo caller puffed out his chest, straining the letters on his Turtle Team shirt. "Over six miles."

Max felt his eyes widen in surprise. Six miles encompassed over half the length of the island. "I'm impressed, you guys. How do you manage to cover that much beachfront every morning?"

There was a brief pause, and then the seniors all burst out laughing. Every one of them. Like a proper team.

"Goodness, Max. Not six miles *a day*," Opal said.

"Do you know how old we are?" Ethel asked.

More laughter followed.

"Sorry." Max held up his hands. "Six miles a week, then?"

Mavis shook her head. "Not quite."

Max cleared his throat. "A month?"

"Honestly, Max." Mavis let out a little snort, and the tiny Chihuahua in her lap flinched. At least it wasn't dressed as a lobster or any other variety of shellfish. "There are eleven of us on the Turtle Team, and we probably have six good hips between us."

"Understood." Max nodded, stifling a grin. He had, after all, seen this crowd do yoga. "But how exactly do the six miles come into play?"

"We walked a total of six miles over the whole summer," Ethel said. "And we marked four nests, which is double the amount from last year."

Mavis nodded. "Molly kept track of it on her fancy spreadsheet on her computer. She said we did really well...considering..."

Mavis's voice drifted off, and Max could sense his reputation slipping back into villain territory. Who wouldn't seem like an antihero in comparison to Molly's lovable mermaid persona?

The last thing he wanted was to make the seniors feel bad, particularly when it appeared that they did more for the community than any other group on the island. The residents of the senior center poured their hearts into Turtle Beach on the regular. When Max thought back to his summers on the island, so many of the most memorable evenings had taken place in the same lobby where he'd been contorting himself into downward facing Dalmatian and pretzel poses every morning, from bingo nights and bake sales to arts and crafts projects and guest lecturers on marine life and beach ecology. Max in no way wanted to imply that the seniors weren't doing enough.

"You've done a wonderful job," he said, even though four turtle nests probably represented less than ten percent of the sea turtle eggs that had actually been laid and buried on the island.

There was no telling where they were all located, and now that summer was coming to a close, the eggs would start hatching soon. Tiny baby turtles would crack through the eggshells and crawl their way up and out of the sand to the water. Without the help of humans watching over the nests, only a small portion would make it to the sea. The beach was a dangerous place for newborn hatchlings. In an ideal scenario, the turtle hospital would know when and where nearly all the nests had been laid, so teams of volunteers could babysit the area when it was time for the turtles to be born.

Four nests was a start, though.

"Next year, we'll be able to cover more territory. I just got a new electric scooter," the bingo caller said proudly.

"It *books*," said the man next to him.

Ethel nodded. "That scooter is like something out of *The Fast and the Furriest*."

Nibbles the Chihuahua's tiny ears pricked forward.

"You mean *The Fast and the Furious*," Opal said, enunciating with care.

Behind Ethel's purple glasses, her eyes rolled. "That's what I said."

Max held up a hand before he lost complete control of the meeting. "I get the picture. Again, great job, and I look forward to seeing this smokin' scooter."

"I'd say you could try it out, but maybe you should master the Jeep first." The bingo caller shot him an exaggerated wink.

Touché.

"Maybe we should move on to SandFest," Max said.

Opal spoke up at once. "Mavis, Ethel, and I have got that completely under control. We're spearheading the Turtle Team's entry this year."

A man wearing suspenders over his Turtle Team T-shirt blew out a breath. "Thank goodness. After last year, I've still got sand in places I don't want to think about."

Max studied Opal and her two friends. Visions of walkers

and hip replacements danced in his head. "I'm not sure if having just the three of you build a sand sculpture is such a good idea."

Mavis waved a hand. "Don't be silly. We're not building it. We're *designing* it."

"A group of students from the marine biology department at the college in Wilmington is going to put it together for us." Opal removed a folded sheet of paper from the pocket of her cardigan. "Here's a sketch of our preliminary design."

Max unfolded the paper. "You drew this?"

Opal smiled. "Yes."

The sketch was magnificent. Drawn in graphite pencil with shading to give it depth and dimension, it featured a sea turtle swimming against the backdrop of a coral reef. Tiny hatchlings dotted the sand around the base of the main sculpture.

Given his status as a SandFest newbie, Max wasn't sure if it was good enough to win, but he couldn't imagine a more perfect design to represent the aquarium and sea turtle hospital.

"Opal taught art at Turtle Beach High for over forty years. She also designed the mural on the exterior of the aquarium." Mavis patted Opal's shoulder.

"This is stunning, Opal." Max tapped the sketch with his pointer finger.

"The kids who are building the sculpture for us just won a sandcastle building contest in Myrtle Beach last June. They really know what they're doing," Ethel said.

"My grandson is a freshman in the program, which is how we snagged them as our helpers." Mavis's eyes gleamed.

Stone cold relief washed over Max. Maybe they had a shot at winning this thing after all.

"Well, then. I approve." He slid the paper across the table toward Opal. "This is exciting. The aquarium could really use that prize money."

Opal took the sketch, folded it back into quarters and tucked it away again. "I'm still working on the final design. I have some ideas that should 'take it to the next level,' as the kids say. It needs to really be a statement piece if we want to win."

"Memorable," Ethel nodded.

"Impossible to ignore," Mavis added.

"Sounds like a plan, but I've got just one very important rule." Max held up a finger. "No mermaids."

He braced himself for an argument, but miraculously, it wasn't forthcoming.

"I wouldn't dream of it." Opal smiled sweetly at him. "You have my word—no mermaids."

Something about this was too easy. Or maybe Max was being paranoid. Still, he couldn't help thinking of one of Uncle Henry's favorite expressions.

Fool me once, shame on you. Fool me twice, shame on me.

Chapter 8

FOR THE REST OF the day, as Molly wrestled with the espresso machine, blended more frozen drinks than she could count, and did her best to play peacemaker between Ursula and Sebastian, she tried to come up with a plan for dealing with her parents during SandFest.

Molly contemplated every form of deception, from feigning illness in an attempt to get out of it altogether to casually wearing her mermaid costume and pretending she was still employed at the aquarium. She just wasn't ready to tell them the brutal truth, probably because she'd yet to accept it herself. But, as she'd had to remind her father again and again, Molly wasn't a child anymore. She was a grown woman. Responsible adults didn't lie to their parents or engage in ridiculous charades to avoid admitting they'd been fired. Or laid off. Or double-fired...or whatever had happened. Honestly, Molly wasn't even sure anymore. All she knew was that overnight she suddenly had a career as a semi-competent barista and a new neighbor she despised.

The best thing to do was to go ahead and fess up now so the sick feeling in the pit of her stomach would go away. Granted, telling her dad up front would allow him several days to prepare his case for moving off the island. But Molly would deal with that on Saturday. Again, she was a grown woman. He couldn't *order* her to pack and move to Philadelphia.

But he can kick you out of the cottage to prove a point.

Plus it would just be really great to feel like her dad approved of her life choices for once. And now that Molly had made such a mess of things, she didn't necessarily approve of her circumstances herself, so trying to get her academic father on board was a tall order. Why had she insisted on antagonizing Max to such a degree? She'd probably been one mermaid cupcake away from getting her job back.

When Molly's shift at Turtle Books ended, she drove home on her vintage turquoise Vespa with Ursula strapped in the pet carrier that sat between the handlebars, copper ears flying in the wind. The puppy smelled like French roast coffee beans, as did Molly's hair, her skin, and her cute starfish print fit-and-flare dress. A dip in the ocean would definitely be in order when they got back to the cottage.

Fortunately, Henry's old Jeep wasn't parked at the beach house next door, which meant that Max was most likely still at the aquarium. Molly changed into a swimsuit with a flippy little skirt and headed to the shore with Ursula's leash in one hand and her cell phone in the other.

Thank goodness she had some privacy. Molly was *so* not in the mood to see Max's smug face. Or his annoyingly muscular body, complete with washboard abs. How did a marine biologist get muscles like that anyway—from wrestling octopuses? Molly didn't have a clue. Nor did she care, she reminded herself. She let her toes sink into the warm sand as she clutched her phone and tapped the contact for her parents' landline.

Ursula romped at the end of her leash, chasing foamy, shallow waves. She pawed at a tiny bubbling crab hole in the sand as the phone began to ring.

"Hello?" Molly's mother answered, breathless. Dotty Prince rarely sat still. When she wasn't busy grading essays for her high school English lit students, she was usually working in her garden. The overflowing flower boxes on the deck of Molly's beach cottage were a testament to her mom's spectacular green thumb.

Was it too much to hope that maybe her mother had a spelling bee or garden club meeting this weekend and her parents wouldn't be able to attend SandFest after all? A mermaid could dream.

"Hi, Mom," Molly said.

Ursula scampered away from the water and pressed her snout to the soft ground. When she looked up at Molly, her tiny nose was coated with fine, sugary sand. The puppy sneezed three times in rapid succession.

"Oh hello, honey! What a nice surprise. We didn't expect to hear from you before Saturday when we leave for the beach. We know how busy you always are with the aquarium and your turtle ladies."

"Turtle Team," Molly corrected as she unclipped Ursula's leash from her collar. What did semantics matter, though? Molly wasn't the Turtle Team's leader anymore.

"I'm glad you called. Your father and I are aware of a recent development down there in Turtle Beach. There's apparently a big change in your life that you forgot to mention." Mom cleared her throat the way she always used to do when Molly got a B instead of an A on her report card or forgot a homework assignment.

Molly's heart immediately fluttered like a nervous bird.

Her parents already knew she'd been fired...

But how?

"It just happened." Molly swallowed. "I haven't had a chance to—"

"Just happened?" Her mom tut-tutted. "Have you forgotten that we still subscribe to the *Turtle Daily*? There's a picture of you with the dog right on the front page."

Molly opened her mouth to defend herself and then promptly closed it. Dotty wasn't upset because she'd found out that Molly had lost her job. This was about Ursula.

"Right. My puppy." Molly squeezed her eyes shut.

Gah. Why had she waited to tell her parents she'd adopted a dog?

Oh right, because her mom and dad were strictly anti-pet. Molly, on the other hand, had always had a penchant for bringing home every stray that crossed her path.

Now that she thought about it, that was sort of how she'd ended up dating The Tourist. She'd been on her way home from work, and he'd been struggling along Seashell Drive with a bicycle rental with a wobbly tire. Molly had given him a ride on the back of her Vespa to Turtle Sports, the local sports rental shop. He'd taken her out for ice cream as a thank you, and boom—fast forward a year later to her broken heart.

She should have just skipped the romance and gone straight to the island's adoption fair where she'd fallen in love with the orphaned Cavalier King Charles spaniel puppy with the huge, sad eyes. Live and learn.

"You know your father is allergic," Mom said.

Actually, he wasn't. Dad just liked to pretend that he was in order to avoid any unwanted interactions with overenthusiastic dogs.

Molly had a sudden flashback to Violet's Dalmatian, Sprinkles, snatching the mermaid cupcake from Max's hand at bingo night. In retrospect, Molly had to admit that Max had been a pretty good sport about it. Her father would have probably called Animal Control.

"We've gone ahead and booked one of the rental beach houses on the bay, so no need to worry about us staying with you at the cottage," her mother said.

Molly should have been relieved. She *knew* she should. But the cottage still belonged to her parents. Molly was simply their unofficial-tenant-slash-offspring. Having them stay in a rental just seemed wrong.

"Mom, that really isn't necessary. Ursula is a total love bug." Molly's gaze swept the shore, but her perfect puppy had bounded out of sight. She had to be somewhere close by, though. Ursula never wandered away.

"Seriously, Mom. You and Dad will hardly know she's here. Ursula is small and sweet." Molly shaded her eyes with her free hand and squinted into the sunset.

Still no sign of Ursula.

Where *was* she?

"As far as puppies go, she's no trouble at all," Molly said, voice trembling ever so slightly.

Surely Ursula hadn't ventured into the water. The puppy

didn't like to get more than just her paws wet. She never left the beach.

Then again, she usually never left Molly's side, either.

"Puppies will be puppies, Molly." Dotty tut-tutted again. "She can't possibly be as perfect as you're making her out to be."

"No, really. Ursula is…"

"Ursula is getting on my last nerve," someone behind Molly said.

She whipped around to see who it was.

Max Miller. *Of course.*

He was walking straight toward her, barefoot, with his dress pants rolled up. Ursula's little pink tongue lolled gleefully out of the side of her mouth and she pawed at the air while Max held her at arm's length.

"Molly?" Dotty's voice drifted from the phone. "Is something wrong?"

"Your puppy is an ecological menace." Max thrust Ursula toward Molly. Up close, she spied a fine layer of sand coating Max's features—from his stern eyebrows all the way down to his broody, kissable mouth.

Molly's breath caught in her throat. How had she failed to notice that her nemesis had pillowy, Tom Hardy lips? It seemed like a detail worthy of attention.

"Molly! What is going on over there?" her mother said, dragging her back to the very problematic present.

"Everything's fine. Just peachy. See you on Saturday," Molly chirped, and then ended the call without waiting for a goodbye.

Max pulled Ursula back toward him. He arched a single inquisitive eyebrow. "Who was that?"

Molly jammed her hands on her hips. "We might be neighbors, but we're *not* friends. You don't get to ask me questions about my personal life, Wilson."

Max's noteworthy lips quirked into a reluctant grin.

Molly averted her gaze. "Stop it. What could you possibly be smiling about right now?"

"You called me Wilson."

Molly's face went hot. "So?"

Max flashed her a wink. "So, you only call me that when you're not mad at me."

No, Molly only called him that when she realized she was attracted to him. Even then, it was an accident. Obviously.

"Your theory is flawed. I'm furious with you. Can I have my puppy back, please?" Molly reached for Ursula, but Max pulled the puppy closer to his chest.

Ursula snuggled shamelessly against him in an absurd display of misplaced affection. Molly was embarrassed on the dog's behalf. (And not one bit jealous, thank you very much.)

"Not so fast." Max's gaze flitted to the iPhone in Molly's hand. "Who are you going to see on Saturday? A date?"

Laughter bubbled up Molly's throat. *As if.*

Max's jaw clenched. "Molly."

Wait a minute. Why was he going all alpha male on her all of a sudden?

"Max," she said simply, biting back a smile. A shiver ran up her spine and she was suddenly acutely aware of her own heartbeat. It boomed in her ears, drowning out everything else—the wind, the waves…even Ursula's needy little whine.

"I—" Max started to say something, but then just frowned and shook his head. "You're quite impossible, you know?"

Her? *She* was the impossible one?

Molly had a sudden urge to kick water right in his face.

Somehow, she managed to resist. "I'll take my dog back, thank you."

"Your puppy was up by the dunes just now." Max handed the Cavalier over and crossed his arms. Molly could have sworn she saw his biceps flex under the sleeves of his pressed oxford shirt. "*Digging.*"

Molly shrugged. "Newsflash: dogs dig."

Something brushed up against her foot in the water, but when she looked down, all she saw was a flash of green. Seaweed, probably.

"You shouldn't let her dig at the beach. Holes in the sand are a hazard to beachgoers of all species," he said.

Living next door to him was going to be pure joy, wasn't it?

"Look at her." Molly glanced at Ursula in her arms. The puppy was gazing down at the water with her ears swiveled forward on high alert. "She weighs less than seven pounds, and she has the attention span of a gnat. Just how large of a hole do you think she can dig?"

"That's hardly the point."

Molly tilted her head. "Isn't it, though?"

Ursula whined again, and she wiggled in Molly's arms, begging to be set free.

Molly felt a little bit wounded, to be honest. Why was her puppy so crazy about Max? It stung.

"As she grows, so will the size of the trouble she gets into," Max said.

So now he was a dog trainer in addition to being a scientist. Could he be any more infuriating?

"Look, I really don't need you to mansplain puppy behavior to me. I get it. You have a PhD, but that doesn't make you—"

Molly broke off, mid-rant, because Ursula was struggling to get down and Max's attention had strayed elsewhere. He was staring down into the water at Molly's feet, oblivious. Honestly, sometimes he really took the whole hot-but-absentminded-professor thing too far.

"Forget it," she huffed. "We're leaving."

Ursula's whining escalated to a caterwaul that was beyond obnoxious. Was it just not possible for Molly to have a single face-to-face interaction with Max that didn't end in humiliation?

Before she could swish past him in the shallow water, he reached out and took hold of her arm. Annoying little goose-bumps broke out on every inch of Molly's skin.

What was happening? Was he about to confess that he was attracted to her, or did he think that romantic chemistry was "scientifically insignificant"? Probably the latter, especially considering that he still couldn't seem to look her in the eye.

But then Molly followed his gaze and immediately realized why Ursula was going bonkers and Max had stopped chastising her.

She gasped. "Turtle!"

At first glance, Max didn't realize the sea turtle—a green turtle, *Chelonia mydas*—was in trouble. It wasn't unheard of for this specific variety of sea turtle to linger in the shallows during mating season. But the turtle floating at Molly's feet was about the size of a dinner plate, too small to be a mating female. And once Max was able to block out the sound of Ursula's howling and see past her flailing paws, he could see that the juvenile turtle was struggling to swim properly. Only one of her front flippers was moving, and she was drifting in slow, laborious circles.

"There's a fish hook in her left flipper!" Molly pointed toward the water.

Max bent over, hands on his knees, for a closer look. Molly was right—and the hook was large, probably from a commercial fishing boat.

"Good eye," Max said as he shifted to stand upright.

Molly glanced at him, surprise splashing across her face. "Thank you."

Max wanted to say something, anything, to convince her that he wasn't, in fact, *all* bad. But now wasn't the time.

"We need to get her to the turtle hospital and get that thing out of her flipper." He tugged off his necktie, shoved it in his pants pocket, and moved to unbutton his dress shirt.

Molly's gaze dropped to his fingertips as he fumbled with the third button. "And you, um, need to get undressed to do that?"

The look on her face reminded Max of how he felt every time he'd seen her in her clamshell bustier. He bit back a smile. After all, turnabout was fair play.

"We need to keep her as wet as possible en route to the

aquarium." Max shrugged the rest of the way out of his oxford and offered it to Molly. "Can you dunk this in the water and wrap it around her shell after I pick her up?"

"Of course." Molly dragged her attention away from his bare chest and took the shirt from his hands. Her face was almost as red as the lobster costume Ursula sometimes wore.

After Max carefully hauled the turtle out of the water, she released her hold on Ursula. The puppy yipped and pranced in wet circles around them as Molly doused his shirt and carefully spread it over the sea turtle like a drippy, wet blanket.

Everything that followed—the mad dash across the sand toward Max's Jeep, loading and unloading the sea turtle until she was safely placed on an exam table at the sea turtle hospital, gathering the necessary instruments to remove the hook—felt like a perfectly choreographed dance. They barely spoke. There was no need—they each knew what to do and fell in step, working together side-by-side, as if they'd done so countless times before.

Max cut the hook in half with wire cutters while Molly held the turtle still. Ursula had come along for the ride, of course, but she remained blessedly quiet. The puppy planted herself at Molly's feet, watching everything that transpired with her ridiculously huge melted-chocolate eyes. After they moved the sea turtle to her own private tub, Ursula finally left Molly's side and curled up by the tank and fell asleep, her tiny chest rising and falling in a drowsy rhythm.

Max pulled off his blue surgical gloves and shook his head. "That is one strange dog."

Molly tucked a pink lock of hair behind her ear. "You mean you consider her a dog now instead of an ecological menace?"

Now that the urgency of the past hour was behind them, Max became acutely aware of just how green Molly's eyes were, and how looking directly into them made him feel like he was drowning all over again—panicked...lost...but determined to live life to the fullest if he managed to survive. "What if we forget about that for now and agree to a truce?"

"A truce?" She let out a laugh that seemed to reach deep into Max's gut and warm him from the inside out.

A truce? What was he thinking?

"Just a temporary one, of course," he said before he could stop himself.

"Of course," she echoed, and this time when she smiled at him, it didn't quite reach her eyes.

Max wanted to reel those last words back in, but it was too late. He raked a hand through his hair, then continued straightening up the surgical area, moving as slowly as possible to buy some time. The silence grew thick between them, weighed down with the things neither of them would say out loud.

The strap of Molly's retro cherry-print swimsuit slipped off of her shoulder. Her cheeks blazed pink as she pulled it back in place.

"It was my parents," she said softly—so softly that Max almost didn't hear her at first. "On the phone earlier. You asked me if I was going on a date this weekend, remember?"

Oh he remembered, all right. The thought of it had made him want to do something utterly stupid, like sweeping her off her feet and carrying her away as if they were in one of the sailor-meets-mermaid watercolor paintings that were always so popular in the art gallery on the Turtle Beach boardwalk. Or worse, cupping her beautiful face and kissing her, right then and there. She would've tasted like sea spray and sunshine, and they would've kissed until the waves threatened to drag them out to sea…

Or until Ursula wormed her way between them, whichever came first.

"Ah." Max nodded. "So they're coming to the island for SandFest?"

"Indeed they are." Molly sighed.

Max sensed there was more to the story. She definitely didn't seem thrilled at the prospect of seeing her family, but he wasn't ready to switch gears quite yet.

"I've heard SandFest is really something." He took a tentative step closer to Molly and felt his mouth hitch into a grin when she didn't back away. On the contrary, she seemed to lean slightly toward him, a cherry pie dream with tousled mermaid hair and sun-kissed skin. "I don't have a date for it either."

Her gaze flicked to his shirtless torso again, traveling over him like a caress. "That's too bad."

The air between them crackled with electricity. Molly licked her lips, and Max suddenly couldn't look away from her perfect pink mouth.

"Unless…" He reached for her fingertips and wove them loosely through his.

Molly's breath hitched, and Max could see the boom of her pulse in the lovely dip between her collar bones. She snuck a glance at him through the thick fringe of her eyelashes. "Unless?"

Max squeezed her hand tight. *Unless we go together—you and me.* He tugged her closer and lowered his head toward hers, until he was whispering against her bow-shaped lips, just a kiss away. "I think we should—"

The door flung open, and suddenly Nate was there, standing between two turtle tubs, gawking at them. "Dude."

Molly jerked her hand away from Max's and crossed her arms. "Nate. Hi."

"Molly! Sorry, I'm just so surprised to see you here. I stopped by to check on Silver." Nate's face spread into a wide grin. "This is so awesome. I guess this means you're back working at the aquarium."

"Oh, well—" Molly said.

At the same time, Max shook his head. "No."

Nate frowned, glancing back and forth between them. "No?"

How could such a basic question seem so loaded? And why did Max's simple *no* suddenly seem like the worst possible answer he could have given?

Molly glanced at him through a veil of unshed tears and looked away. A moment ago, he'd been on the verge of asking her on a date—of *kissing* her—and now Molly wouldn't even look him in the eye.

"You heard Dr. Miller," she said crisply. *Dr. Miller?* Ouch. "Absolutely not."

"We found an injured green turtle on the beach. Molly and I rescued her." Max nodded toward the tank where the turtle swam in happy circles.

"And now she's right as rain, so I should really be going."

Molly brushed past him to gather Ursula into her arms. The sleepy puppy sighed and planted her chin on Molly's shoulder to gaze at Max while she had her back turned to him.

You blew it, genius, Ursula's big brown eyes seemed to say.

Max's stomach hardened. "Aren't you forgetting something? I drove you here. Let me grab my keys and I'll take you and Ursula home."

She couldn't just leave. Max could fix things between them. He *needed* to fix things.

Molly shook her head. "No worries. Nate can give us a ride, can't you, Nate?"

She turned a blinding smile in Nate's direction.

Nate nodded, oblivious. "Sure."

Ursula aimed a pleading look at Max, as if imploring him to do something.

There he went again, anthropomorphizing. Ursula was a dog, not a person, and she certainly had no interest in making sure that Max and Molly went to SandFest together. Max was probably just projecting his own feelings onto Molly's puppy.

He just wished he'd realized how badly he'd wanted the afore-mentioned truce before Molly and Ursula walked out the door.

Chapter 9

MAX WASN'T IN THE mood to go home after Nate left with Molly and Ursula in tow, especially since "home" usually meant sitting on the deck and pretending not to wonder what was going on in the cozy cottage next door.

Molly liked to keep her windows and French doors open so her gauzy curtains danced in the breeze. Max could sometimes hear her television in the evenings. She apparently liked to watch that English baking show everyone was so wild about. Between snippets of conversation about "soggy bottoms" and "saucy puds," he often heard her talking to Ursula, her tone all sweetness and light.

Then he'd open his sliding glass door and step inside his own cottage, with its knotty pine paneling and relics from his childhood, and feel alone in a way he never had back in Baltimore.

Max liked living alone. As an only child, he'd grown accustomed to his own company, particularly after his parents' divorce when he was so often shuttled back and forth between his parents' homes. Around that time—fifth grade—he'd started spending summers on the island with Uncle Henry. Max and Henry both pretended it was in order to avoid an ugly tug of war between his mother and father. Max suspected the truth was quite the opposite—both of his parents seemed too caught up in their new lives to want him around during the summer months. Staying with his uncle at the beach seemed preferable to signing up for summer school just to have a way to pass the time.

He wasn't used to being alone here, though. Not in this house. Not on this island. That's what he told himself, anyway. Because he definitely didn't want to believe his restlessness in the evenings had anything to do with Molly's presence just a stone's throw away. That couldn't be it. In any event, he didn't want to face that kind of emptiness after coming so close to asking Molly out back at the turtle hospital. If Nate hadn't interrupted them, they might have kissed. Max had wanted it so bad he'd nearly tasted it. Molly's lips, bubblegum sweet.

So once he'd checked on the recovering green turtle, whom Molly had begun calling Crush, and Silver the seahorse one last time, Max climbed into the Jeep and drove to the senior center. He'd been on the island for days and still hadn't managed to have a lengthy conversation with his uncle about the aquarium. Their interactions thus far had been limited to yoga classes and bingo, and as far as Max was concerned, there was no time like the present.

It wasn't until Max activated the parking brake in the gravel lot outside the senior center that he realized he still wasn't wearing a shirt. His oxford was currently sitting atop the laundry pile at the turtle hospital, along with a heap of towels that smelled like fish. He probably could have grabbed an aquarium T-shirt from the modest gift shop if he'd thought about it.

Too late now.

No big deal, though. This was a beach town, after all. He'd gotten plenty of ribbing this week about being overdressed. Now, he'd finally fit in. Also Max doubted the retirees would even notice, much less care.

Wrong again.

As fate would have it, Opal, Ethel, and Mavis were sitting in the lobby when Max walked in and they most definitely noticed.

"Good evening, Max." Ethel pushed her purple glasses higher up on the bridge of her nose. "You look…"

"Naked?" Opal suggested.

Ethel shrugged. "I was going to say 'comfortable,' but if the shirt fits…"

"You mean *shoe*." Mavis shook her head.

"No, I mean shirt." Ethel waggled her eyebrows. "Because he's not wearing one."

The three women collapsed into laughter.

Max couldn't help but crack a smile. "I had to give up my shirt for a turtle and I wanted to stop by and see Henry on the way home. I'm going to go see if he's in his room. You ladies try and stay out of trouble, okay?"

Doubtful.

Max held his hand up in a wave and headed toward his uncle's room while the women continued snickering behind his back. He laughed under his breath. Opal, Ethel, and Mavis could be a handful, but they were harmless enough.

The exchange was quickly forgotten, though, when Max knocked on Henry's door and his uncle announced he was on his way out.

"Again?" Max said. "Where to this time?"

"Volleyball league. We have a big game tonight."

It was official: Max's elderly uncle had a more active social life than Max could ever dream of. "You guys have a volleyball league?"

"Every Thursday night." Henry waved toward a wall calendar pinned to his refrigerator door with a magnet shaped like a turtle. Nearly every square was filled with Henry's neat handwriting. "See?"

Max raked a hand through his hair, tugging hard at the ends. "You wouldn't want to skip it just this once, would you? So we can visit?"

"No can do. My team is depending on me, but you're welcome to join us." Henry glanced at Max's torso and frowned. "But only if you put on a shirt so you don't make the rest of us look bad. We're not sixty anymore, you know."

Max's lips twitched. "I'm aware."

Henry grabbed a garish Hawaiian print shirt from his closet that had cartoon sea turtles swimming amongst the hibiscus. "You can borrow this one."

"Thanks." Max slipped it on. The shirt was approximately three sizes too big and looked nothing short of comical paired with his tailored dress pants. He definitely wouldn't be making *anyone* look bad.

"Come on, then." Henry waved Max out to the hallway and clicked the door shut without bothering to lock it.

"So is this beach volleyball or standard court volleyball?" Max asked.

Henry shook his head. "Neither."

What could that possibly mean?

"Intriguing," Max said.

He knew better than to ask questions. His uncle had never been much of a talker, and he wasn't about to waste words on senior volleyball when he had so much other information he wanted to drag out of Henry.

"How are things going at the aquarium?" Henry glanced at him. "Have you figured out the money thing yet?"

Max almost asked if he was joking. How in the world was he supposed to solve the aquarium's financial crisis in just a matter of days? Henry's expression was dead serious, though. And despite the fact that Max had been lured back to Turtle Beach under dubious pretenses, he didn't want to stress Henry out any more than necessary. The older man was already getting winded and they hadn't even reached the end of the hallway.

"Not yet. I'm working on it." Every one of Max's eggs were now in the SandFest basket. A win would only be a temporary fix, but it would help keep the doors open until he could come up with a better plan. "We saved a green sea turtle this evening. It was in the surf right out in front of the house, struggling to swim with a fish hook caught in its fin."

"We?" Henry shot him a sideways glance.

"Molly was out on the beach when it happened." Max cleared his throat. "Her little dog too."

"And Molly helped you, didn't she, even after you fired them both?" Henry shook his head.

This again? If anyone should have been able to understand

Max's actions, it was his uncle. "For the last time, I didn't fire a puppy. You can't fire a person, much less an animal, who's not even on the payroll."

Henry came to a stop outside the senior center's gymnasium. "Molly's a special girl, and her dog is pretty special too. You might want to reconsider."

"I'll keep that in mind, but things have gotten rather—" Max looked away. More seniors filed past them as they lingered outside the gym. "—complicated."

"You'll figure things out." Henry shrugged and charged through the door.

Wait. That was it? No words of wisdom or secret insights into how he'd managed to keep the aquarium up and running all this time?

Max joined his uncle on the far side of a volleyball net that had been strung across the middle of the gym. "Maybe we could figure things out together."

"Enough about the aquarium." Henry plopped into an empty wheelchair and pointed to another available one, right beside him. "Sit."

Max looked at the chair and then back at his uncle. "But I don't need a wheelchair. Shouldn't I save that for someone who actually nee—"

He was cut off when something soft and squishy hit him in the face.

Max staggered backward and fell into the wheelchair. It rolled a few feet until he crashed into one of the posts holding up the volleyball net.

"Interference!" someone yelled.

A whistle blew, and Max looked up to see a woman looming over him with her hands on her hips. She wore a name tag that said BARBARA WALLACE, ACTIVITY DIRECTOR on it in large-print lettering, and she had a red balloon tucked under each arm.

"You just fouled," she said. "Two more of those, and you're out."

A balloon whizzed past Max's head. "I thought we were playing volleyball."

"You are. Wheelchair balloon volleyball—five balloons in play at all times and none of them can touch the ground." Barbara winked, threw a balloon in the air and lobbed it toward him. "Try to keep up."

Max punched the balloon. It clipped the net before barely crossing to the other side. Wheelchairs crashed into one another like bumper cars, rubber tires squeaking against the gym floor. Balloons bobbed anywhere and everywhere.

Try to keep up.

Like everything else in Max's new life, that might be easier said than done.

———

Molly managed to avoid Max for the following two days—not an easy task, considering he'd invaded her happy little corner of the island by moving in next door. She took Ursula out to play on the beach only when the Jeep was absent from his driveway. Luckily, she could hear Max riding the clutch from a mile away, so she usually had time to get inside before he pulled up to Henry's home.

Although it wasn't Henry's home anymore. It officially belonged to Max now. He owned it, unlike Molly, who was practically a squatter in a beach house that still very much belonged to her clueless parents.

Not clueless for long.

SandFest started tomorrow. Tourists had been flocking to the island all morning, and Molly was so busy making coffee drinks that she'd barely had time to think about the fact that she'd almost kissed her nemesis.

Emphasis on *almost.* Thank goodness Nate had stopped by for a prenatal seahorse visit and interrupted whatever terrible mistake she'd nearly made.

Molly flipped the lever for the frother on the espresso machine with a tad bit too much force. She wasn't sure why she was still so angry at Max for his hasty denial when Nate had asked if she was back working at the aquarium. Maybe it was the looming sense of dread surrounding the impending arrival of her mom and dad. Or maybe being back at the turtle hospital had simply made her realize how much she missed her coveted mermaid gig. Who knew, really? But the second Max had answered Nate's question with a firm *no*, something snapped inside her.

Molly had instantly been plunged straight back into reality instead of whatever hazy dream state she'd been lulled into by Max's lopsided grin and the thrill of their turtle rescue. She'd somehow let herself get charmed into *holding hands* with the man who'd fired her twice and wanted to tell her how to raise her puppy. She'd been temporarily blinded by the gentle way he'd treated the injured turtle, and yes, she might have been a tad bit distracted by his bare chest. At least she knew how he'd gotten in such great shape now—by carrying large ocean animals to and fro. Mystery solved.

Milk overflowed from the frother, and Molly jumped back to avoid getting burned.

"Everything okay over there?" Caroline called from the book section of the shop.

"I've got things completely under control," Molly said, flipping various levers and knobs until the machine finally stopped hissing.

"Clearly," her customer, a young mom pushing a jogging stroller, said as milk dripped from the counter onto the floor.

Ursula scrambled to lick up the puddle, proving once again that her work ethic was impeccable. Max Miller wouldn't know a good employee if one kissed him right on the lips.

Molly let out a little cough. *Bad example.*

She finished mixing the drink, poured it into a to-go cup and handed the messily crafted beverage to the customer. She eyed it dubiously and then headed outside to the boardwalk.

Molly took a deep breath. The morning at Turtle Books had been nuts so far, especially since the boardwalk was positioned so close to the bridge connecting the island to the mainland. Things couldn't get much crazier.

At least that's what she thought until the bells on the door jangled, announcing the arrival of a new customer, and Molly glanced up to see Max strolling into the bookshop.

No!

Molly wasn't ready to see him again—not here and *definitely* not now, when she was dressed in a frilly apron and would be forced to smile politely at him while she whipped up whatever coffee drink he demanded, as if she were Suzy Freaking Homemaker. Panic clogged her throat, and she ducked behind the counter, out of sight.

Maybe he'd come for reading material instead of coffee and Molly could somehow slink away without him seeing her. Max was definitely the bookish type. But no, of course she wasn't going to get off that easy. Ursula bounded toward the sound of the welcome bells. Seconds later, while Molly sat crouched on the floor with her eyes squeezed shut, Max loomed above her, clearing his throat.

Molly opened her eyes. Sure enough, there was Max's reflection in the shiny chrome surface of the espresso machine. Ursula, the little traitor, was cuddled in the crook of his elbow. Neither of them appeared to be going anywhere anytime soon.

Molly stood, smoothed down her apron, and pasted a smile on her face. "Hello. Welcome to Turtle Books. How can I help you?"

"Molly?" Max peered over the counter before meeting her gaze. "Were you hiding from me down there just now?"

"Don't be ridiculous." She couldn't seem to stop swallowing. Or looking at Max's mouth and remembering the thrill that had coursed through her when she thought he was going to kiss her.

Stop looking at his mouth!

It was smirking, that lovely mouth of his. He knew she'd crouched out of sight. He'd probably been able to see her reflection in the stupid coffee maker the entire time.

"Hiding? As if." Molly feigned nonchalance as best she could. "I lost something down there, that's all."

My dignity, mainly.

Max's eyes glittered. His gorgeous, gorgeous eyes. "Did you find it?"

Not even close.

"Never mind all that." She waved a hand at Ursula, still nestled in his arms. "You don't have to pretend to like my dog. She's an excellent judge of character. I'm sure she knows exactly how you feel about her."

As if on cue, Ursula licked the side of Max's neck, tucked her head beneath his chin and let out a dreamy sigh.

Max shot Molly a look that said *see?* "I think you might be right. She *is* an excellent judge of character."

Clearly Ursula was suffering from Stockholm syndrome. She'd gone and developed feelings for her oppressor. Molly wondered if there was a doggy therapist somewhere on the island. Doubtful, given the fact that they didn't even have a Walmart.

Molly glared at Max. "What are you doing here?"

Couldn't he simply place his order and go away, already?

Max frowned at the ruffles on her apron. "You work here now? That explains a few things."

"Such as?"

"Your elderly friends have been trying to get me to come here for days." Max leaned closer and lowered his voice. Molly resisted the nonsensical urge to pull an Ursula and lick his neck. "Something tells me they think you and I might be attracted to each other."

"They're pushing ninety," Molly said flatly.

"They're mistaken, then," Max said.

"*So* mistaken." Molly's stomach flipped. She'd always been a terrible liar.

"Agreed." Max's jaw clenched. He wasn't the greatest liar himself, apparently.

She squared her shoulders. "What was it you wanted to order, again?"

Max bent to deposit Ursula onto the floor—*finally*—and the puppy trotted behind the counter and plopped down on the toe of Molly's ballerina flat.

He stood and crossed his arms. "A frozen Milky Way latte, but don't worry about it if it's too much trouble."

"No trouble at all. It's my job now, remember?" She reached into the red and white retro-style refrigerator for the carton of milk and chocolate syrup.

Max looked at her for a long moment while she blended the ingredients for his drink. The laugh lines around his eyes disappeared, and he suddenly looked bone-tired. "Just so you know, I didn't mean to hurt your feelings when I told Nate you weren't back working at the aquarium. He caught me by surprise, and I—"

"Please stop," Molly said. Did they really need to talk about what happened? The last thing she wanted to do was re-live it. "Of course you didn't hurt my feelings. We decided that working together would be a disaster, remember?"

Technically, *he* had decided that. But still.

"You don't still believe that," Max said, and the earnestness in his tone was just too much for her to take. It made her want things—things she'd given up on after The Tourist.

And how was Max any different from Molly's recent disaster of a boyfriend? He'd swooped onto the island as if he belonged there, but what did Molly *really* know about him? Just because her puppy loved him, he had a way with sea turtles, and he did yoga with senior citizens didn't mean he was a good person.

Although now that she thought about it, those were just the sort of qualities that did indeed make someone a catch. No wonder she'd wanted to kiss him.

Not anymore, though. They'd had a moment, and that moment had passed. Period.

"Nothing's changed. I love it here. I have zero desire to work with you—ever." She gave him a tight smile and turned on the blender so whatever he said next would be drowned out.

It churned to life just as he tried to speak. Stubborn as ever, he commenced with yelling over the racket.

Molly had stopped listening altogether, though. Max's voice was nothing but a dull roar, because just over his shoulder, Molly could see a couple of new customers headed toward the bookshop. It was a middle-aged couple wearing matching beachy linen pants with pastel-colored sweaters tied around their necks, like they'd just stepped out of the pages of an L.L.Bean catalog. Harmless as could be…

Or not.

Molly's legs turned to water. Ursula paced in circles and whined, clearly attuned to her sudden state of panic. She swallowed hard.

Mom and Dad.

Chapter 10

WHAT WERE HER PARENTS doing on the island? They weren't due to arrive until tomorrow morning.

Tomorrow, when Molly could break the news about her mermaid job over pancakes and sand castles. Not while standing behind the counter at Turtle Books, making coffee for the man who'd let her go from the aquarium.

It couldn't happen this way. It just couldn't. She wasn't ready. News like this needed finessing.

Molly's gaze flew to Max. "Would you *please* stop talking?"

Miraculously, it worked. He closed his mouth and rolled his eyes. Not ideal behavior, obviously, but it was definitely preferable to her mom and dad finding her working as an argumentative barista when they thought she'd given up a chance at grad school or regular teacher employment to be a mermaid.

She was twenty-seven years old. Being this concerned about her parents' approval was humiliating—almost as humiliating as continually embarrassing herself in front of Max, but not quite. At least Max couldn't evict her from her beach cottage. His ability to throw her life into total disarray only extended so far.

Molly yanked at her apron strings, pulled the telltale garment over her head and stuffed it on the shelf beneath the cash register while simultaneously scurrying out from behind the counter to stand beside Max.

He frowned down at her. "What's happening right now? Where's my dr—"

"I said stop talking," Molly hissed. This was going to end in disaster. She could feel it.

But then the bells on the front door chimed and her parents walked inside the bookshop. *No turning back.*

Her mom spotted her in an instant.

"Molly!" She clutched onto Dad's arm. "Look, hon, Molly's here."

"Um, I think maybe it's time to—" Max pointed at the blender, still whirring away.

"Shhh." Molly grabbed his pointer finger, jerked his hand down and held it in place. Honestly, what about *stop talking* did he not understand?

Ursula made a beeline for Mom and Dad, doing her trademark full-body wiggle that the aquarium visitors had always adored. Her father, not so much. His footsteps slowed and his body stiffened as he prepared for the puppy's exuberant greeting.

"It's okay, Dad. Ursula is a total angel," Molly said.

"*Total?*" Max snorted. "Not quite."

Molly squeezed his hand until his eyes began to bulge.

"She does seem sweet," Mom said, crouching down to pet Ursula with hesitant strokes.

Dad held up his hands. "I'm allergic."

"Actually, you're not, Dad. Dr. Larson said the only things you're allergic to are grass and kiwis, remember?" Molly gritted her teeth. The last thing she wanted to do was antagonize her father before they even got to the job discussion, but her feelings were already hurt on Ursula's behalf. "If you'd just give her a chance, you'd see that she's a very nice dog."

Her father shoved his hands in his pockets and ignored Ursula's overtures. "I'll take your word for it. I'm starting to feel sniffly."

Well, this was going great so far, wasn't it?

Her mother stood, and like a heat-seeking missile, her gaze went straight to Molly's fingertips, intertwined with Max's.

Weird. Why was that still happening? She ordered her hand to let go, but it stubbornly refused.

Mom's hand fluttered to her throat. "My goodness, Molly. Who's your friend?"

"He's not my—"

"Max Miller." Max tugged his hand free and offered it to Molly's parents for a shake. "You must be Molly's folks."

Folks?

She gaped at him. Since when did Mr. Scientist use cute words like that? And why did he seem so eager to meet her parents after she'd made it clear multiple times that he was her mortal enemy?

"Dotty Prince." Her mother grinned as she shook Max's hand. "Your name sounds awfully familiar, and I think I've seen your face somewhere before too."

Molly's dad sidestepped Ursula to greet Max. "Hello, there. Dr. Stan Prince."

"Oh! Now I know why I recognize you!" Mom clapped her

hands. "Your photo was in the paper last week, Max. You're the new director of the aquarium."

The bottom dropped out of Molly's stomach. This entire encounter was getting worse by the second. She really needed to somehow cancel her parents' subscription to the *Turtle Daily*. Either that or stop living a life of subterfuge.

Dad cocked his head. "So you two are an item...and you work together."

"Ahh..." Max glanced at Molly.

She stared daggers at him. *Don't you dare tell them I'm an unemployed mermaid.*

Ursula's back end started wiggling again, signaling the arrival of yet another person on the scene—Caroline, who came bustling toward the shop entrance from the back storage area, juggling a stack of children's picture books in her hands.

"What in the world is going on up here? Why is the blender still going?" Caroline straightened the books and finally looked up. "Oh, hi, Dr. and Mrs. Prince."

"My parents are here early." Molly forced a smile. "Isn't that great?"

Caroline took in Max's presence, the absence of Molly's apron, and cleared her throat. "Super great. And Max is here too. This is all just...great."

"Why *is* the blender whirring away like that?" Molly's dad crossed his arms.

Caroline darted behind the counter to turn it off, causing an avalanche of children's literature in the process. Ursula yipped and darted behind Molly to avoid being conked on the head with *Tale of a Turtle*.

Molly and Max immediately bent to gather the books, nearly bumping heads in the process.

"We were just stopping in for a coffee on our way to check into our rental, but things seem a little chaotic around here," Mom said.

"Sorry, the new girl I hired seems to have vanished into thin air." Caroline gave Molly a strained smile.

Dad harrumphed. "Maybe we should go."

"That might be a good idea." Molly nodded. *Please, please go.* "Things are indeed crazy around here. You know how the island gets during SandFest weekend. Why don't you guys get checked in and we can catch up in a bit for lunch?"

Mom's eyebrows squished together. "But won't you two be busy at the aquarium this afternoon?"

Where to start?

First of all, who said anything about Max tagging along? Couldn't she accidentally hold hands with a man without him automatically being invited to lunch with her parents?

Also, *of course* she wouldn't be busy at the aquarium since she didn't actually work there anymore.

"Um." Molly's head spun. She was going to have to confess to losing her job right here in front of Max. Perfect, just perfect.

"Molly?" her mother prompted.

Was it Molly's imagination, or did her mom's gaze flit to her torso as if wondering why she didn't currently have two clamshells and a green sequined tail covering her lady bits?

"We'd love to have lunch," she heard Max say. "Don't you two worry about the aquarium."

Her mother beamed. "Excellent."

What. Was. Happening.

"How about that nice place on the bay? The one with the grilled lobster?" Dad said, finally perking up now that a fancy meal might be on the table.

"Sounds great. I'll make a reservation. We can sit outside on the deck," Molly said. *Now please go.* Her face was already hurting from all the pretend smiling.

"See you soon." Mom gave them a wave as Dad ushered her out the door and onto the boardwalk.

Caroline turned toward Molly. It was only then that she realized Max had taken hold of her hand again. "I'm not even going to ask what that was all about."

Good, because Molly was fresh out of answers.

Molly handed Max his frozen Milky Way latte—which, after the excessive blending, was no longer frozen and bore no resemblance to a latte. At this point, he really could have passed.

She jammed her hands on her hips. "For someone who doesn't like holes, you just dug yourself an awfully deep one, Wilson."

Wilson. Her use of his erstwhile nickname made Max's heart squeeze, despite the frown on her face.

"Me?" He sucked at his purple jumbo straw. It was like drinking the melted dregs at the bottom of a carton of ice cream that had been sitting out in the sun all day. "If anyone is digging holes for themself it's you. Actually, you made hole-digging look like an Olympic sport just now."

Max had been astounded. And far more intrigued than he wanted to admit.

Molly lifted her chin. Blonde waves, kissed with the barest hints of pink, tumbled down her back. Max wanted to bury his face in her loose curls and take a deep inhale. Those beachy waves would smell of sea air and cotton candy. He just knew it. "Perhaps, but I have my reasons."

A small group of customers walked into the shop, and Molly greeted them as they made their way toward the book section.

"And what might those reasons be?" Max said quietly. To his surprise, he genuinely wanted to know.

All his adult life, the women he'd dated had complained about the same thing—he was too absorbed in his work to care about anything else. Too analytical, too logical.

The accusations weren't without merit. Max liked things to be a certain orderly, predictable way. And he had no interest in meaningless frivolity—great for his career and field of study for a time, but it didn't make him the most desirable social companion. Max knew this about himself.

But Molly was like a puzzle he couldn't figure out. And damned if he wasn't beginning to enjoy poring over the pieces.

"Things with my parents are a little touchy, that's all," Molly said, slipping her apron back on and tying it at her waist with a jaunty bow.

"And yet the reason you want to have lunch at a restaurant with an outdoor seating area is so you can bring this little monster, isn't it?" He cast a pointed glance at Ursula, sitting at his feet with one paw placed gently on the tip of his dress shoes. "Even though your dad clearly isn't fond of dogs."

"She has to come along. I'm her emotional support human." Molly squirted way too much dishwashing liquid into the blender and flipped on the faucet. Bubbles rose to comical heights in the sink. "I told you that already."

"Yes, you did," Max said, but he had a sneaking suspicion it was the other way around. Molly *needed* Ursula. He only wished he knew why.

Among other things that intrigued him about the mermaid next door.

As ever, Molly was tight-lipped on the matter. She scrubbed aggressively at the blender while soap suds wafted all around her. Ursula darted behind the counter to snap at the bubbles.

"I should go." Max had a million things to do at the aquarium if he was going to take off for the afternoon, most notably checking on Crush and Silver. He reached into his pocket for his wallet and placed a ten-dollar bill and one of his business cards with his cell phone number listed on it on the counter. "Just text me and let me know what time to pick you up for lunch."

He headed for the door.

"Wait a minute," Molly called after him.

Max turned and arched a brow. "Yes?"

She batted away at the soap bubbles floating in front of her face. "You're not actually *going*."

Max shrugged. "Of course I am. I told your parents I would be there. It would be rude not to show up."

"Max, you cannot come out to lunch with me and my family. You just can't. Do you want them to think we're a couple?" She laughed as if it was the most preposterous idea she'd ever heard.

Max felt his jaw clench. "They already do. Do you really want to have to explain that we're not, on top of everything else?"

From what he could tell, Molly hadn't told her mom and dad she'd lost her job or that she now worked at Turtle Books. It had also appeared as if Ursula's very existence had caught them somewhat off guard, not to mention the puppy's place of prominence in their daughter's life. There were more lies floating around this place than there were soapsuds.

"Of course I don't." Molly let her gaze linger on his dress shirt and his glasses before flitting to his business card. His name was styled in classic black typeface—Dr. Max Miller. "Believe me, you would be my parents' dream boyfriend."

But not yours. Message received.

"It's one lunch. Consider it my penance for firing you." His lips twitched into a grin. "Twice."

"Aha! So you admit you basically fired me twice. I knew it." Molly's eyes sparkled.

Max shrugged. He didn't quite trust himself to say anything else. He'd already gone against every shred of common sense he possessed and committed to what was sure to be the most awkward lunch in the history of oceanfront dining. He didn't want to know what might come next.

"Okay, then. You can come," she said, as if she were doing him a favor instead of the other way around.

"It's a date." Max winked, just to see if he could make her blush.

Sure enough, her porcelain face went as pink as the mermaid highlights in her hair. "You mean a fake date."

Did he, though?

Did either of them?

———

Later that afternoon, Molly sat on the bayside dock of The Windjammer, Turtle Beach's one and only fine dining establishment. Much to her father's mortification, she'd indeed brought Ursula along. The little dog was currently sitting in Max's lap, happy as a clam, with her ears ruffled by the breeze coming off the water.

Anyone looking on would have assumed that Max was Molly's boyfriend, given the way he'd escorted her to the table with his hand on the small of her back and was now making casual conversation with her parents while her dog kept trying to sneak bites of his shrimp scampi. But that was pretty much the whole point of this train wreck of a lunch date, wasn't it? To make her mom and dad think they were an item?

What were they *doing*? This had never been part of the plan. Molly was supposed to be coming clean with her mom and dad, not letting them fall in love with her fake boyfriend. Once her mom had jumped to the wrong conclusion, it had just been so tempting to pretend it was true—especially after Max started playing along.

But now that it was happening, now that Max was charming the socks off of her family and keeping mum about the mermaid-less state of the aquarium, Molly just couldn't do it. She couldn't tell her parents the truth in front of him. It would have been far too humiliating, particularly since he was doing such an outstanding job of pretending to care about her.

"So you really saved Max's life, sweetheart?" Mom pressed a hand to her chest. "We just assumed you'd met at the aquarium. Never in a million years would we have guessed that you'd resuscitated him."

"You might say she brought me back from the dead." Max flashed Molly a wink.

She took a generous gulp of her chardonnay. "You're exaggerating, darling. There was no resuscitation necessary."

Definitely not. If Molly had locked lips with him in any way, shape, or form, she'd remember. She was having trouble catching her breath just imagining it.

Fake. She clutched her wine glass like it was a life preserver. *This is all fake.*

"Why is this the first we're hearing about Max's dramatic rescue?" Molly's dad asked as he cracked open a lobster claw.

Ursula cocked her head.

"I guess it just hasn't come up," Molly said. Too bad their meet cute hadn't been on the front page of the *Turtle Daily.* If so, her parents would have known all about it. "I don't think the current would have gotten him, though. Max is surprisingly strong. You should see him lift a sea turtle."

Max laughed, and the sound of it sent a shiver coursing through her. She needed to somehow steer the discussion in a less dangerous direction.

"How are things at the aquarium?" Dad dipped a forkful of lobster meat into the tiny pot of butter that sat over the flame of a votive candle next to his plate. "The last time Molly talked to us about it, she was working on ideas for fundraising."

Also dangerous. This entire meal was a conversational minefield.

Molly started talking before Max could cut in and announce that he'd already made budget cuts roughly equal to a mermaid's salary. "We haven't implemented any of them yet, but I have a spreadsheet full of ideas on my laptop at home."

Max let out a cough. "You do?"

"Of course I do, darling." Molly turned toward her mom and dad. "Max is still new at the aquarium, obviously. He's been busy getting up to speed so we haven't had a chance to chat about it yet."

Mainly because he eliminated my position before I had a chance to get a word in edgewise. Molly swallowed. She'd also engaged in a rather aggressive cupcake and bingo campaign, so perhaps she was a tiny bit to blame.

"No time like the present." Max's eyes met Molly's a beat too long for two people who were only pretending to like each other. "Tell me your ideas."

Her mouth went dry. They were really going to do this… here? *Now?*

"Well, for starters, I was thinking we could hold a fancy ball similar to the one the fire department has every year on the Fourth of July—only for ours, we would sell tickets to the public. Turtle Beach doesn't have any sort of black-tie event. I'm sure the senior center would let us use their lobby free of charge, or maybe even their gym."

Max quirked an eyebrow. "I'm familiar with the gym. Unfortunately, I can't imagine people paying good money to dance there in tuxedos and ball gowns."

Of course he couldn't. The man had no imagination or sense of whimsy.

"They would after the Turtle Team and I got finished with it. We could do an Under the Sea theme with blue and green lighting, transparent balloons hanging from the ceiling to look like ocean bubbles, and jellyfish chandeliers. I actually have a mood board on Pinterest with decoration ideas. It would be beautiful." She swallowed, feeling acutely vulnerable all of a sudden. "Romantic, even."

She waited half a beat for Max to agree—an excruciatingly silent moment when the scrape of her parents' silverware against their plates seemed louder than the ocean itself.

"I have other ideas, obviously," Molly said, rushing to fill the silence, in case Max misinterpreted her comment about romance. She'd been speaking in general terms, not about *them*. At least she thought she had. "There's also a grant application I've been working on."

Ugh, she was starting to feel like she was at a job interview… for a position that no longer existed, with the added awkwardness of her parents along for the ride.

"A grant?" Max's forehead creased, surprise etching his features. "Really?"

Molly stabbed at the food on her plate with her fork. Did he have to act so surprised? Again, she wasn't an *actual* cartoon mermaid. "Yes. Really."

At long last, her father chimed in. "You might want to let Max handle that, sweetheart. A grant application would have a much better chance if it came from someone with the letters

PhD after their name." He turned toward Max. "Isn't that right, Dr. Miller?"

Molly's dad laughed—not just a chuckle, either, but a deep belly laugh that had the flame on his votive candle doing a fiery little dance. Her mother tittered and aimed a look in Molly's direction that seemed to say *he's got a point, honey.*

Embarrassment blossomed in Molly's chest. She felt like she might cry all of a sudden. Why had she agreed to let Max come along on this latest exercise in humiliation? She should have known her father would go there. He didn't miss a single chance to try to get her to go back to school and follow in his footsteps.

Ursula hopped out of Max's lap and leapt into Molly's, a bundle of warm fur and unconditional love. Somehow Molly resisted the urge to bury her face in the puppy's soft neck. She didn't dare look at Max. If he so much as snickered, she was going to put an end to this farce and leave. The truth was going to come out eventually.

"Actually, I'm not sure I agree," Max said quietly. "Molly knows a lot about the aquarium."

Molly almost fell out of her chair. No one contradicted her father—certainly not on matters of academia.

Her dad sat back in his chair and blinked a few times. "Oh, of course she does. Molly has always been a bright girl, which is just one of the reasons why we've been encouraging her to recommit to her schooling and earn a higher degree. She can't be a mermaid forever." Dad smiled at her. "Right, sweetheart?"

Beneath the table, Max's warm hand covered hers. Molly snuck a glance at him and he squeezed her fingertips tight. A lump lodged in her throat, preventing her from answering her father's question, which was well enough, because what could she possibly say?

Her dad was right. She couldn't be a mermaid forever. She wasn't even one now.

"So how long will you two be on the island?" Max asked, deftly putting an end to talk of Molly's job. Or lack thereof.

Seagulls swooped overhead and water lapped gently against the side of the deck as the conversation moved on to more benign topics, like SandFest and the weekend's weather forecast.

Stormy, with a one hundred percent chance of awkwardness.

And somehow, Max had become her unlikely shelter from the downpour.

Chapter 11

THE FOLLOWING MORNING, MAX showed up at the Salty Dog pier bright and early, as per his Uncle Henry's instructions.

Given a choice, he would have chosen somewhere more private to share a meal with his uncle and talk about the aquarium, but after a full week on the island, Max had grown tired of waiting for the perfect time and place for a heart-to-heart. If Henry wanted to chat over sunrise pancakes during Turtle Beach's most crowded weekend, then so be it. Max was prepared.

He parked the Jeep in the Salty Dog's oyster shell parking lot, tucked the aquarium's financial ledgers for the last three years under his arm, and headed toward the worn metal gate that led to the pier. Weathered shells crunched under his feet, and in the distance, he could see seagulls diving for fish in the ocean. Waves tumbled onto the shore as the rising sun cast fiery light over the water. The breeze was fresh with the briny scents of Max's childhood—salt and surf. Wet grass and driftwood. Sun-bleached seashells and fine, sugary sand.

The one thing Max *didn't* smell was pancakes. When he reached the top of the wooden steps that led to the pier, he immediately knew why.

"Morning!" Uncle Henry grinned as he walked past Max

carrying a jumbo-sized container of pancake mix. "You made it, good, we could really use the help."

Max looked around. Two parallel rows of long picnic tables stretched all the way to the end of the pier, covered in plastic tablecloths with a sandcastle print. Volunteers who Max recognized as residents of the senior center were busy anchoring the table coverings down with conch shells to prevent them being carried away by the brisk sea wind.

Uncle Henry, Hoyt Hooper, and a man in a cardigan who Max was pretty certain was Mavis Hubbard's boyfriend stood behind a massive grill near the pier's tackle shop and convenience store. All three men wielded spatulas and wore matching aprons with *I Pancake My Eyes Off You* splashed across the front.

Max had been duped. Again. "Let me guess. We're not here to eat breakfast together, are we?"

Henry's brow furrowed as he handed Max an apron of his own. "Did I say that?"

Yes. Yes, he had. But Max didn't bother arguing. He just took the apron, pulled it over his head, and tied it in place.

"You know, if you don't want to talk about the aquarium, you could just say so," Max said. He dumped the financial ledgers onto a nearby beach chair. Why did he bother to keep dragging those things around?

"I'm not saying I don't ever want to talk about it." Henry shrugged. "Although Opal Lewinsky assures me the aquarium will be just fine."

And how exactly would Opal know about Max's operating budget?

Max raked a hand through his hair and forbade himself from asking questions that surely had nonsensical answers.

"We can chat about the aquarium when the time is right," Henry said as he poured an entire gallon of buttermilk into a mixing bowl.

Alarm bells started ringing in Max's head. Just how many pancakes was he expected to make?

"I'm assuming that now isn't the right time," Max said.

"Nope." Henry grinned wide and handed Max a wooden spoon. "Now is the time for pancakes."

Truer words had never been spoken. For the next several hours, Max, Henry, and Mavis's boyfriend—who Max learned was named Larry—mixed up batch after batch for the tourists and locals who poured onto the pier. Down on the beach, sand sculptures went from modest piles of sand to elaborately crafted pieces of art as the teams in the SandFest competition got busy. In order to qualify for judging, the entries had to be completed no later than noon.

Max had planned on having an early morning breakfast with his uncle and then doing what he could to help the Turtle Team and the college kids they'd enlisted to build their entry for the competition. Not that Max knew the first thing about building a sand sculpture, outside of the drip castles he'd made with his uncle during his childhood summers on the island. But it seemed like a big job to leave completely to volunteers, especially with ten thousand dollars in prize money riding on the results.

Too late now. It was midmorning, the sky shone high in the sky, and Max felt like he was sweating maple syrup.

"Thank you," a beachgoer in a bikini said as Max piled her plate with a stack of silver dollar pancakes.

"You're welcome. Enjoy SandFest." Max turned his attention back to the grill where bubbles were already beginning to form around the edges of his next batch.

The woman's coquettish smile grew as she lingered in front of Max's station.

He glanced up. "Can I get you something else?"

She answered with a giggle. "No, I just had to see the real thing for myself."

"Oh." Max's gaze swept the crowded pier. The pancake breakfast was definitely a see-it-to-believe-it sort of affair. "Yeah, this is really something, isn't it?"

"It sure is." She glanced pointedly at his chest and licked her lips.

A ribbon of smoke drifted up from the griddle. Great. Max's six hundredth pancake was burning.

"Well, you have a nice day," Max said, prompting her to move on with a wave of his spatula.

He scooped the blackened lump of batter from his griddle and tossed it into a metal trash can behind him. When Max turned back around, he found Molly standing at the front of his line, pulling a face.

"I've been trying to figure out why you've got the longest queue when everyone on the island knows that Hoyt Hooper makes the best pancakes in Turtle Beach." She gestured toward the charred crumbs clinging to his spatula. "Now I'm *really* curious."

Sweet relief surged through Max's veins at the sight of her.

He hadn't liked what he'd seen at lunch with her parents the day before. Not at all. He'd felt an almost primal urge to protect her—ironic, considering she'd been the one to quite literally save his life. But the desire had been there, all the same.

It still was. Max's fingers itched to toss his spatula over his shoulder, scoop her into his arms, and carry her off into the sunset in a very real, very non-imaginary way, despite the fact that they were supposed to be pretending.

"I have the longest queue?" A grin tugged at Max's lips as he peered past her. Sure enough, a line of people snaked all the way from his station to the steps that led down to the parking lot. By contrast, Henry, Hoyt, and Larry each only had a handful of people waiting in their lines.

"What exactly are you putting in your pancakes?" Molly tilted her head. She was holding Ursula in her arms, and the puppy cocked her head, perfectly mirroring her mistress's expression.

"Just the usual stuff, I assure you." He glanced down at the lettering printed across his apron and back at Molly. "It's true, you know."

She tucked a strand of pink hair behind her ear while Ursula's tail beat against the curve of her waist in a happy rhythm. "What's true?"

Max leaned closer, until the heat of the grill warmed his face. Or maybe that delicious warmth was simply because of Molly's nearness. "I pancake my eyes off you."

She smiled, then appeared to catch herself. "You don't have to say those kinds of things. My parents aren't anywhere near us."

But what if I want to say those things? What if it's the truth?

Ursula's nose twitched as someone walked by with a towering stack of pancakes dripping with syrup and topped with a liberal dusting of powdered sugar.

"I was hoping you could take a quick break so we could talk in private for a minute, but from the looks of things…" Molly cast a dubious glance at his queue, still going strong.

"Done." Max flicked the power switch on the grill to the off position.

"Are you sure?"

Max nodded. "Absolutely."

He walked over to Uncle Henry to let him know he was taking a break. There were a few sighs of disappointment from the pancake seekers in Max's line when they realized he was leaving, which made exactly zero sense. He'd never been much of a cook.

"Where to?" he asked Molly.

"Follow me," she said and turned toward a small side staircase off the pier that led down to the beach.

Ursula squirmed in Molly's arms the minute her feet hit the sand. She let the puppy down and turned to face Max. Her gaze flitted to the words on his apron and she seemed to forget what she'd brought him down here to say.

"Sorry." She shook her head as her lips curved into a grin. "That apron might be the dorkiest thing I've ever seen."

"I already told you." He shrugged one shoulder. "It's true."

The pink swell of her bottom lip slipped between her teeth and she shook her head. "And I told you that you don't have to say those things. There's no one around to hear them."

"Not true. You and I are here." He jerked his head toward

Ursula tiptoeing in circles below. Her faint paw prints disappeared almost as quickly as they formed in the damp sand. "Your needy little puppy is here too. That makes three of us."

Molly looked at him for a long moment, until her gaze softened.

"That's just it—there is no us." She swallowed, eyes sparkling. "Is there?"

Ursula wiggled her way between them, nose pressed into the damp ground. She stopped a few paces from Max's feet and started digging frantically, spraying his legs with sand.

Molly blew out a breath. "Never mind. Clearly there isn't."

"Clearly," Max echoed, but the word sounded hollow, even to his own ears.

Thwack. A fresh wave of dug up sand pelted his shin.

Molly looked down at her dog and back up at Max. She arched an eyebrow, as if challenging him to say something about Ursula's rapidly growing hole.

He crossed his arms, refusing to take the bait, even though it pained him not to mention the digging. Max's jaw clenched harder with every grain of sand that flew in his direction. "You wanted to talk to me about something?"

A group of teenage girls in bathing suits walked past them, lingering beneath the shade of the pier. Max glanced over at them, hoping they might catch the hint and move on. They promptly collapsed into giggles. Max heard the click of a camera phone before they dashed away.

Molly frowned. "What was that all about?"

"No clue." Max didn't know, nor did he care. He just wanted

Ursula to stop digging and the busybody residents of Turtle Beach to leave them alone long enough to have a conversation about the real feelings that seemed to be swirling between them.

Not that Max quite understood what those feelings were, exactly. But looking at the situation from a logical standpoint, he couldn't deny that something was indeed simmering beneath the surface. Never mind that his rational side also told him he'd be a fool to pursue anything real with Molly. Logic could be a real pain sometimes.

"Listen, about yesterday," he said, but before he could finish his sentence, another passerby—a woman walking a yappy little dog—stumbled to a halt to openly stare at them.

Max was going to lose it. Were his pancakes really *that* good? Had they made him a local celebrity?

"Good morning." He forced a smile at both human and dog.

The woman blushed lobster-red. She gave her dog's leash a gentle tug and moved on.

Max's gaze swiveled back towards Molly. He shook his head. "Where were we?"

Ursula backed away from the hole she was digging, barked a few times, and then dove back in.

"We were talking about yesterday." Molly held up a hand. "Let me get this out before we get interrupted again, Pancake King."

Max nodded silently, far more obedient than her puppy, who was still acting like she'd never heard the word *no* in her life.

"Thank you for what you did at lunch. It meant a lot to me… more than I can say, really. But you don't have to keep it up. Truly. I can't keep lying to my family. You and I are even now."

Max's gut churned. "Even?"

"You said you wanted to help me to make up for firing me, remember?"

Oh right. That's why he'd done it. Somehow Max's noble intention kept slipping his mind. "I don't mind spending more time with you and your family this weekend. Wouldn't it be unrealistic if your boyfriend just disappeared?"

"Clearly you haven't met my most recent ex," Molly said. She laughed, but it didn't quite meet her eyes.

A strange combination of jealousy and concern stirred inside Max. *Don't ask. It's none of your business.* "Wait a minute. What does that mean? Did someone hurt you?"

"No." Molly shook her head, cheeks flaring pink. "Well, yes. But not physically. It's not important, really."

"I think it is," he countered. "Feelings matter, Molly."

Her feelings mattered. They mattered more to Max than he really understood. Ursula wasn't the only one digging herself into a hole. Since the moment he'd first set eyes on Molly, Max had been inexplicably drawn to her. And the more he got to know her, the more he realized why. Sometimes Max thought they might be flip sides of the same coin—opposite at face value, but the same in ways that truly mattered.

Molly was sand and sea and windswept dunes. And every time he was anywhere near her, he felt like he was drowning all over again.

She took a deep breath, and when she let it out, there was a quiver in her bottom lip. It was the tiniest possible display of emotion, but it was enough for Max to realize that she was letting down her guard and inviting him in. *Finally.*

Her eyes went glossy and she whispered, barely loud enough to be heard over the ocean's roar—just a single word that thrummed inside Max like a heartbeat. "Wilson."

He forgot all about pancakes and puppies and the fact that she'd reduced him to a town villain with a single signature cupcake and a legion of dogs dressed as shellfish. None of that mattered right now. He just wanted to close his eyes, press his lips to hers and slip under again, to a place where everything was loose and fluid and deep, dreamy blue.

Max planted his hand on the weathered wood piling at Molly's back and leaned toward her. She rose to meet him halfway, eyes glittering like beach glass.

Her gaze dropped to his mouth.

Max felt like he was floating on his back in the middle of the ocean without a care in the world as he reached toward Molly and brushed the sea spray from her lips with a tender touch of his thumb. He wanted to bottle this moment, like a handwritten message cast out to sea, so he could come back to it again and again—the delicious burn of anticipation, the promise of what came next. He remembered an old sea myth he'd read once in one of the dusty hardbound books in his uncle's study: a kiss from a mermaid would protect a sailor from drowning. Some even said such a kiss could grant the ability to breathe underwater. Ridiculous, really. A myth was, by its very nature, false.

But the pounding of Max's heart told him he just might be a believer as his mouth lowered toward hers. Someone groaned, and he realized it had been him, and then there was no more thinking. No more remembering. No more pretending. There was only the softness of Molly's lips brushing against his, and her breathy little sigh of surrender, and the salty sweet taste of relief. Max felt like he'd been waiting to kiss her for years instead of days…possibly even a lifetime.

But apparently, he'd have to wait a little longer.

"Oh, hey! It's you," a voice boomed nearby.

Seriously? *What now?* Had no one on this island ever heard of boundaries before?

Max dragged his eyes open just in time to see Molly leap away from him like they'd just been caught making out under the pier. Which they sort of had…

Almost.

Max gritted his teeth and turned to see who had just interrupted them. A lanky, sandy-haired kid with a surfboard tucked under his arm pointed at Max.

"It's you," he said again. He nodded and his face split into a wide grin. "Nice abs, dude."

Max glanced down at his midsection, which was still thoroughly covered by both a shirt and the *I Pancake My Eyes Off You* apron. His gaze slid toward Molly, but her attention had snagged on something in the distance, beyond the shelter of the pier.

"I'm sorry." Max narrowed his eyes at the stranger. "Have we met?"

"Um, Max?" Molly said. The color seemed to be draining from her face.

"No, we haven't. Not in real life, anyway," the surfer said with a laugh.

What did that even mean?

Ursula, knee-deep in her hole at this point, batted another clump of sand at Max's legs. That was the final straw. He couldn't take it anymore—the digging, the interruptions, the greater population of Turtle Beach stopping to fawn all over his pancakes. Not to mention his constant worry about the aquarium and all the weird activities his uncle kept roping him into. This island was going to be the death of him. Molly probably should have let him drown.

He dragged a hand through his hair, tugging hard at the ends. "Listen, if you don't mind, we were kind of in the middle of some—"

"Max!" Molly blurted, louder this time.

It was official—they were never going to actually kiss, were they?

The surfer, who didn't seem to be in any kind of hurry to get his feet wet, glanced from Molly to Max and back again.

"Yes?" Max asked, as calmly as he could manage.

Molly pulled a face. "I hate to tell you this, but I don't think your pancake queue had anything to do with your actual skills at the griddle."

"I'm not following." How had they gotten back to pancakes?

"Oh, dude." The surfer's eyes went wide. He looked at Molly. "He doesn't know, does he?"

A trickle of dread snaked its way up and down Max's spine. This was going to be worse than being recruited for senior yoga or wheelchair balloon volleyball against his will, wasn't it? *Far* worse.

He had a sudden urge to crawl into Ursula's hole and let her bury him in the sand. "Know what?"

Molly made a little spinning motion with her pointer finger and aimed a meaningful look over Max's left shoulder. Her mouth twitched, like she was trying her best not to laugh.

"Turn around and take a look."

Chapter 12

Seconds later, Molly stood alongside Max as they gazed up at the aquarium's entry in the SandFest sand sculpture competition. The team that Mavis had recruited to build it must have been working since sunup. Situated in all its glory just beyond the pier, the sculpture was truly a sight to behold. How Molly had failed to notice it earlier must have been a testament to her focus on trying to put an end to her pretend relationship with Max...or maybe she'd been a tad distracted by almost kissing him.

Again.

Why did that keep happening?

Never mind. Molly couldn't think about that now—not when Max seemed like he might pass out. He'd gone instantly pale when he caught sight of the sculpture, and now that they were getting a closer look at it, he appeared to be a little green around the gills. Molly wondered if she might need to resuscitate him for real this time around.

"It's me," Max said woodenly.

"Indeed it is." Molly bit down hard on the inside of her cheek to keep from laughing.

The sculpture was a perfect replica of Max himself, albeit with some superhero-like embellishments. Sand-Max stood atop a giant sea turtle, surrounded by dolphins, coral, and a swirling school of tiny fish, giving him a definite Neptune-like vibe. He even clutched a trident that had tiny shells pressed into it from top to bottom in one of his hands. Sand-Max's other hand cradled a baby sea turtle whose shell was covered with overlapping sand dollars. It was an elaborate homage to Max as god of the sea. A hand-painted sign with the name of the aquarium and its entry number in the contest was speared into the sand at the base of the intricate creation.

As lovely as those details were, Molly had hardly noticed them at first. Her attention had immediately gone straight to the sculpture's impressive physique.

Max blinked. "Where's my shirt?"

What shirt? The sculpture was bare-chested, with a definite six-pack. Or eight-pack. Maybe even a twelve-pack. Was a twelve-pack a thing? Molly hadn't stopped to count, but muscles bulged everywhere—from the sculpture's strong shoulders all the way down to his flat, sandy stomach.

"At least they gave you pants," she said, somehow resisting the ridiculous urge to drag the tip of her pointer finger along the indention that ran down the center of Sand-Max's torso. Thank goodness there were rules against touching the entries in the contest.

"Yeah, I suppose it could have been worse." Max scrubbed his hand over his face. "I just don't understand. How…why?"

Molly gave him a sideways glance. "Do you seriously need to ask that question?"

She knew exactly how, why, and most important *who* was responsible. This was the work of the OG Charlie's Angels. Molly would have bet money on it.

It all made sense now—the gigantic line at Max's pancake station, so many stares and whispers when they'd been trying to have a simple conversation. Thanks to Mavis, Ethel, and Opal, Max was the talk of the town.

The older women were nowhere to be seen at the moment, but their fingerprints were all over this. Literally. Molly was pretty sure she saw a thumb-sized indentation in the sand right around one of Sand-Max's oblique muscles. It bore an uncanny resemblance to the inky smudges that dotted Opal's bingo sheet every Tuesday. Molly would know that thumb-print anywhere.

Ursula started wiggling in Molly's arms before she could say anything about the guilty party, and within seconds, a flash of black and white spots bounded into view.

"Sprinkles, stay away from the—" Violet's voice came to an abrupt halt as she jogged to a stop alongside Molly and Max and took in the sand sculpture. She blinked a few times and then slid her gaze toward Max. "It's—"

"Me," Max said flatly.

Violet swiveled her head to gape at the statue again. "And you're—"

"Practically naked." Max's face was turning an alarming shade of red. "You noticed, huh?"

Ursula whined to be put down, so Molly acquiesced and the little Cavalier began chasing Sprinkles in circles around the sand sculpture.

"Great. Let's draw even more attention to this monstrosity," Max said.

"Monstrosity? Hardly." Violet blew out a breath. "It's very flattering."

And not altogether inaccurate. Molly had seen Max's actual bare chest with her own eyes the night they'd rescued Crush. His body had made quite an impression.

"Look on the bright side. At least you're no longer the town super-villain." Violet shrugged.

A crowd was beginning to form around the sand sculpture. A few people seemed to be trying to take stealthy photos of Sand-Max and the real deal side-by-side.

Caroline emerged from the cluster of onlookers and came to stand next to them. "Congratulations, Max. I think you've just been crowned Turtle Beach's unofficial sexiest man alive."

"See? Told you," Violet said.

Max finally tore his attention away from his sandy doppel-gänger. His nostrils flared. Evidently, he'd yet to see the humor in the situation. Or the bright side, despite Violet and Caroline's best efforts. "If you'll excuse me, I need to go track down a certain trio of octogenarians."

I'll bet you do.

"See you later," Molly said, wiggling her fingertips in a little wave.

But Max had already turned away.

—⁓—

For three women who'd never had trouble standing out in a crowd, Mavis, Ethel, and Opal had suddenly become difficult to track down.

Max searched for them at the picnic tables on the pier while simultaneously trying to avoid tourists wearing Sand Fan T-shirts who wanted to snap selfies with him, but his efforts on both counts were unsuccessful. From the Salty Dog, he went straight to the senior center, and for once the hub of Turtle Beach's social scene was a ghost town. There wasn't a walker, cane, or yoga mat in sight. The island's senior citizen population was apparently just as invested in SandFest as everyone else, possibly even more so.

Max swung by the aquarium on the off chance the women had tried to find him there and give him a heads-up about the sand sculpture, but of course that was a pipe dream. All he found was a mob of Sand Fans who'd come to the turtle hospital hoping for a glimpse of the island's real-life sea god. Max hid in a supply closet until Nate came to tell him the coast was clear.

"Thanks," Max said, back aching from being crammed between a mop and bucket for the better part of twenty minutes.

"No problem." Nate shook his head. "It's been wild here all morning. You might want to keep a low profile for the rest of the day."

"I plan to, just as soon as I have a word with the leaders of our Turtle Team. You haven't seen Mavis, Ethel, and Opal around, have you?"

"No, but the children's sandcastle contest is going on right now down at the dog beach. You might check there." Nate jerked his head in the direction of the turtle hospital. "I've got to get back to work. We've got tours going all day. Everyone on the island is dropping in to visit the turtles. This has been our busiest day of the year."

Max crossed his arms. "Seriously?"

Nate nodded. "Seriously."

"Okay. Well…that's good, I guess." This wasn't quite the way Max wanted to get the aquarium out of the red, but he'd take whatever win he could get, no matter how personally embarrassing it was.

Still, his volunteers had some explaining to do. The fact that they seemed to be going out of their way to avoid him only made things worse.

On his way out, Max grabbed a baseball cap with the aquarium's logo on it from the gift shop, along with a pair of neon-yellow plastic sunglasses—the best disguise he could come up with on short notice. Fortunately, it seemed to work. No one batted an eye in his direction when he got to the dog beach.

The crowd here was a bit smaller than it had been down at the pier, mostly families. And dogs, of course. They milled about in a canine free-for-all, running from sand castle to sand castle, noses pressed to the ground. The sand creations were modest compared to the ones in the big contest closer to the heart of the town. These were genuine kid castles, with wet, drippy turrets and lopsided moats filled with sea water. Nostalgia tugged at Max's heartstrings as he took in the scene. It reminded him so much of the summers he'd spent on the island with Uncle Henry.

There'd been fewer people on the beach back then, and definitely fewer dogs. But crossing the bridge from the mainland to Turtle Beach was always a bit like stepping back in time. Life was simpler here…slower. As a kid, Henry had always felt like he could breathe here—as opposed to back home, where his parents were constantly at war with each other. On some level, he knew that's why he'd come back. It had been a long time since Max had allowed himself to slow down and take a deep breath. Over the past few years, he'd somehow let himself forget why he'd started working in ocean conservation to begin with. Moments like this and seeing Turtle Beach at its homey, small-town best were potent reminders.

But when Max's gaze snagged on a trio of walkers parked in front of one of the wooden benches facing the ocean, he remembered what he was doing there and why he was disguised as a tourist. His reasons weren't remotely homey or nostalgic.

He stomped across the sand—dodging dogs, sand castles, and children hopped up on maple syrup and adrenaline as he went— until he stood in front of the Charlie's Angels' park bench with his arms crossed over his now-infamous chest.

"Ladies." He narrowed his gaze at the three women.

They were all wearing Sand Fan shirts, matching gauzy yellow skirts, and floppy wide-brimmed straw hats. Mavis's sun hat had the words TALK TO THE SAND stitched around its brim in swirly calligraphy. Opal's hat said RESTING BEACH FACE. The letters on Ethel's spelled out CHEERS BEACHES. Mavis's Chihuahua was perched in the basket of her walker, wearing a tiny yellow and pink tutu. On an ordinary day, Max would have laughed. Alas, a day on which thousands of people stood by the water gawking at his sandy, shirtless lookalike was anything but ordinary.

"Hello, Max," they all said in unison, blinding him with smiles so big that his cheap plastic sunglasses didn't stand a chance.

Ethel inspected him over the top of her signature purple

bifocals, gaze lingering on his sunglasses and baseball cap. "I see you've finally given up on your formal attire and embraced the island look…from the neck up, at least."

"It looks like you stopped mid-makeover," Opal said as she passed a thermos to Ethel.

If it contained any form of alcohol, Max wanted in. Now.

"This isn't a makeover. It's a *disguise*." He gritted his teeth. "Thanks to you three, I'm getting mobbed everywhere I go."

Mavis flashed him a satisfied smirk. "I told you my grandson and his friends knew what they were doing."

She glanced at Ethel and Opal on either side of her and then the three women exchanged high fives.

"That sculpture is *not* what we agreed on," Max said, directing the full power of his irritation at Opal.

"I told you the design wasn't final. I very specifically said that I was working on something that would take it to the next level." She shrugged. "Then you came waltzing into the senior center without your shirt the other night and bam, inspiration struck."

Mavis nodded. "Just like lightning."

"We gave the team your picture from the *Turtle Daily* along with a shirtless photograph of Chris Evans and told them to combine the two images into a turtle-saving ocean god. Genius, don't you think?" Ethel poured whatever was in the thermos into a small paper cup. It smelled like airplane fuel.

Max pinched the bridge of his nose and took a few of the calming breaths Violet was always talking about in yoga class so he wouldn't do something he'd regret—like fire his entire team of volunteers. "That sand sculpture is inappropriate."

"Inappropriate?" Mavis barked out a laugh. "I think the word you're looking for is *hot*."

Opal nodded. "*En fuego.*"

"That's it. I'm cutting you three off." He grabbed the thermos and tucked it under his arm. Nibbles the Chihuahua let out a tiny growl.

Ethel's face fell. "That's not nice, Max. We're celebrating."

"The celebration's over," he said. A nearby corgi lifted its leg perilously close to Max's foot. Even the dogs were on the Charlie's Angels' side. "The three of you deliberately went behind my back on this. Do you have anything at all to say for yourselves?"

Opal, Mavis, and Ethel all looked at each other. Opal was the first to speak up.

"You're welcome," she said with a grin.

"That's it? *You're welcome?*" Max sighed. "I was thinking more in terms of an apology."

"But we're not sorry," Mavis said.

"At all," added Ethel.

"If we hadn't changed the design, we might never have gotten this." Opal reached into the pocket of her gauzy yellow skirt and pulled out a shiny blue ribbon. It fluttered in the wind.

Max went still. "Is that—"

"Grand prize, baby!" Mavis did a fist pump.

Ethel pointed at the thermos, still tucked under Max's arm. "Can we have our whiskey back now?"

"Unless you'd rather we decline the prize money, since you're so unhappy with our grand-prize–winning design?" Opal blinked innocently at Max.

She wasn't fooling him for a second. There was nothing innocent about these women.

But right then, Max couldn't have cared less. "We *won?*"

"Sure did." Mavis gave Opal's knee a tender pat. "Thanks to Opal."

"And your abdominal muscles," Ethel said.

"You missed the judging. It was right after the pancake breakfast. Where have you been, anyway?" Mavis asked.

He'd been all over town looking for them, sure they'd been trying to avoid him. Max should have known they'd have no shame.

"Never mind. It's not important. I'm sorry I missed the announcement." He handed the thermos to Ethel.

"We told you that we had everything under control." Opal shrugged a slender shoulder. "Although honestly, Max. You worry too much about the aquarium's finances. Everything is going to be fine."

Max's throat grew thick. He couldn't believe it. They'd *won.* Between the ten-thousand-dollar prize and today's ticket sales, the aquarium would be in decent shape for the next few months. He could spend his days coming up with a long-term plan instead of putting out fires. It wasn't a permanent solution, but for now…

This changed everything. Maybe Opal was right. Maybe everything really would be okay.

"I don't…" Max shook his head. He felt like a tight band had just been removed from his chest and he could take his first full inhale in days. "I don't know what to say."

"Say cheers." Ethel lined up four small paper cups in her walker basket and poured a round from the thermos.

Max took one of them. "Cheers!"

He downed the whiskey in a single glorious swallow.

"*And* say that you'll give Molly her job back." Opal sipped delicately from her cup. "Starting first thing tomorrow."

"Ursula too." Ethel poured another three fingers' worth of liquor into his cup.

Max arched an eyebrow. "Are you three trying to get me drunk so I'll agree to rehire a mermaid and her four-legged sidekick?"

They were like *The Golden Girls* on steroids. God help him.

"No, you're going to rehire her because she deserves it and now you can afford to pay her salary," Mavis said.

Opal took another dainty sip from her cup. "So long as we hand over the prize money. If you don't give Molly her job back, who knows what we'll do with it."

"You're blackmailing me now?" Max laughed.

Mavis, Ethel, and Opal didn't. They were dead serious.

"Oh, so you *are* blackmailing me." He drained his whiskey.

"Don't be silly. It's not blackmail, just strong advice," Mavis said.

"Potato, potahto." Ethel shrugged and refilled his cup again.

Max shook his head to protest. In the distance, he spotted two Dalmatians trotting among the seagrass in the dunes. They looked like exact mirror images of each other. He'd had two small shots of alcohol, and already he was seeing double.

"You need Molly, and you know it," Opal said quietly.

She was right. He did need Molly, in more ways than one. Max had been seriously impressed with her fundraising ideas at lunch yesterday. And weirdly enough, he just knew they'd make a pretty fantastic team. At work and…elsewhere.

But it would have been nice to make the decision to hire her on his own instead of being forced into it by Rose, Blanche, and Dorothy.

"Do we have a deal?" Opal tilted her head.

"What happens if she says no?" Max said. Molly wasn't any more predictable than the three members of her elderly fan club.

"She won't." Ethel waved a hand. "Molly loves the aquarium."

But she didn't exactly love *him*. Things had thawed between Max and Molly since the initial firing, but he wasn't convinced she'd jump at the chance to work with him. Every time they grew closer, something always seemed to get in the way.

"Fine. I'll do it." He tipped his cup back and let the whiskey slide down his throat with a slow burn. "But the dog stays home."

He had to draw the line somewhere. Also, Ursula might be cute, but she was a troublemaker. Max would *not* allow himself to be strong-armed into putting a dog on the payroll. It was bad enough that he was letting his bonkers team of volunteers dictate his business decisions, particularly after they'd brazenly objectified him for the sake of the island's sick and injured sea turtles.

A passerby walking a Newfoundland with wet sand matted in its shaggy coat stopped to stare at him. Oh joy, he'd been recognized.

"It was for a worthy cause," Max said to the stranger, slurring his words ever so slightly. Then he turned his attention back toward his blackmailers. "I repeat, I'm not hiring the dog."

Mavis shook her head, and Ethel snorted with laughter.

"Keep telling yourself that, Sandman." Opal smirked.

Either Max was drunk, or Nibbles the Chihuahua smirked too.

—⁓—

The sand sculpture of Max had proved to be a formidable distraction, but by evening, Molly was once again wilting beneath the pressure of the lies she'd told her parents.

She reminded herself that she was a grown woman in charge of her own destiny, and she didn't owe anyone an explanation for her life choices. Also, she hadn't outright *lied*, had she? She'd only misled them a bit?

Nope. Those were just technicalities. She was a liar, full stop. If she'd been wearing pants instead of her favorite floral smocked sundress, they would have indeed been on fire.

It was time to face the music. Mom and Dad were both sitting on the deck of the beach house, facing the ocean as the sun went down. In the kitchen, Molly opened a bottle of rosé with trembling hands. She'd given Ursula a doggy bone stuffed with peanut butter in an effort to persuade the puppy to ignore her father. So far so good. The bone was nestled between Ursula's paws as she stretched out, frog-style, in a sunbeam on the opposite side of the deck from her dad. If there was ever a good time for Molly to fess up and throw herself under the bus with minimal damage, that time was now.

She carried the opened bottle of rosé and three wine glasses out to the porch. The sun was just beginning to dip below the horizon, causing the sea to look like liquid gold. Sand sculptures dotted the shore as far as the eye could see, and everything seemed softer and hazier than it had in the bright light of day. Molly remembered that the Charlie's Angels always called this time of day the "magic hour." She hoped they were right and she'd somehow magically come out of this conversation unscathed.

"Cheers!" Molly set the bottle and glasses down on the picnic table in the center of the deck and began pouring. "It's been such a nice weekend so far, hasn't it?"

Her father nodded wordlessly as she handed him his wine.

Mom reached for hers and smiled. "Absolutely lovely. We really enjoyed meeting Max yesterday. We were hoping to see him this afternoon, but I suppose he's been busy at the aquarium?"

"Yes, I'm sure he has." Molly sat down in the chair closest to Ursula, who was busy trying to shove her entire tiny snout into the center of her bone to get to the peanut butter.

In fact, Molly was sure of nothing of the sort. She hadn't seen Max at all after he'd gone off in search of Ethel, Opal, and Mavis. Which was fine, really. She'd gotten exactly what she'd wanted. No more pretend boyfriend muddying up the waters and confusing her about what was real and what wasn't. No more Max inserting himself into her family time with her parents. She should be thrilled. And she was...so, *so* thrilled.

"What's the matter, sweetheart? You look sad," her mother said.

"Nothing's wrong." Molly forced her lips into a grin, but the furrow in her mom's brow grew deeper. She took a deep breath. "Actually, there's something I wanted to talk to you two about. A few things, really."

Her father brightened. "You've decided to go back to school."

He said it as a statement of fact rather than a question...as if following in his footsteps was Molly's destiny and getting started on the road to tenure was just a matter of time.

"No." She shook her head. *Gosh, no.*

Her mother waved a hand. "Honey, let it go for now. Molly seems to be doing great. She's obviously moved on from her last relationship."

Molly swallowed. Had she?

"Molly's happy at the aquarium and Max seems like a fine young man." Mom shrugged. "Who knows? Maybe she'll end up being second in command. He certainly seemed impressed with her fundraising ideas."

Molly swirled the rosé in her glass, a furious little rose-colored riptide. It was like she wasn't even there. "I don't actually want to be second in command."

She *liked* being a mermaid, and she was tired of having to defend that choice. So much so that she forgot for a second it was no longer her job to defend.

"And Max isn't quite as wonderful as you think he is." *Here we go.* Molly set down her glass with a clunk. She needed a clear head for this discussion. "In fact…"

"Oh, look!" Her mother stood to bend over the deck's railing and peered down at something below.

"Mom, please. I'm trying to tell you guys something important," Molly said.

Her mother leaned further over the railing. "Yoo-hoo, Max! We're up here."

Molly flew to her feet. "Wait. Mom, no."

Max was here? Of course he was. He lived right next door. Why, oh why, had he chosen now to insert himself into her mother's line of vision?

"You should have told us that Max was joining us," her father said. "We could have waited to open the wine."

"But he's not. He lives next door, that's all." Molly gestured toward Henry's beach house, but just as she did, Max appeared at the top of the stairs leading up to the deck.

At least she thought it was Max. It certainly looked like Max, albeit a much looser, more relaxed version of him. He was wearing the same pressed khakis and button-down shirt from this morning, but his pants had gone uncharacteristically rumpled and his shirtsleeves were rolled up to the elbows, giving Molly a tantalizing glimpse of his strong turtle-hoisting forearms.

Ugh, how pathetic was she—ogling her nemesis's forearms?

She shifted her gaze to Max's face, shielded by the brim of one of the baseball caps they sold at the aquarium gift shop. He smiled at her in a very non-nemesis sort of way, and the plastic neon-yellow sunglasses he was wearing went crooked.

"Why didn't you tell us that Max lived right next door?" Dad asked.

"I guess it just didn't come up," Molly said. The truth had gotten lost somewhere among all the pretense.

"Hi there, Molly." Max leaned nonchalantly against the railing. "Molly the mermaid."

She opened her mouth for a snappy comeback, because really? He was mocking her unemployment now, right in front of her parents?

But then he stumbled a bit on his way to greet Ursula with a stream of ridiculous-sounding baby talk. The puppy promptly abandoned her stuffed bone to flop down, belly-up, at his feet.

Wait a minute.

Something was definitely off. Was Max *drunk?*

He crouched down to give Ursula a good scratch and then stood to greet her parents, neither of whom seemed to notice anything out of the ordinary. But Molly knew Max well enough to realize that the loosey-goosey personality currently on display wasn't his ordinary one.

"Nice glasses," she said with a smirk.

"Thank you. I got them at the aquarium." Max pushed the glasses up on his head and his gaze leapt toward Molly's. "Where you and I both work."

What was he doing?

"Can I speak to you inside for a second, Max?" Molly jerked her head toward the French doors that lead to the beach cottage's interior.

"Don't forget to grab a wine glass for Max while you're in there, sweetheart," her mother said.

Ha. As if he needed it.

Molly spun on her heel, marched toward the French doors, and hauled them open. Ursula sprang to her feet and followed. Max fell in step behind them much more slowly and languidly, as if being poured from a bottle. Once he was finally inside, Molly shut the doors with a firm click and led him to the kitchen.

Max began opening cabinets, one right after the other.

"Excuse me, but what do you think you're doing?" Molly said.

"Looking for the wine glasses." He peered into the cabinet where Molly kept Ursula's treats. The puppy dropped her bone on the tile floor with a clatter and began spinning in hopeful circles.

"Something tells me that a wine glass is the last thing you need." Molly rolled her eyes. "Where have you been for the past few hours?"

"At the dog beach with Mavis, Ethel, and Opal."

Uh-oh. Molly crossed her arms. "Did they happen to have a thermos with them?"

"They certainly did." Max fumbled with a box of puppy biscuits. Treats spilled onto the floor and Ursula yipped as if she'd just won the canine lottery. "How did you know?"

Molly slapped the dog treat cabinet door shut. "Trust me. I've been there. Never again. Those women can drink anyone under the table."

"But I'm not under the table. I'm right here." Max gave her a thoroughly charming, lopsided grin as he weaved a little on his feet. "And I'm fine."

"You don't look fine. You look…" Molly's gaze swept him up and down.

He looked sort of adorable, actually. His slightly disheveled state reminded her of the times she'd seen him with his guard down—at the dog beach when she'd rescued him, and again the night they'd saved the sea turtle together…even this morning under the pier when he'd almost kissed her. Moments when he'd dropped the professor act and she'd gotten a glimpse of the real him.

"Yes?" he asked, ducking his head to force her to look him in the eyes.

Molly took a sharp inhale. She couldn't think with him so close like this. It was disorienting, like trying to walk on dry land after hours at sea.

"You look like a mess and you smell like a distillery." Lies, both of them.

He smelled like salty ocean and cool island breeze, like summer itself. Something deep inside Molly made her want to just tip her face back and soak up the sun.

But she couldn't. She *shouldn't*. This was supposed to be a truth-telling mission. Her parents were leaving tomorrow, and she was running out of time to do the right thing.

Max looked at her long and hard, until her cheeks went warm. The beating of her heart seemed even louder than Ursula's teeth crunching away at her pile of dog biscuits. "I thought you were going to say I look like Captain America. Or rather, he looks like me. That's what your Turtle Team said."

They weren't wrong, but that was totally beside the point. Molly planted her palms on Max's chest, intent on pushing him away. For some dumb reason, they just stayed there.

She bit her lip. "Please stop calling them *my* Turtle Team. I don't work at the aquarium anymore, remember? Pretending that I do is just making everything harder."

"That's just it. I wasn't pretending out there a few minutes ago. We *do* both work at the aquarium…or we will, as of tomorrow. I want you to come back." He pressed a hand to his heart. "*Please* come back."

They were the words Molly had been hoping for since she and her friends first conceived their ill-fated costumes and cupcake assault on bingo night. This was it. She'd won. She could go back to doing what she loved best. Max had even said *please*, which for him was borderline begging. Wonders never ceased. Molly should have been elated beyond all measure.

Then why did she suddenly feel so…so…hollow?

"Molly?" Max regarded her with a penetrating gaze. "I was really hoping you'd be happy about this."

"I am. I just…" She shook her head. "Why now?"

"The grand prize money from SandFest gives the aquarium some breathing room, and who am I kidding? The visitors miss being greeted by a mermaid. Your throne has been sitting there empty, and…"

"You mean mermaid grotto?" Molly forced herself to breathe. This was *real*. She was in shock, that's all. She just needed a minute to take it all in.

"Mermaid grotto. I stand corrected…again. I also want to go over that spreadsheet of yours and start working on some of your fundraising ideas. They're good, Molly. I know we can do this. With the prize money, we've bought ourselves some time. Now maybe we can get the aquarium back on track. Together." He grinned a boyish grin—open, vulnerable, unguarded.

Molly could have kissed him. In fact, it was taking every last shred of her self-control not to.

Max tilted his head. "What do you say?"

Yes. *Of course* her answer was yes. A small part of her wished this wasn't happening after he'd been drinking, but she couldn't look a gift horse in the mouth. This was her chance to get her life back. Besides, Max could have chosen to do anything with that prize money. He wouldn't ask her to come back if he didn't truly think she needed to be there. She was important, glittery fishtail and all.

"I say yes." Molly grinned from ear to ear. She couldn't quite help it, and before she could stop herself, she threw her arms around Max and hugged him tight.

"Thank you," she whispered into the warm crook of his neck, and then she realized what she was doing: hugging her boss.

That's what Max was now—her boss. Although over the past couple of days, he'd started to feel like more. Molly knew it was silly to hope that part of the reason he wanted her to come back to the aquarium was because he might be developing feelings for her. And yet...

She hoped all the same.

Was her mother right? Molly's pulse boomed in her ears. Was she really ready to move on and let someone get close to her, someone who didn't have four legs and a tail?

This could be a disaster waiting to happen, a tiny voice in the back of her head whispered. Molly tried her best to ignore it. She wanted to savor the moment and hold it close, but for some odd reason, it felt like water slipping through her fingers.

"Don't thank me. We need you there." Max removed the sunglasses from his head and tossed them onto the counter. Then he raked a hand through his already disheveled hair, leaving it ravaged. "I'm so glad you said yes. I was mildly worried I'd have to tell Opal, Mavis, and Ethel that I'd screwed this up and you'd said no. Is it weird that they sort of frighten me?"

"It's not weird at all. They may look harmless but when they get an idea in their heads, they can be downright terrifying. You should definitely be afraid of them." Molly laughed, but then her thoughts snagged on something he'd said. "Wait a minute, though. Why would the Charlie's Angels know you were offering me my job back?"

"Oh. Well..." A furrow formed in Max's perfect brow. "They sort of think they blackmailed me into it."

She blinked. "What?"

"They didn't, obviously. I mean, not technically. It's not important, though. I want this." He gestured to the space between them. "I want *us*."

Molly wasn't sure if they were still talking about the aquarium or if they'd ventured into more personal territory. Feelings kept rushing in like the tide, blurring the line she'd so carefully drawn in the sand. But did the subtext really matter anymore?

He'd had to be *blackmailed* into rehiring her. She knew this moment had been too good to be true.

Molly's disappointment must have been evident, because Max's grin slowly slid off of his face. "Molly? Is everything okay?"

"Everything is just peachy," she lied.

Everything was a hot mess, but she wasn't about to admit it, or else she might talk herself out of a job again, just like she'd done at bingo night. She was simply going to have to swallow her pride and show up at the aquarium tomorrow in her costume with a smile on her face and glitter in her hair.

"Are you sure?" Max searched her gaze until she had to look away.

"Absolutely. I can't wait to start again tomorrow. But you should probably go." She bent to pick up Ursula, her security blanket. The only significant other Molly would ever need. "You might want to take some ibuprofen and go to bed. I need to get back to my parents."

The corner of Max's mouth quirked into a half-grin. "I can stay if you like."

He was utterly clueless, and Molly wasn't inclined to explain to him why she found it less than flattering to hear that her job offer had been orchestrated by her meddling senior citizen friends. Just the thought of it put a lump in her throat.

"It's okay, really." She tightened her grip on Ursula. The puppy craned her neck to lick Molly's cheek. "I'll see you tomorrow."

"See you tomorrow," Max said with a nod.

And then he left, just like she'd asked. He exited through the front door instead of going back to the deck, which was a relief. There was no way her parents—the newly self-appointed president and vice president of the Max Miller fan club—would have let him go. She took a deep breath and returned to the deck, still clutching Ursula and more confused than ever.

"Where's Max?" her mom asked as Molly shut the French doors behind her.

"He needed to get home, but he sends his apologies." Molly swallowed. "And just so you guys know, he's not my boyfriend. He never was, and he never will be. We're coworkers…and neighbors, but that's all. Honestly, we don't even like each other that much."

There, she'd said it. It felt good to get the truth out in the open. Max was nothing to her.

Molly had to focus on the waves tumbling onto the shore in the distance so she wouldn't have to see the look of disappointment on her mom and dad's faces, but at least she'd fessed up and told the truth. No more lies.

Except when she finally forced herself to look up, her parents appeared to be wearing twin expressions of amusement. They exchanged a glance and her father's mouth slid into a rare grin as he sipped his wine. Her mom let out a quiet laugh.

Molly blinked. "What's so funny?"

"You are, dear." Her mother stepped forward to cup one of Molly's cheeks. "There's definitely something going on between you and Max. Your father sees it, and I see it too."

Molly shook her head, ready to object. But when she tried to set the record straight, the words just wouldn't come.

A smile danced on her mother's lips. "We're just wondering who it is you're trying to fool—us or yourself."

Chapter 13

"So you're sure you're not mad?" Molly winced at Caroline as she sipped her frozen Milky Way latte at Turtle Books the following morning.

Molly was situated on the customer side of the counter, back where she belonged, with Ursula curled into a ball in her lap. The aquarium didn't open until noon on Sundays and her parents had already headed back to Philadelphia bright and early this morning, so Molly had a few hours to kill. She thought it best to break the news of her newly reinstated mermaid status to Caroline in person, especially since she was giving her friend zero days' notice that she'd no longer be working as her barista.

"I'm not mad in the slightest. I'm thrilled for you." Caroline pulled a face. "No offense, but you're a much better mermaid than you are a barista."

"No offense taken," Molly said, scowling a little at the espresso machine. She'd miss seeing Caroline for hours a day, but that stainless steel monster...not so much.

Ursula plopped her chin on the counter, and Caroline reached across the counter to give her a pat. "Also, during your last shift I went to go shelve some books and when I came back up here, I found you pretending not to work here. So again, not a huge loss."

Right. Molly had forgotten about that. A lot had happened over the past few days. "Ugh, I'm sorry. That was bad."

"It's fine. I get it. You always get a little nutty around your parents."

"I do, don't I?" During the past twenty-four hours, she'd pretended she'd never lost her job and she'd let them believe she and Max were in a relationship. She'd tried to correct that last one, though. It wasn't her fault that they hadn't believed her. "I've just always wanted to make them proud, but also stay true to myself."

Caroline's eyebrows crept up to her hairline. "Staying true to yourself by pretending everything is okay when it isn't?"

"Believe me, I see the irony." Molly finished off her drink and set her cup down on the counter with a determined thud. "But today's a new day. I've already scheduled a meeting with the Turtle Team this afternoon so we can get to work on fundraising. I finally have my life back and I want to make sure I keep it."

"And what about Max?" Caroline said.

Molly focused intently on the back of Ursula's furry little head. "What about him?"

"How does he fit into your reclaimed life?"

"He doesn't." Molly did her best to feign indifference, but it was a tall order. She'd been so surprised when Max had told her he wanted her to come back to the aquarium. So deliriously happy. Then when she'd realized it hadn't been Max's idea, she'd felt exactly like she had when he'd fired her to begin with—like a joke. Unnecessary. How had Max put it, exactly?

Scientifically insignificant.

Molly's chest tightened. She buried her hands in Ursula's soft fur.

This was exactly why she'd sworn off dating. After her messy breakup with Steve, more commonly referred to as The Tourist, she'd designed her life so as never to have the rug swept out from under her ever again. She'd had enough of being humiliated, and now she'd gone and let it happen again. And she and Max weren't even romantically involved...

They *weren't*, regardless of whatever her mom and dad might think.

"Max is my boss," she said definitively. Never mind that she'd almost kissed the man...twice. "That's it."

"Exactly. You're going to be working together every single day. It just seems like that might be—" Caroline paused, appearing to weigh her next word carefully. "—complicated."

"Nope. Not complicated at all." Molly slid off of her barstool and clipped Ursula's leash onto her collar. "I'll simply be completely businesslike and professional."

"While wearing a clamshell bra."

"It's a bustier," Molly corrected.

Caroline held up her hands. "My bad. A *bustier*...while you're working with Max the shirtless god of the sea."

"I'm pretty certain he'll be wearing a shirt to work," Molly said, even though she desperately wished the memory of that provocative sand sculpture wasn't burned into her mind with such startling detail.

"Okay, well, good luck with all of that." Caroline flipped a switch on the espresso machine and grabbed a coffee cup from one of the pegs on the wall. It was made from hand-crafted yellow pottery with a clay turtle insignia in its center.

Molly had a whole set of those turtle mugs in the kitchen at the beach house. Practically everyone on the island owned at least one of them. She wondered if Max drank his morning coffee from the same type of mug that she did. She could picture him leaning against the railing of his uncle's deck, sipping black coffee while gazing broodingly at the sea. Of course the coffee would be black. Cream and sugar was frivolous. Unnecessary. Maybe even scientifically insignificant. Max would probably give up his dress pants and crisp oxford shirts before he'd drink his coffee sweet and blonde.

Which begged the question—why was Max shirt*less* in this imaginary scenario? Every time she pictured him now, his customary button-down was conspicuously absent.

Molly blinked hard, banishing the picture from her mind.

"Thanks for wishing me luck, but being a mermaid is what I do best." Or that had been the case before Max had entered the picture. It was like riding a bicycle though, wasn't it? A frown tugged at Molly's lips. *Small yet crucial detail—mermaids don't have legs and they definitely can't ride bikes.*

Bad analogy.

She cleared her throat. "Everything's going to be great. Easy peasy."

Exactly. Easy peasy.

Molly nodded to herself as she waved goodbye and led Ursula to the boardwalk. But as the puppy trotted alongside her, glancing up at Molly every now and then as if she knew the answers to all of life's big questions, a familiar three-word phrase kept spinning through her mind.

Famous
last
words…

————

The amount of optimism that stirred inside Max as he waited for Henry's percolator to do its thing on Sunday morning far outweighed whatever actual difference the aquarium's recent ten-thousand-dollar windfall would afford. His head told him not to let his guard down. He still had a monumental problem on his hands—a problem that would require an equally monumental solution. And Max's problem equaled a heck of a lot more than ten grand. Mountain, meet molehill.

Today was different, though. Dare he think it? Special. It was Molly's first day back as the aquarium's resident mermaid. At long last, he wouldn't be fielding questions all day from visitors who'd been hoping for an "Ariel experience," as someone had put it last week…as if Max ran a theme park instead of a public aquarium.

No matter. The important thing was that Molly would be there when he went in to work today. And even though they'd yet to spend a single day working side by side, Max couldn't help feeling that Opal was right. Everything was going to be okay.

Max added a celebratory spoonful of sugar to his coffee. The percolator was a bona fide relic, and Max was tired of starting his day dark and bitter. Maybe a dash of sweetness was just what his life needed. Preferably, sweetness in the form of a mermaid with cotton-candy-hued streaks in her hair and glitter on her skin. But the coffee was a start. A few hours later, he strolled into the lobby of the aquarium feeling like a new man...

And he was immediately greeted by a wiggling Cavalier King Charles spaniel dressed in a lobster costume.

Max stared down at Ursula. He'd had a few whiskey shots with the Charlie's Angels before he talked to Molly the night before, but he hadn't been so hammered that he couldn't recall their conversation. He remembered every last detail, from spilling the dog biscuits to Molly throwing herself into his arms when he'd told her he wanted them to work on saving the aquarium together. What he didn't remember, however, was telling her that she could bring Ursula to work.

Because he hadn't.

The puppy squirmed at Max's feet, and the ridiculous googly eyes on her lobster costume spun round and round. Max sighed. There was no way he could send the dog home without looking like a total jerk. Perhaps he could just talk to Molly and gently remind her that Ursula didn't work here. In fact, there were rules against this sort of thing—actual laws that forbade random animals from entering public aquariums.

Ursula peered up at him with her huge, sad eyes. Max shook his head.

"I'm not going to pet you," he said quietly. "You shouldn't even be here."

At the sound of his voice, Ursula's tail beat against the floor with a cheery *thump thump thump*.

"Please don't. I mean it, Ursula."

When the little Cavalier refused to budge, Max gritted his teeth, picked her up, and carried her across the lobby to the mermaid grotto.

Having come through the employee entrance in the corner of the lobby near the Seahorse Dude Ranch, Max was facing the back of Molly's grand throne. He could only see her blonde and pink curls tumbling over her shoulders and her dazzling emerald green fishtail wrapped around the base of the throne as he approached. Her singsong voice rose above the chatter of guests. She seemed to be saying something about angelfish and halos that had no basis in reality.

Should Max talk to her about that? Or were they simply going to ignore science altogether in this little corner of the aquarium? Max suddenly realized that having a mermaid on the staff was going to be complicated—even a mermaid for whom he was developing a soft spot.

Who was he kidding? His growing feelings for Molly were going to make this situation *especially* complicated. But they'd moved beyond their initial skirmish, hadn't they? They were on the same team now.

Ursula shifted in the crook of his elbow until one of her lobster antennae came dangerously close to poking Max in the eye. Okay, so maybe there were still a few obstacles they'd need to deal with. Mainly the one that had four legs and a tail.

But then Max rounded the corner and got his first full-on glimpse of Molly the mermaid at home in her grotto, and all of his breath seemed to bottle up tight in his chest. It had been a while since he'd seen her in costume. Somehow he'd forgotten about the ropes of pearls and the sparkly pink starfish that were part of her mermaid look. Today, she even had a delicate starfish painted on her cheek in glittery copper-colored paint. Little silver bubbles rose from the seahorse's snout toward the corner of Molly's eye, adorned with sweeping purple eye crayon.

A line of children stretched from the mermaid grotto all the way to the front entrance to the aquarium. As Molly greeted each little boy and girl, she painted a fanciful sea creature of choice on their cheeks. Turtles, octopuses, seahorses, and starfish, all whipped up in mere seconds from a palette she held in her left hand and slender lavender paintbrush in her right. Then she'd pose for photos with the child while flashing a blinding smile, or sometimes pinching her nose and holding her breath to act like she was comically swimming underwater.

Max was confused. Weren't mermaids by their very nature supposed to be able to breathe underwater? He needed some sort of manual to keep up with this nonsense.

But his confusion was secondary to a lot of other feelings wrestling for attention inside him—fascination, awe, and a longing that made his head spin. She was the missing piece to the puzzle that he'd inherited from Uncle Henry. She brought life and laughter to the aquarium. Mermaid magic. He could see it already, in a single glance. No wonder the town had taken her side after he'd fired her.

The lobster in his arms barked and wagged her tail. Max cleared his throat, suddenly having no idea what to do with himself. He felt wholly out of place, like a boring, colorless relic in a world that had instantly turned rainbow bright. He had a fierce pang of sympathy for his uncle's percolator. Dr. Max Miller, marine biologist and champion of all things logical and quantifiable, suddenly found himself falling under the mythical spell of a pretend mermaid.

Or perhaps he'd been falling all along.

Molly's gaze, luminous and lovely, flickered toward his.

"Good morning," he said stiffly.

"Good morning," she said in return.

And then she gave him the same bright smile that she bestowed on her adoring public, but it seemed just a little too fixed. Too superficial. Too *practiced*.

So Max headed to his office, where things were black and white and far easier to understand. It wasn't until he got there that he realized he still had the unwelcome puppy tucked into the crook of his elbow.

—⁘—

The dog remained glued to Max's side throughout the day, either curled into a sleepy ball in one of the chairs opposite his desk or trotting at his heels as he moved about the aquarium. For the most part she was easy to ignore, despite the lobster costume and the snuffly noises she made while she was sleeping. The snoring was actually a little cute, although if pressed, Max wouldn't have volunteered that particular nugget of information.

Mostly, he went about his business while Ursula dozed across the desk from him or regarded him with very direct, very intense eye contact. The only waking moment when Max didn't seem to be her preferred object of attention occurred when he ventured to the turtle hospital area. Ursula trotted alongside him as if she had every reason to be there. Once inside the warehouse, she moved from one big tub to the next, nose twitching as she sniffed the air. Max could have sworn he saw Crush, the recently rescued green turtle, bang one of her flippers against the side of her tub in acknowledgment of the little dog's presence down below.

But that was impossible…

Okay, perhaps it wasn't impossible so much as highly unlikely. Sea turtles did possess a keen sense of smell, both in and out of the water. It was partly how female turtles navigated their way onto dry land to bury their eggs. But sea turtles in captivity mostly responded to smells that they associated with prey, such as squid, jellies, and shrimp. Besides, Crush was a green turtle and ate mostly plants—not Cavalier King Charles spaniel puppies.

It was funny, though. Ursula did seem oddly fascinated by the turtles, especially considering that she couldn't see them. Max would have thought she'd prefer to watch the shark tank or any of the other more visually stimulating displays than sniff the fishy, turtle-scented air in the hospital. But what did he know about dogs?

Not much. That was veterinary medicine, not marine biology, fuzzy felt lobster claws and googly-eyed antennae notwithstanding.

On the way back to his office, Max passed the conference room and his steps slowed at the sight of a collection of aluminum walkers once again piled up near its entrance. The Turtle Team must have been reassembled.

But that wasn't right. They weren't scheduled to meet again until the end of the month. The date and time were circled on Max's desk calendar…in Sharpie. As far as he was concerned, the Charlie's Angels needed as much supervision as Ursula did. Maybe even more.

Max peered through a crack in the vertical blinds of the conference room's wide window, and just as he suspected, he spied a group of senior citizens wearing tie-dyed Turtle Team T-shirts. Molly sat at the head of the table, dressed in her mermaid finery. Pink boxes of familiar-looking cupcakes covered the entire surface of the polished walnut conference table.

Max squinted. Oh yes, indeed, they were the same cupcakes from bingo last week. Mermaid Marshmallow Cream and Sidekick Snickerdoodle. Max's stomach grumbled, to his immense annoyance.

He glanced down at Ursula. "Did you know about this?"

She wagged her tail.

Max rolled his eyes at himself. He was talking to a dog. A dog that had clearly betrayed him, but a *dog* nonetheless.

His head told him to walk away. Molly was the leader of the Turtle Team and she knew what she was doing. But Max couldn't help himself. He needed to know what they were up to before he ended up half-naked on a billboard somewhere.

"Good afternoon, everyone," he said as he swung the door open and walked inside.

"Hello, Max. So nice of you and Ursula to join us." Opal Lewinsky's mouth twisted into a smirk.

Ethel and Mavis snickered like two schoolgirls.

That's right. Laugh it up. The puppy was trotting around like she owned the place, just as they'd predicted. At least someone found it amusing.

Max cleared his throat. "I would have been here earlier, had I known about the meeting."

Molly blinked up at him. She had a cupcake in her hand and a tiny dab of frosting on her upper lip. Max had an immediate, inappropriate urge to bend down and kiss it away. "Max, hi. I didn't realize you'd want to attend. Henry usually wasn't interested in our meetings."

"Well, I am." He pulled out a chair and sat down. The happy chatter around the table came to an abrupt halt.

"That's great." Molly sat up a little straighter, squaring her shoulders. "So, so great."

Nothing about her posture indicated that having him join the meeting was great in the slightest. What he couldn't figure out was why. He thought they'd forged some sort of unofficial truce. He'd had lunch with her parents. They'd shared a moment under the pier.

But what was it she'd said right before they almost kissed?

There is *no us…is there?*

"This meeting wasn't on the schedule," Max said flatly.

The members of the Turtle Team glanced back and forth between him and Molly as if they were watching a match on center court at Wimbledon.

Ursula leapt into Molly's lap, planted her chin on the table, and refused to look at Max. The puppy had clearly chosen a side.

"I know it wasn't." Molly's voice was crisp, sending Ursula's copper ears swiveling back on her head. "But I thought I'd call one right away since you mentioned we should get to work on fundraising ideas."

He'd definitely said that, but he'd meant the two of them. Not the island's entire senior citizen community.

Max looked at her for a long moment and she looked right back at him, neither of them willing to stand down.

"So let's hear it," he heard himself say. "What have you come up with?"

It was a challenge, and they both knew it. There was no way Molly and her team had had time to get anything planned. She hadn't even been back at work for a full day yet.

But to Max's surprise, he was wrong.

"We've already secured a date for the Under the Sea Ball, just three weeks from now. The senior center has agreed to let us use their gymnasium free of charge. We're also planning a more immediate event—a sea turtle release," Molly said. Then her tongue darted out and licked away the dab of frosting on her lip.

Max went momentarily dumbstruck. "Pardon?"

"A turtle release," she repeated. "I talked to Nate this morning and he said that Crush is doing well enough to be released back to her natural habitat. The team and I thought we could make it into a party this weekend. We can invite everyone to come watch and cheer Crush on as you and Nate carry her back into the sea. Violet has agreed to make special turtle cupcakes and donate all the profits to the aquarium. We can sell T-shirts, plush turtles, and other souvenirs."

"It'll be so much fun," Ethel said.

Opal nodded. "And a turtle release will bring more awareness to the aquarium and turtle hospital."

They were right. It was a fantastic idea. *Then why are you so annoyed?* Max gritted his teeth and smiled. "Where exactly do you have in mind?"

"The dog beach. There are lots of benches there, and everyone on the island knows exactly where it is," Molly said.

Oh, joy. The dog beach—the site of Max's near-drowning. His favorite place.

He glanced at Ursula, and the little Cavalier hopped off of Molly's lap and strutted out of the conference room toward Max's office.

"What do you think, Max?" Opal said, nudging a mermaid cupcake toward him.

Max's mouth watered, but he didn't dare pick it up. "I think it's a great idea, but do you think we've got time to get everything organized and ready by this weekend?"

He didn't want to keep Crush in the hospital any longer than necessary. The turtle's well-being was more important than the sad state of their financial affairs.

Molly nodded. "Absolutely."

"Sounds like a plan." Max stood, no longer sure whether his presence was really necessary. "But keep me updated with the details, please."

Molly's eyes flashed. "Of course. I wouldn't dream of making any sort of nefarious plans involving the aquarium behind your back. I definitely wouldn't want you to think you knew the entire story and then ended up feeling blindsided. Or worse yet, hurt."

Ethel turned toward Mavis. "Did I miss something? What's going on?"

"I don't have the foggiest idea," Mavis said.

But Max did.

Molly was upset about the comment he'd made about the Charlie's Angels forcing his hand regarding her employment. No wonder things had seemed strange between them all day. Why hadn't she said anything?

Perhaps because you'd just offered her the chance to get her job back and she didn't want to rock the boat?

Max took a deep inhale. "Molly."

They needed to have a conversation about the blackmailing. He could explain. And he would, but he'd have preferred to do so in private, not with the entire Turtle Team as audience.

"Max." Molly arched a brow.

"Last night, I didn't mean—"

But before he could complete that thought, Ursula came strutting back into the room, tail wagging like a little white flag and carrying something in her mouth. The puppy strode directly toward Max and spat her treasure at his feet. The round white object rolled until it bumped into the toe of Max's dress shoe and came to a stop.

"Oh, dear." Mavis gasped.

"That's not what I think it is, is it?" Opal said.

Ethel rubbed at her purple glasses with the hem of her Turtle Team T-shirt. "It can't be. Max, what is it?"

Max glanced up at Molly—who for once looked properly horrified at her dog's behavior—and fixed his gaze with hers. "It's exactly what it looks like. A sea turtle egg."

Chapter 14

"FOR THE LAST TIME, it wasn't a *real* egg." Molly rolled her eyes as she arranged a pile of stuffed turtle plushies in a pyramid on one of the picnic tables that Violet's brothers Joe and Josh, both police officers with the TBPD, had dragged onto the beach early Saturday morning.

The turtle release was scheduled for ten o'clock, an hour away, and Molly and the Turtle Team had been at the dog beach for hours already, getting everything set up.

Beside her, Violet stacked pink boxes of cupcakes. Chocolate Turtle Drizzle, dripping with caramel and piled high with chocolate shavings. Molly had already eaten one for breakfast.

"Are you sure?" Violet asked. "In the version of the story that I heard, it was a genuine sea turtle egg."

"I'm positive. It was a replica of a sea turtle egg from the model nest in the aquarium's beach ecology wing. Ursula probably thought it was a ball she could play with." Honestly, why was everyone on the island still talking about this? It had happened almost a week ago.

Six whole days, during which Max had returned to his original grumpy demeanor every time they came into contact with one another—particularly when Molly had Ursula in tow. Which was 99.9 percent of the time, obviously.

Gone were the lingering glances and the flirty little comments that had begun to slip into their conversation. Since Ursula spat the egg at his feet, Max definitely hadn't had any trouble pancaking his eyes off of Molly. They'd also been going back and forth for days over what to do about the grant application Molly had been working on. Max wanted to send it in with a bunch of dry, boring numbers about sea turtle nests and the island's efforts toward conservation. Molly thought the application needed a bit of pizazz—something special and interesting to set it apart from all the other scientific entries. She just couldn't figure out what. The fact that she and Max couldn't agree only added to the tension between them.

Molly told herself that was for the best. She wasn't interested in a relationship with anyone but her dog. She just wasn't sure why she had to keep reminding herself that was the case.

"Maybe you're right. Ursula might have thought it was a ball. Sea turtle eggs actually look a lot like Ping-Pong balls," Violet said. "Sprinkles *loves* those."

Violet glanced toward the water where her boyfriend, Sam, was walking their matching Dalmatians. Molly couldn't tell the two dogs apart. Sprinkles was always on her best behavior around Sam. He had a way with dogs. He'd even trained his own rescue Dalmatian, Cinder, to be an official fire safety demonstration dog.

See? a little devil on Molly's shoulder whispered in her ear. *Some men aren't all that bad. Some of them even love dogs just as much as you do.*

And then she looked up to see Max crossing over the dune, scowling at Ursula, who'd found a perfect spot in the shade to do some digging in the sand. The devil on her shoulder took a swan dive straight into the ocean.

"I'll be right back," Molly said to Violet under her breath.

Violet shrugged. "No rush. I think the sales table is ready to go. We're just waiting on Caroline to get here with the boxes of iced coffee, and the Charlie's Angels should be here any minute to help with the customers."

Excellent. Everything was perfectly under control…with the notable exception of Molly's puppy.

She hustled across the sand as fast as she could manage in her mermaid costume. For once in his life, Max wasn't dressed in his usual dress pants and crisply ironed shirt. In his sea turtle hospital tee, board shorts, and flip-flops, he looked like a bona fide local. It should have been difficult to pick him out of the crowd, but as usual, Molly's entire body had gone on high alert the moment he'd crested the dune. Awareness flooded her senses every time he was anywhere in her vicinity. Even this past week, when they'd both been doing their best to avoid one another, she could always tell when he stepped foot inside the lobby. It was beginning to get annoying.

Equally annoying was how good he looked in beachwear— laid back, casual. *Chill*, even. Which was completely laughable, of course. Max didn't have a chill bone in his irritatingly chiseled body. Did his T-shirt really need to hug his biceps so closely?

Says the woman dressed as a mermaid…

They reached Ursula at the same time, which meant that Molly couldn't reprimand her dog. Doing so in front of Max would have been embarrassing, either to Ursula, Molly, or, more probably, both of them.

"Hi, Max," she said, smiling as if her puppy wasn't currently engaged in the behavior that seemed to bug Max more than sand stuck in the lining of his swim trunks.

He scowled down at Ursula and then lifted his gaze to Molly. "What's she doing here?"

Wow. Rude. "Max, this is the dog beach, remember? If anything, we're encroaching on Ursula's territory."

"Today, it's really more of a turtle beach," he countered.

Molly shook her head. "Definitely not a thing."

Ursula dug faster, paws flying.

Max picked her up and held her at arm's length. The little dog let out a whine and pawed ineffectually at the air.

"Please." Max thrust Ursula toward Molly. "Can you please get her to behave, just for the next couple of hours? Once Crush is safely back in the water, Ursula's reign of chaos over the dog beach can continue."

Molly gathered Ursula in her arms. "Fine. But come on, Max, look around."

She gestured toward the crowd of people pouring onto the shore from the wooden steps of the beach access. There were already more camp and lounge chairs than she could count set up along the sand, and eager spectators were still arriving in droves. Molly hadn't expected nearly this big of a turnout. Realizing that so many people on the island wanted to cheer Crush on as she made her way back to the sea tugged at her heartstrings in a major way.

It also made her stand up a little straighter and taller when confronting Max. This whole thing had been Molly's idea, and so far, it looked like a big success. Couldn't he overlook a tiny puppy-sized hole in the sand?

Max's gaze swept the shore. "It's a madhouse."

"Exactly. We're going to make a fortune." She shot him a triumphant grin. "And the sea turtle hospital is getting some major exposure. There's even a photographer here from the *Turtle Daily*."

Max's frown deepened, par for the course. "Let's just hope everything goes okay."

"It *will*." Did he know how to relax? At all? The T-shirt and board shorts combo were clearly just false advertising. He was still wearing an imaginary shirt and tie. "We've got everything totally under control."

Max's eyes flashed over to her again. They were as blue and tumultuous as the deep end of the ocean. "The last time someone said that to me, I ended up immortalized half-naked in sand for all the world to see."

"I can promise you that won't happen again." Molly crossed her heart between her two clam shells.

She couldn't, in fact, promise him anything of the sort. There was no telling what the Charlie's Angels might do from one minute to the next. But Molly wasn't about to tell Max that. He seemed tense enough already.

Also Molly definitely would have noticed if another scantily clad homage to her boss had popped up on the dog beach. So far, the coast was clear.

"The Charlie's Angels are in charge of the sales table. From the looks of things, they'll be too busy to cause any trouble," Molly said.

"And this one?" Max deigned to reach out and scratch Ursula under her cute little chin. "What's your plan for keeping her out of trouble?"

Alas, Molly didn't have one of those. Yet. "I'll keep her with me while I paint faces. Would that make you happy?"

"You could always take her home, you know." He made a big show of checking the time on his waterproof smart watch. "There's still time."

Molly tightened her hold on Ursula. "I can't. She needs me."

The set of Max's chiseled jaw relaxed a bit. And this time, when he looked at her, she caught a glimpse of the man who'd charmed her parents and almost kissed her under the pier…the man who she'd almost believed was real. Until she'd found out who'd really been behind her rehiring.

"Are we still pretending Ursula's the one who needs you and not the other way around?" he asked in a low voice that scraped her insides raw.

He was doing it again—acting like he cared. About her messy breakup, about her feelings, even about her puppy. And it would have been so easy to let her guard down again and admit that maybe, just maybe, Molly liked having Ursula with her at all times because the puppy made her feel like her old self again instead of the girl who'd been cheated on.

But she couldn't. It was almost shameful to admit how much The Tourist had hurt her and how broken she'd felt when Opal had shown her his engagement announcement.

Opal had just happened to be in Charleston for the weekend visiting friends when the announcement had appeared in their local paper. She'd come straight back to Turtle Beach to deliver the news to Molly in person, because that's what kind of friend she was.

Molly should have been able to bounce back. She had a full life, and after all, it happened to other people all the time. Being lied to wasn't the end of the world.

Just the end of hers.

Somehow, putting her trust in the wrong man had made her feel like her parents had been right all along. Maybe she really *was* making a mess of her life. Then she'd adopted Ursula, a pure and perfect bundle of unconditional love and loyalty, and things just felt...*better*.

She couldn't say all of that to Max, though. She'd sooner die.

"Ursula has separation anxiety," Molly said.

"Separation anxiety?" His eyes flickered, like a beach bonfire under a moonlit sky.

Molly felt warm all over. "It's a thing. Look it up."

"No need to look it up. I'm familiar with separation anxiety." He glanced at the puppy and then back at Molly. "I'm just not sure Ursula is the one who has it."

They were done here. Her personal life was truly none of his business...now that he was no longer her pretend boyfriend, anyway.

Good grief, how had things between them gotten so complicated?

"Aren't you supposed to be playing Uber driver to a sea turtle right about now?" Molly lifted an eyebrow and shot a meaningful look at his smart watch. "You should probably go get Crush before she gives you a one-star rating."

He let out a quiet laugh and for a second Molly thought he was going to invite her to go with him. She didn't realize how badly she wished he would until he'd already turned to go.

—⁓—

Nate had Crush ready to go by the time Max got to the aquarium. They'd been working on logistics all week, scheduling everything down to the minute in order to place as little stress as possible on the sea turtle. Just like they'd practiced, he'd placed a transport board on the exam table next to Crush's tank. All they had to do was lift the turtle out of the water, strap it in place, and carry the board to the back of the Jeep.

The plan was for Max to drive back to the dog beach while Nate sat shotgun, swiveled toward the rear so he could keep an eye on Crush. But just as they got the turtle situated, Nate crossed his arms and cast a sheepish look at Max.

"Don't take this the wrong way, boss." He sighed. "But maybe I should drive. I think it might give Crush here a smoother trip."

"Fair point." Max handed Nate the keys.

His intern hadn't been kidding. The Jeep practically floated down Seashell Drive, which might have seriously wounded Max's pride if he hadn't been more concerned about Crush than he was his own ability to drive an antique stick shift.

The turtle did great, though. When they arrived at the dog beach, Violet's brothers—Joe and Josh, officers with the Turtle Beach Police Department—had arranged for Nate to drive the Jeep straight onto the packed sand, even though cars usually weren't allowed on the shore. While Max and Nate prepared to carry Crush into the sea, Joe and Josh organized a path that ran straight from the Jeep to the ocean, cordoned off with yellow police tape. With the crowd effectively parted, Max took hold of Crush's shell by grabbing hold of her carapace just behind her head with one hand and near her hind flipper with the other. Nate mirrored his position on Crush's opposite side.

"Ready?" Max fixed his gaze with Nate's over the top of the sea turtle. "We lift on three and head straight into the surf."

"Got it." Nate nodded. "Ready."

Adrenaline hit Max hard in those final moments before they lifted Crush from the back of the Jeep. His heart raced, and he was sure he could have heard the frenetic beat of his pulse in his ears if not for the roar of the crowd as they chanted the turtle's name.

Crush, Crush, Crush.

The number of people had tripled in the short time he'd been gone. Everywhere he looked, there were people in aquarium T-shirts and kids with turtles painted on their cheeks clutching sea turtle stuffed animals. The photographer from the *Turtle Daily* crouched at the shoreline with his big telephoto lens aimed straight toward the Jeep.

Max had never seen anything like it, certainly not back in Baltimore. Molly had been right. The scene playing out in front of him was incredible. It made Max fall in love with Turtle Beach all over again.

Molly did this. It was her idea. She *made this happen.* Max no longer cared if they made a dime. Seeing the community come together to cheer for a sea turtle was special, whether they made a profit or not. He scanned the crowd in search of Molly—even just a quick flash of her emerald sequins—but he couldn't find her in the madness.

They were running out of time, though. Max wanted to get Crush into the water as quickly as possible.

He tightened his grip on the sea turtle's carapace and started counting in a loud, clear voice so Nate could hear him above all the noise. "One, two, three."

The crowd broke into applause as they heaved the turtle between them and carried her toward the ocean. Out of the corner of his eye, Max saw Ethel, Opal, and Mavis shaking blue and green pompons above their heads. Dogs barked, humans cheered, and just as Max felt a rush of foamy water swirling around his ankles, he caught sight of his uncle grinning at him and shooting him a double thumbs-up as if he'd just scored the winning spike in wheelchair balloon volleyball. Max's throat closed up tight.

This. This right here was why he'd come to Turtle Beach. Crush's flippers waved in the air, like slow-motion angel wings, and the moment seemed to imprint itself on Max, just like the night he and Henry had stumbled upon the mother sea turtle burying her eggs in the sand.

Max was vaguely aware of the photographer from the paper snapping photos as he and Nate waded into the sea. They stepped gingerly past the first sandbar until the water came up to their knees, and then they carefully lowered Crush into the ocean.

The turtle's flippers went into overdrive the second she realized she was back in her proper home. Max and Nate exchanged a glance. The intern's smile was so big that it nearly split his face in two.

"It's time to let her go," Max said.

With a mutual nod, they removed their grip on the turtle's carapace. A wave hit right afterward, knocking Max slightly backward on his feet. But Crush sliced right through it, like a warm knife through butter. In a split second, she was gone. Headed home to the blue depths of the sea.

Back on the shore the crowd whooped and hollered. Max jammed a hand through his damp hair and let out a breath.

"Yes!" Nate raised two fists in the air, and then scooped up two handfuls of water and splashed Max's shirt.

Within minutes, the shallows of the dog beach turned into a party. People waded into ankle-deep water, splashing each other and dancing along to music blaring from a nearby TBFD fire truck. It sounded like songs from the fifties, along the lines of the music they played at the skating rink above the post office. Then the familiar notes of "Happy Together" started, and he realized the fire department was playing *The Turtles' Greatest Hits.*

Max laughed to himself as he waded back to shore. *Nice touch*, he thought. It had Molly's name written all over it.

He'd probably been too hard on her earlier. She'd put so much effort into making today a success, and she'd succeeded beyond his wildest dreams. But just when his feet landed on dry beach, he finally found her again—standing by the dunes with the pompon-wielding Charlie's Angels as Ursula dug frantically at the sand.

To her credit, Molly appeared to attempt to intervene. She begged and cajoled and at times dragged Ursula away from her hole. But the little Cavalier couldn't be stopped.

Max told himself to let it go. And he tried to do just that. He really did. But by the time he reached the dune, his jaw hurt from gritting his teeth so hard. A muscle ticked in his cheek. The effort it took to keep biting his tongue nearly killed him.

"Oh, Max. There you are." Molly leapt in front of Ursula and the hole, as if that simple maneuver would keep him from seeing it.

Actually, it was more effective than he wanted to admit, given that she was wearing her mermaid costume. Max could barely drag his attention away from her.

Until sand flew from behind her back, pelting him on the legs. Ursula's signature move.

Molly pretended not to notice, but her smile hardened in place. "Can you believe this turnout? Fantastic, right?"

Max leaned to the side to peer around her. All that was visible of Ursula was her dainty backside and feathered tail. She was tipped nearly vertical, straight into her hole.

"Oh, boy," Mavis said under her breath.

"Molly." Max crossed his arms.

She heaved a sigh, and a pink lock of her hair tangled itself in her mermaid crown, an elaborate, bejeweled creation crafted from shells, pearls, and polished bits of beach glass. "She can't help it. She's a puppy, and this is *her* beach."

He held his tongue, rather enjoying how flustered she was getting.

"Are you going to go around policing all the children who dig holes, too?" Molly planted her hands on her hips, drawing his attention to her curves.

Nice try, but he was still worried about Ursula's hole. If she didn't stop soon, she might bury herself. Max jerked his head toward the dog and tried to warn her, but Molly kept talking.

"I didn't think so. Just admit it—you really do hate dogs."

The tick in his cheek kicked up a notch. "But I don't."

Mavis, Opal, and Ethel stood watching the exchange with their arms at their sides, pompons drooping, as if they couldn't decide who to cheer for.

Molly regarded him through her thick fringe of mermaid lashes, tipped with glitter. "So it's just Ursula who gets under your skin?"

Ursula didn't get under his skin. *Molly* did. Okay, maybe her dog did too, but in a wholly different way. The puppy couldn't be blamed for Max's sleepless nights, though. It was Molly's face that Max saw when he closed his eyes and listened to the ocean's roar through his open windows. It was her voice he heard calling out to him when he dreamed of the waves pulling him under.

Wilson!

Max swallowed as Molly stared at him, waiting for an answer.

"Um, guys? There's something you really need to see," Opal said, breaking the loaded silence between them.

Molly's gaze didn't waver. Her eyes remained glued to him, and somewhere in their sapphire depths, he saw a hint of vulnerability. She cared what he thought about her and Ursula. She might not want to, but she did.

"Hello?" Opal waved her pompons in Max's periphery. "Can you two even hear me?"

Mavis snorted. "Maybe they need hearing aids."

Ethel shrugged. "If so, I know a good doctor."

"They don't need a doctor. They need to get a room, if you catch my drift," Mavis said under her breath.

"*All of you,*" Opal yelled. She pointed toward Max's feet with a mighty shake of her pompons. "Look!"

Molly glanced down and gasped. Her hand fluttered to her throat. "Oh, no. Not again."

Max was almost afraid to look. His jaw clenched preemptively as he dragged his gaze to the sand where, for once in her life, Ursula sat serenely at his feet...

With a turtle egg nestled in her tiny jaws.

Chapter 15

To Molly's horror, the egg was real this time—a genuine, rare, unhatched sea turtle egg. Not a Ping-Pong ball, a model egg, or a dog toy, but the real deal.

Molly had only seen a handful of actual sea turtle eggs before, but if there'd been any doubt in her mind as to its authenticity, the look on Max's face would have cleared that right up. He seemed even more shellshocked than he'd been when he'd first seen his sand sculpture at SandFest. One of these days, Molly really was going to have to resuscitate him.

"No one move," Max said.

Molly and the Charlie's Angels went still as stone. Ursula blinked, but otherwise remained remarkably calm.

Max crouched down and placed his hand in front of her mouth, and the puppy gently set the egg down in his palm. It was round and white, just like the model egg she'd stolen from the display at the aquarium. But without even touching it, Molly could tell that this egg was far more delicate. Its shell seemed almost translucent.

Ursula wagged her tail, clearly proud of herself, as Max studied the egg, eyes shining with wonder.

"I don't understand." Molly shook her head. She didn't want

to think about what would have happened if Ursula had bit down and cracked the egg. Thank goodness she hadn't. "Where did it come from?"

"She must have dug it up," Max said.

His gaze flew to Molly's, and her heart felt like it might pound right out of her chest. Everything seemed to move in slow motion as their little group turned to examine the spot where Ursula had been digging moments before.

And there it was...a nest full of eggs, just like the one in Max's hand. Seventy, eighty, maybe even one hundred of them! Definitely too many to count at first glance.

The eggs were piled on top of one another at the bottom of the hole Ursula had been digging, deep enough that the sand was damp and darker beige than the fine powdered sand at the surface. Molly couldn't believe her little dog had dug a hole that big. Had she somehow known that there was a clutch of eggs buried in that spot?

No, that was impossible. Ursula was just a puppy.

Elated to be the center of attention, the little Cavalier wiggled her entire body as she pranced around the perimeter of the nest. Her tiny black nose was frosted with sand.

"That's right, you found the turtle eggs." Molly gathered Ursula into her arms. The dog didn't seem like she was about to remove another egg, but Molly didn't want to take any chances. "You're a canine *genius*."

Max bent over to inspect the nest. He kept shaking his head, like he couldn't believe what he was seeing.

With great care, Max placed the egg in his hand back inside

the hole. Then he stood and ruffled the fur on Ursula's head. "Good girl, Ursula. Now we know there's a nest here, and we can take care of it. You're a good dog."

Molly's throat clogged with emotion. She wasn't even sure why. Hadn't she been trying to tell Max that Ursula was good this entire time?

Still, it did something strange to her insides to see him beaming at her dog like that. She felt a little woozy, like she'd been out in the sun too long.

Max jammed a hand through his hair, leaving it disheveled. His absentminded professor vibe was strong today. Molly definitely didn't hate it. "We're going to need to re-bury the eggs. Then we can mark the nest and surround it with stakes and caution tape to protect it. Nate and I can run back to the aquarium and get the supplies."

"We'll stay here and babysit the nest while you're gone," Molly said.

Ethel, Opal, and Mavis all nodded. They started spreading out, forming a barrier around the nest with their walkers and pompons while Max knelt in the sand and gently covered the exposed eggs.

Ursula preened in Molly's arms until Max stood, brushed the sand from his hands, and flashed her a wink. The dog was clearly besotted. Molly couldn't altogether blame her.

"You don't really think she knew the nest was down there, do you?" Opal studied Ursula's sweet face. The puppy sneezed, spraying sand everywhere.

"She does like to dig," Ethel said, wiping damp sand from her purple glasses with the hem of her Turtle Team T-shirt. "She was bound to stumble upon a sea turtle nest at some point."

"Unless," Max said quietly as he glanced from Ursula to the nest and back again.

"Unless what?" Molly's breath quickened. Of everyone assembled, the last person she'd expect to get on board with the genius theory was Max. But she couldn't deny that he'd suddenly started looking at Ursula in a whole new light.

Max drew in a long breath and then shook his head as if he couldn't believe what he was about to say. "Unless she's scent tracking sea turtle eggs."

Opal's eyes went wide. "You mean, like, on purpose?"

"Yes." Max shrugged. "It's a possibility. Dogs scent track all sorts of things—drugs, bombs, missing people."

"I read a story on the internet a while back about dogs that can sniff out medical problems, like low blood sugar and cancer. Some dogs can even predict seizures." Molly was breathless at the idea that Ursula could possibly rank right up there with these talented canine Einsteins.

The Charlie's Angels all turned to look at Max, clearly expecting him to shoot down this crazy-pants theory.

But to Molly's complete and utter delight, he didn't.

"Think about it." He shrugged again. "She always sniffs the air when she's in the sea turtle hospital. Since Molly's been bringing Ursula to work since she got her, the pup is well acquainted with the scent. She could be naturally tracking it out in the world."

Molly's head spun. If Max was right, this could be huge. It

could also mean that Ursula had *earned* her place at the aquarium. She might even have a more important role there than Molly.

Mavis and Ethel both frowned in Ursula's direction. Except for Molly, the only other believer seemed to be Opal. And even she looked a tad dubious.

Molly tried not to feel wounded, but really? They should have been Ursula's biggest cheerleaders. They already had the pompons and everything.

"But how do you know for certain that's what Ursula is doing?" Mavis asked.

"Because he's right. Max is a scientist, and Ursula is an ecological hero." *Not* an ecological menace. Big difference. Huge. "Isn't she, Max?"

She wanted to hear him say it. She might even need him to embroider it on throw pillows so she could sell them on Etsy.

"She could be, but like Mavis and Ethel said, we don't know that for certain." Max gave Molly one of the lopsided smiles she'd missed so much lately. Her heart did a little somersault in her chest. "But there's one surefire way to find out."

By the time Max and Nate made another mad dash to the aquarium, returning with stakes, spools of neon nylon tape, and a triangular sign that read Sea Turtle Nest, Do Not Disturb, the party at the dog beach had cleared out.

Max was grateful for the peace and quiet. His thoughts were screaming loud enough without the added distraction of the music, crowds, and barking of countless canine beach bums.

Little Ursula could scent track sea turtle eggs. Who would have thought?

Certainly not Max. Even now he told himself not to get his hopes up. Common sense—not to mention Max's prevailing sense of logic—told him that the Cavalier's discovery of the nest was just a happy accident. Daydreaming about the aquarium's sea turtle nesting identification program resting on the tiny shoulders of a spoiled spaniel puppy wasn't prudent. He shouldn't have mentioned scent tracking at all until he'd had a chance to go back and examine all the spots where he'd seen Ursula digging. Molly was already acting as if her dog was Lassie reincarnated. He didn't want her to be disappointed if he'd been wrong.

Who was he kidding? She wouldn't just be disappointed. Molly would be devastated. Max definitely should have kept his thoughts to himself. Wasn't that one of the fundamentals of the scientific method? A hypothesis required rigorous testing before it could be considered truth. Scientists knew better than to trust hunches or intuition.

But thinking back on Ursula's past behavior made goosebumps slide along the back of his neck, especially the way her little nose quivered whenever she was in the sea turtle hospital. She'd been relentless about digging that hole today. Max just knew she'd been attracted to the smell of the eggs. It had to be true.

The Charlie's Angels entertained Ursula, the star of the hour, while Molly and Nate helped Max drive stakes around the nest and mark it off with the neon tape so beachgoers would know to leave the area alone.

"I wish there was a way to know when the eggs might hatch," Molly said as they tied off the last bit of tape.

"The incubation period lasts anywhere from forty-five to seventy days." Max studied the freshly patted down sand and shook his head. "Unfortunately, without anyone seeing the turtle tracks after the nest was initially made, there's no way of knowing how long the eggs have been down there."

"The dog beach is pretty popular. There's usually a lot of early morning activity. I'm surprised no one noticed anything." Molly sighed.

"Odds are the eggs have been there a while. Turtles usually nest in these parts from May to August. We're nearing the tail end of that window," Nate said as he gathered the leftover supplies.

"We should probably round up volunteers and start a schedule for watching the known nests on the island overnight. If we can have a team in place when the hatchlings make their way up through the sand, we can help them get to the water safe and sound." Max glanced at Molly.

"I already have a spreadsheet with names of volunteers," she said. *Of course* she did. "I'll start making calls tomorrow."

"Great." Max nodded and tried not to picture himself on a moonlit beach with her head on his shoulder. They were talking about plans for an ecological mission, not a date.

Even so, just thinking about spending the night sitting beside her with their toes buried in the sand and listening to the ocean's gentle lullaby while they waited for the baby turtles sent warmth coursing through his veins.

Molly's eyes found his, met, and held. He wondered if she was

thinking about the same thing—the same imaginary intimacy—
but he didn't dare hope. With the SandFest win and Ursula finding
the nest, there'd been quite a few miracles in Max's life lately. The
longer he stayed in Turtle Beach, the more he felt like his life
was shifting from shades of grainy black and white to full-blown
color. Wishing for more felt greedy…borderline dangerous, even.
Especially where Molly was concerned.

But Max wished all the same. Oh, how he wished.

"So what now?" Molly blinked, a lush sweep of her glitter-
tipped eyelashes. "You said you had a plan to find out if Ursula
could really scent track sea turtle nests."

Indeed he did. "Now we take Ursula back to the scenes of her
previous crimes, so to speak."

"You mean the places where we've seen her digging recently.
Ursula is a turtle savior. I firmly object to the use of the word
'crimes,'" Molly said.

"Duly noted." Max clamped his lips together to keep from
laughing at the fact that Ursula's status had now been upgraded
from *genius* to *savior*.

"If you guys don't mind, I'm not going to be able to come
along." Nate pulled his phone out of his pocket to check the
time. Max wondered where he could possibly be going. Twilight
surfing? A skateboarding convention? "I've got dinner with my
grandparents tonight. My grandma is making chicken pot pie."

"That's so sweet." Molly pressed her hands to her heart, perilously close to clamshell territory. "Have a nice time with your
family. Don't worry, the five of us can handle things from here."

"Actually…" Opal shook her head.

"Oh, right. What was I thinking? The six of us, counting Ursula." Molly's gaze flitted to Max. "She totally counts."

"In this specific circumstance, I agree," Max said.

Opal let out a *pfft* sound. "Of course she counts."

Mavis nodded. "'Duh,' as the kids say."

"I think the kids stopped saying 'duh' in 1999," Ethel said with a snort.

Mavis glared at her.

"She has a point, dear." Opal passed Ursula back to Molly. "But whether or not this little sweetheart counts as a person wasn't what I was referring to."

Molly hugged the puppy to her chest. "Oh, what did you mean, then?"

"Nate isn't the only one who has plans. We've got to get going, too." Opal glanced at Ethel and Mavis. "Right?"

Ethel's forehead crinkled. "We do?"

Mavis gave Ethel a sharp jab with her elbow. "Yes. We do. We have plans tonight, remember?"

"Ouch." Ethel grimaced. "What are you—"

"We have that *thing*," Opal said.

She and Mavis stared meaningfully at Ethel until she finally got the picture.

"Oh, right. That thing." Ethel nodded and then turned toward Max and Molly. "Yep. We've got to go. It looks like you're just going to have to go check out the potential turtle nests on your own."

"Together," Opal said.

"Alone," Mavis added. "Just the two of you."

To say subtlety wasn't their strong suit would have been a massive understatement. He and Molly were definitely being set up.

Max's gaze slid toward Molly. They hadn't been alone together—*properly* alone—in days. And now they were going to be spending a perfect late summer sunset walking on the beach together.

For purely scientific purposes.

Obviously.

Molly narrowed her eyes at the three older women. "Seriously? I hope you know we can see through this charade."

"I have no idea what you're talking about, dear," Opal said. "We've really got to go. Hoyt Hooper is already on the way to pick us up in the senior center's van."

They packed up their pompons, pointed their walkers toward the beach access, and waved goodbye before Max or Molly could get another word in edgewise. Nate escorted the women off of the sand.

Max took a deep breath and glanced at Molly. The sun was already beginning its slow descent, casting a halo of hazy, diaphanous light around her hair. "What do you say?"

Ursula let out a quiet woof, and Molly's expression softened as she looked up at Max. The glitter on her face made him think of stardust and supernovas. Somewhere underneath it all, deep down where it counted, they were the same—just two souls made from flames.

"Let's go."

Chapter 16

FROM THE DOG BEACH, they went back to the shore where their houses stood side-by-side and let Ursula sniff and paw at the sand. Once she homed in on a specific area and started digging a hole, Molly scooped her up and kept her leashed while Max probed the nesting site with a rod to see if he could locate an egg chamber.

Molly could barely breathe the first time he performed the delicate task. Max placed the tip of the probe between his feet and pushed down on it, hoping to find a spot where the sand gave way and the probe would sink down with ease, indicating the presence of a nest cavity. It was slow, precarious work. Max explained that if he went too quickly, he might accidentally damage an egg. He handled the probe so gingerly that it almost seemed like he wasn't moving at all.

Then all of a sudden he'd looked up, face splitting into an impossibly wide grin, and Molly had known—the nest back on the dog beach was no accident. Ursula could indeed sniff out sea turtle nests.

Max had dropped the probe, stepped back from the nesting area and raised his fists in the air. Molly launched herself at him, wrapping her arms around his neck, and he scooped her right off of her feet while they both screamed in victory. Ursula barked and barked, running in circles around them until her leash was wrapped tight around Max's legs and Molly's mermaid tail, anchoring them together and threatening to topple them both. Even then, Molly hated to let go. She wanted to stay right there, with her face pressed into Max's strong neck and their hearts crashing wildly against one another while the ocean crashed against the shore.

But Ursula had just gotten started. She located three more nests in the area where Molly and Max lived. It took them hours to probe, stake, and properly mark off the nest sites. Halfway through the project, Molly climbed the steps of her beach cottage and returned wearing her favorite gauzy white shirt and jean shorts instead of her mermaid tail and carrying a basket stuffed full of watermelon slices, torn up bits of rotisserie chicken, and pimento cheese with crackers—all the ingredients for Molly's favorite beach picnic.

Once the nests had been found and marked, they spread a blanket onto the sand and dove into the food, famished. Ursula fell asleep in Molly's lap, while cold watermelon juice dripped down Molly's chin, her hands, and her arms. She was a sandy mess, but she couldn't remember being this happy in a long, long time.

"Should we pack it in for the night?" Max stole a glance at her once the picnic basket sat empty between them.

Not yet. Please, not yet. "Already? Don't we still need to go check out the area under the Salty Dog pier?"

Neither one of them had mentioned that particular spot, the site of their most recent near-kiss. Molly wondered if they'd been tap-dancing around it or if Max had simply forgotten. When his eyes met hers, she knew he hadn't. Memories shone back at her from his irises, forget-me-not blue.

Then he shifted his gaze to the ocean and cleared his throat. "It's getting late. Are you sure you want to go out there tonight?"

"Definitely. It's the only place where Ursula possibly alerted that we haven't checked." She hedged, just in case he was purposefully avoiding revisiting that specific location with her on a moonlit night, mere hours after she'd thrown herself at him and clung to him like a barnacle. The only reason they were even sitting there alone together was because Nate had had a craving for chicken pot pie and the Charlie's Angels had been up to their old matchmaking tricks. "If you're up for it, that is."

"I'm most certainly up for it," Max said. The hint of gravel in his voice made her feel slightly less like a barnacle. More like a clingy wisp of seaweed.

Molly inhaled a ragged breath. She really needed to stop thinking in terms of ocean analogies. Hashtag #mermaidproblems.

Max's gaze dropped to the puppy in her lap. "You don't think Ursula is too tired, do you?"

At the sound of her name, the Cavalier's ears twitched. She opened her eyes, and when she spied Max grinning down at her, she sprang to her feet, tail fluttering in the ocean breeze.

"You've awakened the beast." Molly laughed. "Ursula is an extremely light sleeper."

"I guess that means we don't have a choice." Max shrugged one strong turtle-wielding shoulder. "We *have* to go to the pier."

"Have to." Molly nodded and did her best to pretend she

was thinking about scent tracking and sea turtle egg chambers instead of things she definitely shouldn't be contemplating, like kissing her full-time boss/part-time nemesis under the pier while the moon drew the tide in like magic.

She was just caught up in the thrill of the moment, that's all. She wasn't *really* beginning to think she had feelings for Max. Her mind was playing tricks on her, elated by Ursula's triumph.

That's what she thought was going on, anyway.

The Salty Dog was almost deserted when Max chugged the Jeep into the parking lot. Only the die-hard fishermen were still clustered at the far end of the pier, hoping for some late-night action. They stayed eerily still beneath the soft glow of the curved antique lamp lights, making quiet conversation.

Molly walked Ursula on the leash she usually used at the aquarium. It was beach-glass blue with little sea turtles printed on it, which seemed rather poignant now that her special talent had been *unleashed*, so to speak. The Cavalier pranced ahead of her, and Max walked alongside, carrying the supplies they'd need if they located another sea turtle nest.

Once they'd descended the weathered wooden steps of the pier and made their way beneath the jetty, Ursula started straining at the end of her leash. Her nose twitched, and her ears swiveled to the tiptop of her head.

Molly was awash with anticipation, heart pounding as her puppy led her back to the place where she and Max had stood on the morning of the pancake breakfast. Ursula pressed her nose to the ground, running in circles until she found the exact spot she was looking for and pawed frantically at the sand.

"Good girl, Ursula!" Molly showered the puppy with praise and gave her a bit of chicken she'd set aside from the picnic.

"She's done it again," Max said, shaking his head. "That's *five* nests today."

"I think you owe Ursula a major apology." Molly gathered the Cavalier in her arms while Max went to work locating the egg chamber.

He pushed his glasses farther up on his nose and pressed the rod gently into the sand. "An apology?"

"For all of those mean things you said back when you fired her," Molly prompted.

"I guess I was hoping you might have forgotten about that." Max shot her a crooked smile.

"Never." Molly rested against one of the wooden posts nearby to watch Max work. The feeling of the rough pine against her skin took her straight back to the moment when Max had leaned close and brushed his lips against hers. It had been *right here.* "I remember everything."

Every little thing…the salty taste of him, the breathy sigh that had escaped her, the way her knees had gone weak—like she'd been a character in a swoony mermaid story instead of a real person.

It had been real, though, not a story. And not pretend, no matter how many times she'd tried to tell herself otherwise.

I remember everything.

Max paused and studied Molly as if he were trying to commit the moment to memory. Or perhaps he was just trying to see inside her head, to see if her recollection of what had almost happened there matched his.

She licked her lips. The only thing that stood between her and Max and the kiss she couldn't seem to stop thinking about was Ursula, snuggled tight in Molly's arms. Molly told herself to put the puppy down, but she couldn't seem to make herself move.

Max's eyes blazed in the moonlight. "Have I ever told you how much I love it when you look at me like that?"

Warmth pooled deep inside her. "Like what?"

"Like you want to call me Wilson."

Heaven help her, she did. The word had been right there on the tip of her tongue.

"It's kind of cute how much you enjoy being compared to a volleyball," she joked, but she didn't laugh.

Neither of them did. It wasn't a moment for laughter. It was a moment for quickened heartbeats and apologies. For honesty.

I'm sorry I keep pushing you away. I just don't know how to do this anymore.

Things were so much easier back when she'd been mad at him. She didn't know what she was going to do now that he would no longer be reprimanding Ursula at every turn.

"Max, I…" she started to say, but then a thought came crashing into her consciousness—a thought that was too important, too urgent to ignore.

She gasped as everything clicked neatly into place. Ursula, the sea turtles, the aquarium…

"Molly?" The easy grin on Max's face faded away. "What is it?"

"The *grant*," Molly said.

They'd been arguing about it for days, bouncing back and forth between ideas about the application but unable to agree on anything. As per usual. Every time Molly tried to suggest infusing any sort of creativity into their proposal, Max looked at her like she was Ursula digging a hole on the beach.

"What about it?" Max said slowly.

"Don't you see? This is it!" Molly waved a hand toward the nest that Ursula had just located, and she pressed a smacking kiss to the top of her puppy's furry head. "We'll write about how we've got a dog in Turtle Beach who can scent track sea turtle nests. The grant committee will love it."

Max rubbed the back of his neck. He didn't automatically agree like she'd hoped he would, but he didn't protest either. And he definitely wasn't looking at her like she'd just dug a hole on his precious beach.

"We're going to get that grant, especially when they find out what we're going to do next." Molly flashed him her biggest and brightest smile.

He went still, looking less like Wilson all of a sudden and more like Dr. Max Miller, PhD. "I'm almost afraid to ask, but what are we going to do next?"

"Molly wants to try to train a team of dogs to sniff out sea turtle nests on the beach," Max said to his uncle the following morning at the Turtle Beach Senior Center.

Henry barely looked up from the Scrabble board that lay on the table between them. "You don't say."

Max sighed. Was his uncle even listening?

At least they weren't having this conversation while bending themselves into nutty yoga positions. Max had known better than to bring up the grant during class earlier today. He'd tried—yet again—to pin Uncle Henry down for a time when they could have a proper heart-to-heart about the aquarium and, more specifically, the grant. His uncle had told him to come back at eleven o'clock, neglecting to mention that eleven o'clock just happened to be the start time for the senior center's annual Scrabble competition.

The funny thing was that Max hadn't even been surprised. He'd walked into the lobby, taken in the sight of a dozen tables set up with two-person, head-to-head Scrabble games and knew there would be a seat with his name on it. Nothing shocked him anymore.

Except maybe how thoroughly his uncle was currently beating him. It was borderline humiliating, really. But for the first three turns, Max hadn't drawn a single vowel tile. How was he supposed to make a decent word from a handful of M's and a ragtag collection of other consonants?

The game doesn't matter. That's not the real reason you're here, remember?

He slapped down a sad three-letter word worth less than ten points and finally drew two vowels—an E and an A.

"Your turn, Uncle Henry," Max said. He spun the rotating game board so it faced his uncle.

Henry immediately laid down a word that used each and every letter on his rack, building on the C that Max had just put down.

"Read 'em and weep, Maxie boy. Schmooze." Henry's bushy eyebrows did a little dance. "S-C-H-M-O-O-Z-E, on a double-word space. That's seventy-four points. Plus I used all my letters, so I get a fifty-point bonus."

Super. Max was now operating at a deficit in excess of one hundred and fifty points, *and* he'd yet to glean his uncle's opinion on the grant application.

It wasn't as if Max thought that training other dogs to scent track sea turtle eggs was a bad idea. On the contrary, it was great. But the grant application was due in ten days. Could they really develop a proper training program and write up a proposal of how they could implement it in such a short period of time?

Possibly...

If they lived someplace other than Turtle Beach.

Grant applications were tricky, especially for state-funded conservation grants like the one Molly wanted to apply for. They'd need to write an abstract and a summary that listed their stated program goals and objectives. Plus they'd need to include a detailed background of the aquarium and sea turtle hospital, as well as the qualifications of the grant applicants. Most important, the application required specifics concerning methods and implementation, which meant they'd need to conduct at least a few real-life training sessions to test out their procedures before they could write the proposal.

The grant committee would expect to see solid evidence of an ecological program that would make a significant impact on the community. Where were these dogs that Molly wanted to train and who was going to teach them?

Max hadn't dared press her for specifics last night. She would have no doubt reminded him about Turtle Beach's booming canine population. But Max had met a good number of the dogs on the island. Most notably, he'd met the dogs that belonged to Molly's friends. Did she really think they could train Nibbles the Chihuahua and Violet's bouncy Dalmatian to scent track turtle nests?

Max just couldn't see it. And as far as Molly's dog training skills went…

He knew better than to voice an opinion in that regard. They both knew she doted on Ursula, but the puppy had learned a skill that very few dogs around the world had mastered. Molly was clearly doing something right, whether intentional or not.

Max had told her they needed to slow down and sleep on the idea before committing to it. He'd been as kind as possible, but when she'd realized he wasn't completely sold on the plan, her face had fallen. The disappointment in her eyes had reminded him so much of the way she'd reacted to her father's comments at lunch during SandFest that an ache had formed deep in his chest.

They'd finished marking the nest by the pier and walked back to their side-by-side beach cottages in awkward silence. The moon overhead had been little more than a sliver.

When Max had woken up this morning, the ache in his chest was still there. As were his doubts.

Max jotted down Henry's seventy-four-point score—plus the fifty-point bonus for using all of his letters—and spun the game board back around. He studied the letters on his rack while Uncle Henry drummed his fingers on the table, making Max's tiles jump in place.

A few tables down, Opal Lewinsky and Ethel Banks were engaged in a heated argument about whether or not *vajayjay* was a real word.

"Use it in a sentence," Ethel demanded.

Max closed his eyes. *Please don't.*

"What's the matter?" Henry asked.

"Nothing. I'm fine," Max lied.

Henry harrumphed. "You can't play Scrabble with your eyes closed."

Max decided to just cut to the chase. If anything, it would make it easier to ignore the vajayjay debate. "Did you hear what I said earlier? Molly wants to apply for a state conservation grant to focus on developing a program for training dogs to scent track sea turtle nests."

"I heard you just fine." Henry shrugged. "I just don't see why you're so torn up about it. You said that Ursula taught herself to sniff out nests. It stands to reason that other dogs can learn to do the same thing."

"Right, but—"

Uncle Henry cut him off. "But you just want to micromanage the grant application when Molly is the one who found out about the grant in the first place."

Was that what he was doing?

All at once, he felt like he was back at his old job in Baltimore, listening to the board of directors tell him that the reason he'd been passed over for a promotion was his lack of work–life balance. Old habits died hard.

Max shifted in his seat. "Uncle Henry, the grant is worth almost a million dollars. If we got it, the aquarium and the sea turtle hospital would be funded for the foreseeable future."

"And you don't want to go with Molly's idea, even though you regretted firing her. And even though you brought her back as soon as you could. And even though she organized that wonderful turtle release yesterday, and her little dog is going to make a bigger impact on this year's sea turtle hatching season than the entire staff of the aquarium put together." Henry held up his hands. "That's about the sum of things, am I right?"

Max sat back in his chair as if he'd been physically punched directly in the place where his chest ached.

"Actually." Max swallowed. "You kind of are."

"Then I think you know what to do," Henry said.

Maybe he did. But could things really be that simple?

"It's your turn. Are you going to make a word or not?" Uncle Henry nodded toward the Scrabble board. Case closed and discussion over, apparently.

At least this time, he'd actually listened to Max and offered some advice. Even if the advice had been difficult to hear.

Max stared at the letters on his rack until they seemed to arrange themselves into a word—a word that made Max's breath bottle up tight in his chest.

He picked up the tiles and carefully laid them down.

M-E-R-M-A-I-D. Mermaid.

If Max believed in signs, he just might have thought the universe was trying to tell him something.

Chapter 17

TEN DAYS. THAT WAS it. That's all the time they had.

Whenever Molly glanced at her calendar, a little flare of panic bloomed in her chest. Technically, she had *less* than ten days to get the dog training sessions up and running, because she'd need time to get everything properly written up before submitting the paperwork to the grant committee.

Miraculously, Max had suggested that Molly write up the entire thing on her own. It had been the absolute last thing she'd expected when Max had walked into the aquarium just after lunch and requested that she descend her mermaid throne to speak to him privately in his office. Frankly, she'd been fully prepared for him to tell her that they wouldn't be doing the dog training program at all. He'd seemed more than a little dubious about her idea last night, and his reaction had taken the wind out of her sails after such a great day. She'd suddenly had zero interest in kissing him under the pier again. All she'd wanted to do was go home, climb into her starfish pajamas, and watch the *Great British Baking Show* with Ursula. It had been patisserie week, her favorite.

This afternoon had been a completely different story, though. Max returned from wherever he'd run off to earlier in the day and given Molly total control over the grant application. It was her baby. Molly would be the author of the proposal, even without the letters PhD after her name. Now, mere hours later, she stood on the sidewalk in front of the Turtle Beach Fire Department's station on Seashell Drive, ready to make her first executive decision.

Molly smoothed down the skirt of her daisy-print smocked sundress. She couldn't very well turn up at the firehouse in her mermaid costume, so she'd darted home to change before the appointment she'd scheduled right after Max had given her the good news. Ursula trotted at the end of her leash, tail wagging as they pushed through the firehouse door.

"Molly, hi." Griff Martin—Caroline's brother and a firefighter with the TBFD—grinned at her from his station at the dispatch area. He bent to greet Ursula. "You too, you sweet little thing."

Ursula writhed in ecstasy as Griff rubbed her belly.

"Hi, Griff. Nice to see you," Molly said, glancing around the immaculate firehouse. "We've got an appointment with Sam. Is he around?"

"You're in luck. He just got back from a call. We had a small fire across the bridge. The rig just pulled into the apparatus bay ten minutes ago." Griff pushed a button and called Sam's name over the intercom system.

Molly barely had time to thank him before Sam appeared with his Dalmatian, Cinder, at his side. He held up a hand in greeting. "Hey!"

"Hi," Molly said as Ursula bounded toward the black-and-white-spotted dog.

Molly always had to do a double-take when she saw Cinder. The Dalmatian's resemblance to Violet's dog Sprinkles was uncanny. Spot for spot, they were identical. Both of them even had the same heart-shaped nose. The only way to distinguish one Dalmatian from the other was to pay close attention to their personalities. The dogs weren't quite the polar opposites that they used to be, but Cinder was still far more composed than Sprinkles would ever be. Case in point: Cinder would never *ever* snatch a cupcake from Max's hand…

Unless Sam told her to do it, which was precisely why Molly needed Sam's help.

"Why don't we go chat outside so the dogs can play?" Sam said.

"Sounds great."

The firehouse had a fenced-in yard out back with a barbecue pit and a real lawn of bright-green St. Augustine grass—a rarity in a beach town where most yards consisted of sand and sea oats. Molly let Ursula off of her leash and she immediately began climbing all over Cinder and tugging gently on the Dalmatian's ears. The spotted dog had the patience of a saint.

"You're probably wondering what was so urgent that I needed to meet with you as soon as possible," Molly said as she took a seat opposite Sam at the long picnic table on the firehouse's back patio.

Sam's eyebrows rose. "I'll admit that I'm rather curious."

"I'm here to offer you a part-time job in the evenings for the next week and a half." She offered him an apologetic grin. "For which I can pay you exactly zero dollars. Also, the task involved might be borderline impossible."

"When you put it that way, how can I refuse?" He laughed,

and then he appeared to turn her words over in his head. "How impossible, exactly?"

Molly was simply being honest, but thanks to Violet, she also knew that Sam enjoyed a challenge. Although what she was about to propose might test that theory. "You're probably more equipped to answer that question than I am. What I'm hoping to do is train some of the dogs on the island to scent track sea turtle nests."

Sam tore his gaze away from Ursula and Cinder, who'd begun chasing each other around the barbecue pit. He looked at her as if she'd just sprouted an *actual* mermaid tail. "And you want to accomplish this in a week and a half?"

"Honestly? More like a week." Molly winced. "I know it sounds crazy, but Violet said you trained Cinder to be a fire safety dog all on your own. She told me that Cinder even makes your bed in the morning and turns on your coffee maker."

He pulled a face. "I've tried to get her to stop with the household chores, but it's not working. I think she just likes it."

Weird. If Ursula suddenly started cleaning the house, Molly would have no complaints.

"I never trained her to do those things, just the fire safety stuff," Sam said.

Molly nodded. "I get it. I never trained Ursula to track sea turtle eggs, but she found five nests yesterday."

Sam glanced at Ursula and then back at Molly. "That's seriously impressive."

"If we can teach other dogs to do the same, the aquarium might have a chance at winning a very generous grant. Frankly, we really need the money. The dogs don't need to be completely trained in a week, but we need to at least be able to prove that we're on the right track." Now that she was saying all of this out loud, the plan seemed completely far-fetched. No wonder Max's initial reaction hadn't been as positive as she'd hoped it would be.

The way that Sam was looking at her now didn't help.

"Things like this take time." He sighed. "And yeah, I know how to get a dog to do basic obedience and a series of specialized fire safety behaviors, but I've never trained a dog to recognize and identify scents before."

Molly's heart sank all the way down to her ballerina flats. Sam was the one and only dog trainer she knew. Without him on board, the proposal seemed hopeless.

"Except smoke," Sam added with a shrug.

And just like that, a little zing of hope coursed through Molly once again. "Smoke is totally a scent. That counts."

The corner of Sam's mouth quirked into a half-smile. "So we're really going to do this?"

"If Ursula can find sea turtle eggs, I know we can teach the other dogs to do it too." Molly reached into her handbag and pulled out a small notepad and a turquoise pen. The pen was topped with a plastic sea turtle and had the words TURTLE BEACH AQUARIUM AND SEA TURTLE HOSPITAL printed on it. "Tell me exactly what you need. I'll get everything together and we can start tomorrow evening."

"The most important thing is the sample smell," Sam said.

"Oh." Molly bit her lip. "I can't dig up sea turtle eggs. We think Ursula familiarized herself with the smell from being at the turtle hospital so often."

He shook his head. "It's okay. We don't need actual eggs. In fact, it might be better if they learn to identify sand where sea turtle eggs are present."

"Maybe I can remove a bit of sand from one of the nests that Ursula found. I'll need to check with Max first, but would that work?" Sand surrounding the egg chamber helped incubate the turtle eggs, but perhaps if a small amount would do the trick, she could safely remove a sample.

"We don't need much—just enough to fill a few small scent containers, depending on how many dogs we're trying to train." Sam held his finger and thumb a couple of inches apart to indicate the size of the scent containers.

Doable. *Totally* doable. Molly was starting to feel better already.

"I can get the scent containers if you get the sand," he said.

Molly jotted down *turtle sand*. "What else do we need?"

"Dog treats. Tiny bits of turkey hot dogs tend to work great, especially if you cut them up and microwave them so they dry out."

She nodded. "Turkey hot dogs. Got it."

"We'll need dog-training clickers, but I've got plenty of those," Sam said.

"Super." Molly looked at her short list. "I can definitely get these things ready by tomorrow."

Sam tilted his head. "Aren't you forgetting something?"

"What?"

He laughed. "The dogs."

Oh, right. The dogs.

———····———

The following morning, Molly presented Max with her detailed plan to train a group of six dogs to scent track sea turtle nests for her grant proposal. The amount of work she'd done since yesterday afternoon was astounding.

She already had a proper dog trainer lined up, a team of volunteers with dogs who were willing to commit to nightly training sessions for the next seven days, and over twenty pages written on the grant proposal. All she needed from him was some sand, apparently.

"Sand?" He squinted at her from behind his glasses. She was already dressed in her mermaid costume for the day. Max wasn't sure he'd ever seen a mermaid carrying a file folder containing grant documents before. In fact, he was certain he hadn't, but it was a sight he could get used to. "I'm not following."

"We need sand from one of the turtle nests, as close to the egg chamber as possible. Just a tiny bit, I promise. We're going to use it to help get the dogs familiar with the scent."

That made sense, although Max wasn't at all crazy about disturbing one of the nests.

"I was thinking that maybe you could collect a sample from the nest at the dog beach and then you could stay and watch class." She tilted her head. "What do you think?"

Ursula—who currently occupied one of the office chairs on the opposite side of Max's desk—panted and her mouth stretched into a wide doggy smile, as if delighted at the prospect of Max attending class. He was anthropomorphizing again, and he wasn't even sorry.

"You realize if you say no, you're going to permanently seal your reputation as a dog hater." Her eyes narrowed into an exaggerated glare.

Max smoothed down his tie. He still hadn't found time to replace his Baltimore wardrobe, but thanks to the island humidity, his dress shirts were decidedly less crisp than they'd been when he'd rolled into town.

He grinned. "We can't have that, can we?"

Not when dogs just might end up saving the aquarium, he thought.

"So you'll come?" Molly's entire face lit up.

Max hadn't been expected to be included. When he'd told her he was turning the entire project over to her, he'd meant it. The plan had been to stay away and let Molly do her thing, lest she think he was trying to micromanage things.

He liked that she wanted him there, though. He liked it more than he wanted to admit, even to himself.

"I wouldn't miss it," he said quietly.

The rest of the day passed in a blur. A speed boat in the intracoastal waterway accidentally hit a three-hundred-pound loggerhead and called the hospital for help. The animal needed emergency surgery, requiring Max to go down his list of volunteer veterinarians until he found one who could make a trip to the island right away. After a harrowing afternoon, the turtle was finally resting comfortably in an open-air tank in the warehouse.

Max had to rush to get to the dog beach in time to collect the sand sample before Molly's training class was scheduled to begin.

He yanked off his tie, stuffed it into the glove box of the Jeep, and made his way across the beach access and onto the shore. A group of dogs and handlers—most of whom were clearly residents of the senior center—had already begun to gather closer to the water. Molly and Ursula stood next to a Turtle Beach firefighter and a stoic Dalmatian with their backs to the sea.

The black and white dog looked *exactly* like Sprinkles, but according to what Molly had told him this morning, she was a specially trained fire safety dog named Cinder. Max still half-expected the Dalmatian to make a beeline for him and grab onto his pant leg like Sprinkles still did if he tried to sneak out of yoga before murder victim pose was over.

Cinder stayed put, though, while Max knelt down at the edge of the sea turtle nest that they'd just marked off yesterday. Since this one had been the telltale nest where Molly's puppy had sat down at his feet with the egg in her mouth, Max liked to think of it as "Ursula's nest."

He used his hands to sift gently through the sand to prevent damage to the eggs with a shovel. When he felt the packed sand begin to give way, Max knew he was close to the chamber, so he scooped a fistful of sand into a sandwich baggie and sealed it shut. With any luck, it would reek of turtle eggs.

"Great, you're here," Molly smiled down at him as he made his way to his feet. "Come on over and you can meet Sam and the others."

Sam and Cinder made an impressive pair. The Dalmatian's

focus on Sam never wavered, not even when Ursula snuck up behind Cinder and pounced on her tail.

As for the other canine students…

Max tried his best not to let his spirits sink. He pasted on a smile and made every effort to imitate Molly's bubbly effervescence as she introduced him to each potential search team. But as he shook hands and smiled, a nagging question kept spinning round and round in his head on a loop.

These are the dogs that are supposed to save the aquarium?

It was a ragtag bunch, to be frank. Mavis was there with Nibbles, of course. For once, the Chihuahua wasn't perched in Mavis's walker basket, and the poor dog acted as if she'd never set foot on the actual ground before. She couldn't seem to keep all four paws on the sand at once, but kept hopping into the air and jerking her paws up as if the shore was made of lava.

Next in line was Hoyt Hooper with his googly-eyed pug, who at least appeared to be a cohesive unit in their matching Hawaiian shirts. But the pug, named Bingo, was wearing aviator-style goggles that fogged up every time Bingo panted.

"I worry about him getting sand in his eyes," Hoyt said.

Max was at a loss.

"There's certainly a lot of it out here." He looked right and left. The shore stretched for miles in either direction. "But it looks like Bingo is well protected."

"Max, this is Hoyt's son, Hoyt Jr., and his Golden Retriever, also named Hoyt." Molly rested her hand on Hoyt Hooper's broad head—the dog, not either of the humans named Hoyt, obviously.

The dog's face had gone completely white with age, but still, weren't Golden Retrievers supposed to be highly trainable? Maybe Hoyt would be their star pupil.

Max clung to that tiny shred of hope as Molly led him down the line, introducing him to Clover, Ethel Banks's corgi, and a giant white poodle named Betty White. Then they reached the final handler/pet team and Max blinked. Hard.

"Hello." Larry Sims, who Max remembered from the SandFest pancake breakfast, held out his hand. "Skippy and I are thrilled to be part of this effort to save sea turtles."

Max went numb as he shook Larry's hand. He frowned down at Skippy. "But that's a—"

"A cat." Molly nodded. Her smile went a bit strained around the edges. "A cat on a leash. Yes. Yes, he is."

Larry puffed out his chest. "Skippy's a Persian, and he can do anything a dog can do."

Max opened his mouth to respond, but he seemed to have lost the ability to speak. He glanced at Molly.

A cat? Really?

He'd definitely missed this significant detail when she'd shown him her neatly typed proposal this morning.

"Skippy is a last-minute substitution. Violet volunteered to come and train Sprinkles, but she got a last-minute order to bake one hundred cupcakes by tomorrow morning. I didn't think five dogs would be enough, and Larry graciously agreed to step in with Skippy," Molly said.

Max took another glance at the cat, who looked like a puff of gray fur with startling sea-blue eyes. She let out a loud meow, prompting an explosion of barks from her fellow trainees.

Max could practically feel the grant money slipping between his fingers like sand through a sieve.

"All right, folks." Sam clapped his hands, and the dogs quieted down. "Let's get started."

For the next hour, Sam showed the handlers how to introduce their pets to the sample scent. Every time a dog touched its nose to one of the small metal containers where he'd stored the sand that Max had excavated from the turtle nest, the handler said "turtle," clicked the training clicker, and gave the dog a treat. In the beginning, chaos reigned. Unsurprisingly, Skippy's presence proved to be a major distraction. But Max had to hand it to the Persian—she was the first animal to earn a reward for smelling the sample scent.

Max tried to get a read on Sam, but if their dog trainer was frustrated with the situation, he didn't let on. He was as cool and unflappable as his Dalmatian. For this Max was grateful, because by the time the training session ended, Molly's eyes had grown shiny with unshed tears.

She held it together while she told everyone goodbye and reminded them to meet back at the dog beach tomorrow night at the same time. But once Betty White, Bingo, Clover, Nibbles, Skippy, and the three Hoyt Hoopers crossed the dune and were out of sight, a lone tear slipped down Molly's cheek.

Chin quivering, she turned toward Max. "This isn't going to work, is it?"

Max could have been honest right then. He could have told her no, it wasn't going to work—not even if she'd had months to train her sad little group of volunteers. He could have gone back on his promise and said they needed to switch gears and do something more conventional for the grant proposal. He could have done the professional thing and put the aquarium first.

But doing so would have broken Molly's heart.

So instead, he cupped her face in his hands and told her not to cry. He brushed the tear from her cheek and smiled into her eyes. And then Max lied through his teeth.

"You've got this. It's all going to be okay."

Chapter 18

"THANK GOODNESS," CAROLINE SAID the following Friday morning when Molly walked through the door of Turtle Books. Ursula strained at her leash to get to Sebastian, but the cat leapt to the tallest bookshelf in the travel section and flicked his tail. "I was about ready to send out a search party. Where have you been all week?"

Where to start?

Molly sat down at the counter and gathered Ursula into her lap. "I'm sorry I haven't been by all week, but things have been crazy busy at the aquarium. Plus I'm finally putting together that grant proposal I've been wanting to write for ages, and it's required a lot more energy than I expected."

Understatement of the century. Molly had been walking around with a gnawing sense of dread in the pit of her stomach for five days running. Her only saving grace was that Max hadn't yanked the grant application away from her. He'd been stunningly supportive, showing up at every training session and effectively acting as a cheerleader to the search teams. And in the moments when Molly's confidence started to crumble and she let her anxiety show, he promised her that everything was going to be just fine.

She kept waiting for the dam to break...for him to point out that they were over halfway through the training period and thus far—other than Cinder, who was already a trained working dog, and Ursula, the class wunderkind—only one dog had successfully identified and alerted to a turtle sample on command.

One dog on *one* occasion.

The entire class had whooped and hollered when Betty White had pressed her nose to the correct sample container and then lowered herself into an immediate sit position—the signal that Sam had taught the dogs to use when they needed to alert their handlers. Molly had whooped and hollered right along with them, but deep down, she couldn't help but wonder if it had simply been a lucky guess.

"I know all about your sea turtle tracking project." Caroline slid a frozen Milky Way latte across the counter toward Molly. "Violet's been giving me updates when she comes in to drop off cupcakes for the bakery case. For the record, I'm deeply hurt that you didn't ask Sebastian and me to participate. He'd make a way better search cat than Skippy the Persian."

Molly regarded Caroline as she took her first sip of her coffee drink. She had to hold back a moan when the chocolate, caramel, and espresso flavors hit her taste buds. It had been way too long since she'd had one of these.

"You're joking, right? You don't really want to try and train Sebastian," Molly said.

Caroline bit back a smile as Sebastian purposefully knocked a book from the shelf with a swipe of his paw. "What do you think?"

"Okay, good. You scared me for a minute." She set her cup

down. Ursula whined in Molly's lap, clearly displeased that no one appeared to be paying any attention to her.

Caroline opened the glass jar full of dog treats that she kept on hand for canine customers and slipped one to Ursula. "No worries. Sebastian and I are happy to leave the turtle egg saving to Skippy and Larry."

"That's the thing." Molly cleared her throat. "I'm not sure there's going to actually be any egg saving going on."

"What do you mean? Your dog is a genuine turtle hero. Everyone on the island is talking about it." Caroline offered Ursula another treat. Sebastian hissed as she crunched loudly on it.

"That's definitely true." Molly pressed a kiss to the top of her puppy's head. There'd been so much going on the past few days that she sometimes lost sight of how the training class had started. "I'm just worried about what will happen if she's the only one."

A man approached the counter to order a plain drip coffee and buy a copy of the latest hardback legal thriller from the fiction table. Molly polished off her latte while she waited for Caroline to ring him up.

After the customer had gone, Caroline refilled Molly's cup. "Here. You really look like you could use more chocolate."

"Thanks." She took a long pull from her straw.

"Why are you stressing yourself out so badly over whether or not you can train other dogs to do what Ursula does? It's a pretty amazing feat. Maybe your dog is just special and that's that." Caroline reached across the counter to scratch Ursula's dainty chin.

"*Of course* she's special." Hadn't Molly been saying as much since the day she'd adopted her? "But the grant is worth almost a million dollars. What if I mess it all up?"

Caroline's gaze narrowed. "You've been talking to your parents, haven't you?"

"Maybe." Molly groaned. "Okay, yes. I have. You wouldn't have believed how proud my dad sounded when I told him I was heading up the entire grant effort. It was the best conversation we've had in a long time."

Caroline sighed. "But now you feel pressured to win the grant, not only to save the aquarium but also to please your folks, am I right?"

Molly nodded. "Exactly, except you also left out the part where I'll feel like I let Max down if I'm unsuccessful."

"You won't be letting *anyone* down, Molls. Ursula alone is going to make a big impact on the island's conservation efforts. Anything else is just icing on the cake." As if to prove her point, Caroline reached into the bakery case for a cupcake and set it down in front of Molly. It was one of Violet's special Sidekick Snickerdoodle cupcakes, decorated to look like Ursula.

"I'm not sure I can eat that after having two frozen lattes," Molly said. "But I love that Violet's still making these. I thought they were just a one-off for bingo night back when I was still fired."

"They were. Violet brought them back by popular demand because everyone in Turtle Beach is so proud of your smart little dog."

Molly felt the tension in her shoulders ease just a tiny bit. "Really?"

"Yes, really. And we're proud of *you* too, Molly. All of us."
Caroline's mouth curved into a knowing grin. "Even Max."

"Don't be so sure—I begged one of the local firemen to help
me train five dogs and a cat to sniff out sea turtle nests on the
beach. When I stop and think about it, it sounds legitimately
crazy pants."

"Exactly." Caroline dropped the snickerdoodle cupcake into
a pink bag with Violet's Sweetness on Wheels logo and handed it
to Molly. "No one on the entire island would take something like
this on. Only you, Molls. That in and of itself is pretty special and
don't you forget it."

Ursula's nose twitched in the direction of the bakery bag.
Sometimes Molly wondered if her favorite British baking show
might be a bad influence.

She smiled at Caroline. "Thank you, and I'm not just talking
about the coffee and cupcake."

"Anytime. Now go be a mermaid. I'll see you later this afternoon for the Under the Sea Ball planning meeting."

Go be a mermaid. At least that was something Molly had
a decent handle on. Plus the Under the Sea Ball was already
coming together. The Turtle Team just needed to go over a few
final details.

Something miraculous happened just a few minutes later
when Molly arrived at the aquarium for her mermaid shift—
something *almost* as miraculous as Betty White correctly identify-
ing the scent of sea turtle eggs. Silver the seahorse at long last gave
birth to over a thousand tiny seahorse babies.

The blessed event happened just after Molly finished changing into her glittering fishtail. She rounded the corner into the lobby with Ursula trotting alongside in her lobster costume and found Max and Nate staring intently at Silver's tank, their faces just inches from the glass.

"What's going on?" Molly asked.

Max's gaze swiveled toward her. The grin on his face was so boyish and goofy that her heart felt like it was being squeezed in a vise. "Seahorse babies. Come see!"

She mermaid-stepped toward the tank and nudged her way in between Max and Nate. Teeny-tiny seahorses floated everywhere, like an explosion of confetti. Each one was smaller than a grain of rice, with tiny little snouts and curlicue tails.

Her hand flew to her throat. "Oh my gosh, they're precious. How many do you think there are?"

"So far I've counted four hundred and twenty-three," Nate said.

Molly and Max laughed, but when Molly glanced at Nate, his expression was dead serious.

Max grinned at her, and when they switched their attention back toward the tank, she felt his hand reach for hers. They stood there quietly watching the newborns float in the water, dainty little miracles. The moment was complete and utter joy, and the warmth in Max's fingertips made Molly feel like everything truly would be okay. It was crazy how so much hope and newness could be wrapped up in a thousand tiny packages.

"I'll go move the newborns to the rearing tanks," Nate said.

He pushed through the door to the aquarium's behind-the-scenes area. Molly expected Max to follow, but he stayed put.

Through the glass walls of the seahorse tank, they could see Nate on the other side. He reached into the aquarium with a glass beaker and began scooping out some of the floating babies and moving them into smaller tanks.

"He's literally getting rid of the baby and the bath water." Molly glanced at Max. "Why doesn't he use a net?"

"Because newborn seahorses can't be exposed to air. They'll swallow it and it'll lead to fatal buoyancy problems." Max pointed at the four smaller tanks in the wall where Nate was carefully relocating the newborns by submerging the beaker into the tank's clean water and waiting for the babies to make their way out. "The newborns are moved into smaller tanks with brighter lighting so they can spot food more easily. Also if they're not removed from the tank with Silver, he might eat some of them. These little guys are really fragile, and we want as many as possible to thrive."

Ursula stood on her hind legs in an effort to get a better look at what had captured everyone's attention. Max released Molly's hand to gather the puppy in his arms. He lifted her up and held her in front of the tanks so she could see. Ursula went wide-eyed at once.

Molly couldn't take her eyes off of the two of them. They couldn't have looked more adorable together if Max had gone full-on dog dad and worn Ursula in a baby sling on his chest. She could never have imagined Max treating her puppy with such tenderness back when he'd fired them. So much had changed since that terrible morning.

Molly swallowed hard and turned back toward the collection of tanks in the seahorse dude ranch.

"Did you know that the proper term for newborn seahorses is 'fry'?" Max said quietly.

Molly shook her head.

He shrugged and that goofy, boyish grin made a comeback. "I'm starting to prefer 'babies.'"

Molly's heart did a full-on flip-flop and she realized she'd been wrong just now. Yes, so much had changed since the morning Max had fired her and Ursula. But more than that, *he'd* changed. She wasn't sure if it was Turtle Beach or the aquarium or being so close to his uncle again, but Max was becoming a different man...a good man. A man who just might be able to make her forget all about her no-dating rule.

No. This is not *the time. You have far too much going on right now to lose your focus.*

So she did her best to put those forbidden feelings in a box and lock them up tight, like a sunken treasure chest. She pasted on a bright mermaid smile, greeted aquarium guests, and painted seahorses on children's faces.

But while she presided over the planning meeting for the Under the Sea Ball, Max strode into the conference room with handfuls of pink and blue bubblegum cigars. He passed them out like a proud dad, and despite every effort to keep her treasure chest of feelings buried in the deepest possible part of the ocean, Molly felt it rising up to the surface.

Then its rusty old padlock fell away, and the lid creaked open...just enough for her to catch a glimpse of the riches hidden inside.

Max had never thought he'd be in a position where all his hopes for his professional future would rest on the shoulders of a poodle named Betty White, but alas, here he was.

The dogs, plus Skippy, were due to arrive at the dog beach for the final night of scent training class in just a few minutes. It would be their last chance to show promise and give Molly some good data to work with before she put the finishing touches on the grant proposal and turned it in. Max couldn't stand still. If he didn't stop pacing, he was going to wear a trench in the sand.

"Can I give you a hand?" he asked Molly. Surely there was something constructive he could do.

She glanced up from the park bench where she was unpacking the little metal tins she'd prepared that contained small amounts of packed sand—some from the sea turtle nests and others from neutral places on the beach. "Do you want to help me spread out the scent samples?"

"Sure." Anything to get his mind off of the fact that thus far, Betty White and Ursula were the team's saving graces. And in an hour, their time would be up.

Max didn't know for certain whether or not the grant team would dismiss their proposal outright if only two dogs on the island had shown any real promise, but he didn't feel good about the odds. If they could get lucky enough for even one more dog to alert to the hidden turtle sample tonight, their proposal might have an actual shot.

Molly had worked so hard. The entire proposal was written and ready to go out tomorrow morning, just in time for the noon deadline. All she had to do was plug in the final numbers. Max did his best to give off a supportive, confident air as she instructed him on where to put the sample tins.

There were eight samples in all, with only two containing sand from the sea turtle nest. Max had excavated fresh sand from close to the egg chamber just half an hour ago so the scent would be as fresh and strong as possible. He and Molly placed the tins in random spots around the dog beach, while Sam and Cinder waited by the dune for the teams to arrive.

Tonight's class was to be a test of sorts. One by one, each team would search the beach. The handler would follow the dog's lead, letting the pup sniff the ground and any scent tins they came across. The goal was for the dogs to immediately sit down when exposed to the correct sample scent. If they barked too, even better.

Max would take a silent sit. He'd even take a meow at this point—from any of the trainees, not just Skippy.

"I think we're ready." Molly wrapped her arms around herself. She was wearing a Turtle Team T-shirt, her hair was piled into a messy pink and blonde bun on top of her head, and her nails were painted a shimmery, iridescent mermaid-blue.

She looked as lovely and quirky as ever, but she seemed a little lost. Max knew she had to be nervous about tonight, but he wasn't crazy about the way she kept crossing and recrossing her arms as if trying to hold herself together.

Then he realized what was missing.

"Where's Ursula?" he said.

"Sam and I decided she probably shouldn't be here tonight. We didn't want her accidentally giving hints to the other dogs."

"Throwing them a bone, so to speak?" Max said.

"Max Miller. Did you just make a dad joke?" Molly poked him gently in the ribs. "You must really be invested in those sea-horse babies."

He held his finger and thumb a fraction of an inch apart. "A little bit, yes."

She laughed. In the distance, Max could see the teams lining up at the beach access and Sam issuing instructions for their test. A thought crossed his mind, one that he'd been tossing around for a while and trying not to act on.

"Speaking of infant sea life," he heard himself say, "are you busy tonight around ten p.m. onward?"

Smooth. Real smooth. He was trying to ask her on a date of sorts, and he couldn't manage to avoid mentioning marine biology.

Molly studied him for a moment and her lips curved into a promising smile. "The only thing ordinarily on my agenda at that time of night is sleeping, but what did you have in mind? I'm intrigued."

"Would you like to babysit the turtle nest on the beach by our houses with me? The hatchlings are due to arrive soon." Max cleared his throat. Why did he feel like a teenager trying to invite a girl he liked to the prom? He was suggesting she join him for a quasi–work-related activity.

On the beach...

In the moonlight.

His chest clenched as he waited for her to respond. Then a loud cheer erupted on the other side of the beach, dragging their attention to Bingo the pug, sitting completely still—goggles and all—in the exact spot where Max had put one of the sample tins that contained sand from the turtle nest.

"Look!" Molly grabbed onto Max's arm. "He did it. Bingo alerted!"

They looked at each other, eyes wide and frozen for a split second, until Molly threw herself into Max's arms.

It was almost too much—her softness, her scent, her joyful energy—like trying to hold sunshine in his hands. Max closed his eyes and held her tight, until she finally backed away to meet his gaze.

The dizzy smile on her face changed into something more private, like a secret she'd been holding onto just for him. "And yes to tonight. Let's babysit a turtle nest together."

Max felt himself exhale. "It's a date."

———

"Just calm down," Molly told Ursula as they walked down the steps of the cottage toward the beach below. The ocean looked inky-black under the night sky. The moon hung high overhead, shining bright like a pearl. "I don't know for sure if this is a date."

Ursula scrambled her paws so fast that they almost ran right out from under her. Down on the sand, Max held up a hand and grinned. Molly's stomach fluttered, beating with the excited wings of a thousand summer butterflies.

Okay, maybe it was a date. Max had said so himself, after all. Molly just didn't want to get her hopes up about anything. Her track record with dates wasn't exactly stellar, and with discovering

Ursula's special talent, the birth of the seahorse babies, and the enormous success of today's training test, so many miraculous things had happened lately that she knew she had to be headed for a fall. The good luck streak couldn't last forever.

Being a professional mermaid, Molly thought a lot about luck, probably more than most people. She liked to memorize fun facts and myths about mermaids to help create her narrative when talking to the guests, especially the kids. She knew that for every legend about mermaids being harbingers of good luck, there was another, darker myth that said mermaids were cursed. They were temptresses who liked to toy with sailors' hearts and lure them off course.

Molly had never felt like much of a temptress, but sometimes she wondered if luck and good fortune worked like the tides. Nature was full of patterns. It was one of the most beautiful and mysterious things about science—the fivefold symmetry of a starfish, the perfect swirls in a seashell, ripples in the wet sand that perfectly mirrored one another. Like the ocean ebbed and flowed, it only made sense that bad times would be followed by good, and so on and so on.

She'd been waiting so long for the good times to come again that she'd almost given up. And now that they were here, she was almost afraid to breathe lest they slip through her fingers.

Every single dog had alerted at class earlier today. Every. Single. One. Skippy, not so much. But Molly was happy to give the search cat a pass. She'd had real results to plug into the grant proposal, and she'd been so excited to get the numbers in place that she'd finished the paperwork and sent it off early, just an hour ago. And now her toes were sinking in the sand as she walked toward Max with her heart in her throat—on a *date*.

"Hi, there," he said, looking more like his sand sculpture lookalike than Molly had ever seen him before. He wore khaki shorts that were a little frayed at the edges, and one of his regular white button-downs but it was rolled up at the sleeves and unbuttoned a few inches, so she could see the hollow of his throat.

Molly liked this loose, relaxed version of Max. Quite a lot. It made her feel things…*volleyball*-type feelings.

"Hi." She swallowed hard as he bent down to rub Ursula's belly. "This was a great idea. I've never seen a sea turtle nest hatch before."

Max stood and pointed toward the nest they'd marked off that was situated farther up on the dunes, directly between their houses. "I was thinking that one might have been laid earlier than the others. The sand up there looks really natural and undisturbed. But of course, there's no guarantee. Odds are we'll sit out here all night long and nothing will happen."

That didn't sound so bad, frankly. "I think I could live with that."

His eyes met hers, and Molly forgot about luck and grants and all the silly things she'd let get in the way of getting to know him better. She even forgot about The Tourist. Life before Max had come to the island felt a million miles away.

"Same here." He held out his hand.

Molly took it, and with fingertips entwined, they made their way to the nest. Ursula tugged at the end of her leash, nose twitching, but Molly made sure she didn't get too close.

"Here we go." Max gestured toward a blanket on the sand, anchored down on one corner with an ice bucket containing a bottle of rosé and two glasses. A dog bowl filled with water next to a large bone with rawhide knots on either end held down the opposite side of the blanket. The other corners were weighted down with small piles of seashells.

Definitely a date. Molly's smile felt like it bloomed from inside out.

They settled onto the blanket, facing the ocean. The sea was a blank slate, not a boat or a ship in sight. A few late-night beachgoers walked past, but after about half an hour or so, the shore went quiet save for the gentle lullaby of the sea. Ursula tucked herself into a ball around her bone, and her tiny form rose and fell in a sleepy rhythm. Molly's head found its way to Max's shoulder.

"You know what? I think Opal, Ethel, and Mavis might be right," she murmured. "You're not so bad after all."

He chuckled, and it moved through Molly like an electric current. "Are you sure, or is this just the sand sculpture going to your head?"

Molly lifted her face to his and looked him straight in his sea-blue eyes. "It's not the sand sculpture. It's all you, Wilson."

His gaze dropped to her mouth, and this time, Molly didn't wait for him to kiss her. She took control of it all on her own. Nothing was going to get in the way of this moment. Not again. She rose up on her knees, placed her hands on either side of his chiseled face, and lowered her mouth onto his.

Max's hands went straight into her hair and his lips were hot and ready...as if he'd been waiting for this to happen since the moment they'd first tried to grab hold of each other in the swirling riptide at the dog beach. Maybe they had. Maybe this entire summer they'd been reaching for one another, desperate for contact, only to slip apart time and time again.

Finally coming together, finally feeling the warmth of his mouth and their hearts crashing against each other should have been a relief. But it was more than that. It was like drowning… like sleeping deep underwater only to find that you could still breathe, still live while at the same time completely losing control.

"Molly," he whispered. Her name was a prayer on his lips. A plea.

She could only whimper in response.

"Open your eyes," he said gently. "Look at me."

She did as he said. His eyes were darker than she'd ever seen them, like a tempest.

"I want us to be together. I want us to give this a try—for real this time." His thumb caressed her cheek in a tender circular motion. "Would you be my date to the Under the Sea Ball?"

"I would love that." She grinned.

His gaze drifted to her mouth and just as they were about to kiss again, Ursula jolted awake, leapt to her feet, and let out three sharp barks.

"Shh, little puppy." Molly turned to quiet the dog down, and then she saw it—a tiny turtle hatchling poking up through the sand.

She blinked. Stared harder at the nest. Two more hatchlings popped up, tiny flippers waving at the air.

"Max." She fisted his shirt in her hands. "It's happening!"

But he was already moving, already getting to his feet. Molly grabbed Ursula, held her close, and followed.

"What do we do now?" she whispered.

The first three hatchlings were fully emerged now, crawling toward the water.

"We just watch and make sure no one gets turned around. Sea turtles are born with an instinct to move in the brightest direction. They're drawn toward the moonlight over the ocean."

Molly nodded. "Right. That's why the Turtle Team puts up signs every year asking people to turn off their porch lights at night if they live on the beach."

"Mainly, we're here because if people are around, predators are less likely to swoop in and take them," Max said.

"So we're like turtle bodyguards."

He laughed, his voice soft as velvet in the darkness. "Yes."

Max took her hand again and squeezed it tight as the nest overflowed with hundreds of baby sea turtles crawling their way home. They didn't need anyone to show them where to go or what to do. They just knew.

Move in the brightest direction.

As instincts went, it was spot on. Maybe that's what Molly needed to do from here on out. Or at least keep moving. She'd spent far too long doing her best to stay still.

Chapter 19

MOLLY SPENT THE ENTIRE day of the Under the Sea Ball with the Turtle Team at the senior center, transforming the gymnasium into a magical underwater oasis.

Hoyt Hooper Jr. and Sr. manned the helium tank, blowing up balloon after balloon and stringing them together in vertical clusters that stretched from floor to ceiling so they looked like bubbles rising to the top of an aquarium. The Charlie's Angels raided the senior center's kitchen and emerged with a dozen big glass bowls they'd filled with blue Jell-O and gummy fish candies so that the table centerpieces looked like whimsical fish tanks. Opal still had the old projector she'd used in her classroom when she taught art at Turtle Beach High. She dragged it out of the back of her closet and used it to project luminous underwater images onto the walls and ceiling—ethereal jellyfish, wavy seaweed, and angelfish with huge wing-like fins. Ursula chased them back and forth as they slow-danced across the ceiling.

Caroline, Violet, and Molly spent most of the afternoon on ladders, unscrewing the industrial fluorescent lighting and replacing it with bulbs tinted light blue and lavender. Violet brought boxes and boxes of cupcakes in special ocean-themed flavors. Day at the Beach, which had been frosted, rolled in graham cracker crumbs, and topped with a tiny umbrella to look like a shady spot on a sandy shore. Clamshell Cupcakes, topped with icing and vanilla sandwich cookies that had been propped open on one side to hold a tiny white edible pearl. And—Molly's personal favorite—Shark Attack, with blue frosting piped into tiny peaks to resemble waves, topped off with gray fondant shark fins and filled with a fresh strawberry jam center. A bit gory, but definitely in keeping with the theme.

The transformation took hours, but all the work had definitely been worth it. The gymnasium was flat-out unrecognizable.

"This place looks beyond dreamy." Violet sighed. "I can't wait for everyone to see it."

Caroline pressed a hand to her heart. "I feel like I'm in the lost city of Atlantis."

"Is that a real place or a myth?" Violet's forehead puckered. "I forget."

It was definitely a myth. In fact, those dreaded words—*scientifically insignificant*—danced on the tip of Molly's tongue. But she swallowed them down. What was the harm in dreaming on a night like tonight?

Wait a minute. Molly's gaze flitted toward the windows, where the lavender sunset sky was deepening to a rich velvety blue. *Why is it getting dark already?*

She took her phone out of the back pocket of her skinny jeans and checked the time. Six o'clock? Max was supposed to pick her up in just an hour and she still needed to go home, feed Ursula, and get cleaned up. The sparkling tulle dress she'd splurged on from her favorite boutique in Wilmington was hanging on the outside of her closet door, ready and waiting.

"I totally lost track of the time. We've got to go." Molly fished Ursula's leash out of her handbag and clipped it onto the puppy's collar. "See you all in just a little bit."

As she zipped home to the beach cottage on her Vespa, she couldn't help but notice how calm the ocean was tonight, reflecting the star-swept sky like a glass mirror so that everything—land, sea, sky—glittered like diamonds. She'd spent so much time hiding from romance, from *love*, that she'd forgotten that sometimes life really did look and feel just like a fairy tale. Or maybe even a long-lost utopian city under the sea.

So it seemed fitting that when Max knocked on her door an hour later, he looked like an altogether dreamy combination of sea god meets Prince Charming. He wore a deep-blue tuxedo with smooth black satin lapels and a bow tie that made his eyes sparkle like sapphires.

"Molly." He clutched his chest. "You look…"

His voice drifted off as he took in the sight of her. Once she'd put her new floor-length dress on, she'd worried it might have been too much. After years of dressing as a mermaid, she'd gone in the total opposite direction and chosen a gown for the ball that was airy and light, crafted from miles of diaphanous powder-blue tulle. The bodice was covered in shimmering beaded embellishment and had a deep v-neckline overlaid with a wisp-thin layer of pale-blue netting.

"You don't think it's too princess-y, do you?" she asked.

"Not at all. It suits you," he said, voice thick in a way that made Molly's heart pound hard in her chest. "You don't look like a princess. You look like a queen—queen of the mermaids."

His gaze swept slowly over the pearl headband holding back her hair in a loose, tousled updo. A shiver made its way up and down her spine. They hadn't even gone anywhere yet, and this already felt like the best date Molly had ever been on, hands down.

Max reached for her hand, brought it to his mouth and brushed his lips against her skin. Gently...*reverently*. Why had she waited so long to let herself have feelings for this man?

He smiled, eyes crinkling in the corners. "Where's our chaperone?"

Molly blinked, and then realized he was talking about Ursula. "Actually, she's staying home tonight. I've got her all situated in a puppy pen in my bedroom with a plush dog bed and a Kong toy stuffed with peanut butter. I left Netflix on for her, so by the time we get back, she should know how to bake a proper Bakewell tart."

Molly was babbling. She couldn't help it. She saw Max every single day, but not like this. There was something so raw and open about the way he looked at her. Things between them would be different after tonight. She *wanted* them to be different, and perhaps that's what made her most nervous of all.

"You're sure about this?" Max's smile turned soft, tender. "I wouldn't want her to feel anxious or vulnerable on her own."

Molly felt the corners of her mouth turn up. They weren't talking about Ursula anymore, were they? "She'll be fine. She's ready for this."

More than ready.

"Okay, then." He waved toward the deck and the cool night air with a flourish. "We have a ball to get to. Shall we?"

To Molly's delight, Max was rendered speechless when he got his first glimpse of the makeshift ballroom. He looked around for a full minute, taking in the balloon bubbles, the Jell-O fish tanks, and the moving pictures on the cool blue and violet walls, and then turned to Molly and shook his head. "Are you absolutely sure we're in the senior center's gym right now? Because this looks nothing like the place where I play volleyball on Thursday nights."

"You play in the senior center's wheelchair balloon volleyball league?" How did she not know this?

"I do, yes." He looked mildly embarrassed.

She gave him a playful shove. "That's all kinds of adorable, Max. I'll bet your Uncle Henry loves having you on the team."

He shook his head. "I doubt it. I'm pretty terrible at it, and I kind of just ended up on the team by default."

"Oh, really?" Molly smirked. "Keep telling yourself that."

He arched his left eyebrow. "What does that mean?"

"It means that your uncle has been playing you. Senior yoga? Flipping pancakes at SandFest? Scrabble tournaments? The wheelchair balloon volleyball league? You don't honestly think you just stumbled into all of those activities, do you?" The situation was so obvious to Molly. Henry just wanted to spend time with Max. Couldn't he see that?

Max thought for a minute and then shook his head. "My gosh, you're right. All this time, I thought he was just trying to avoid talking about the aquarium. But I think it might have been his devious way of getting me to do things with him."

"Devious…" Molly tilted her head. "Or sweet?"

"Both. Those things aren't mutually exclusive," he said, but there was far more than just a hint of affection in his voice.

"It worked. You totally fell for it."

"What can I say? Sometimes I let charm override my good judgment." He winked at her. "I'm human like that."

Molly felt a rush of affection for him right then, like an ocean wave knocking her off of her feet. She wanted to twirl in his arms on the dance floor and kiss him beneath Opal's magical floating jellyfish.

Before she could tell him those things, the Turtle Team descended on them. Mavis, Ethel, and Opal oohed and ahhed over Molly's dress and how handsome Max looked in his tux. True to form, the Charlie's Angels wore matching 1940s-style evening gowns with full ruffled skirts and opera-length white gloves. They might be pushing ninety, but they knew how to dress to make a statement. Molly could only hope to be that stylish at their age. Larry Sims stood quietly beside Mavis, looking dapper in a tux with a ruffled shirt and ultra-wide cummerbund. Sam and Violet were both dressed in black and white, Dalmatian-enthusiasts to their very cores. Violet was thrilled to report that over seventy people had already shown up, and according to Caroline, who was manning the entrance, ticket sales were through the roof.

They snapped selfies and group photos together while they still had a fraction of elbow room, and just as Max was about to dive into one of Violet's Shark Attack cupcakes, Molly's favorite song began playing on the gymnasium's sound system: Bobby Darin's "Beyond the Sea".

She gasped. "We have to dance to this!"

"Let's all go," Opal said, pointing her walker toward the dance floor.

Mavis, Larry, and Ethel fell in step behind her with their walkers.

"Come on." Violet grabbed Sam's hand. "We can't let them show us up."

"Absolutely not." Max set his cupcake down on a nearby table and guided Molly to the very center of the dance floor, his hand warm on the small of her back.

Max spun her around and around as she tipped her head back and took it all in—the decorations, the crowds, the love the community had for the aquarium. Soft purple shadows moved over Max's face, shapes from an underwater world. When the song ended, he lowered her into a preposterously low dip as the Turtle Team cheered. It was all so perfectly ridiculous. Molly wanted the night to go on forever.

And then the music switched to a slow song, and Max held her close. When her lips brushed against his neck, his grip on her hand tightened. She closed her eyes and melted into him as he murmured into her hair.

"Molly, I…"

The chime of an incoming email on Molly's cell phone interrupted whatever he was about to say. Her eyes flew open. The noise had come from her tiny beaded evening bag, dangling from her wrist by a delicate chain.

She blinked as if waking from a dream. "So sorry. I thought I turned that off. Let me just put it on silent real quick."

Emails were one thing. She definitely didn't want the phone to ring and completely spoil the evening's fanciful mood.

"No problem." Max flashed her a grin and released her from their dance hold so she could open her evening bag.

It was barely big enough to hold a smartphone and a lipstick, the only two items nestled inside. Molly slipped her phone from the bag, but when she went to switch it to silent mode, a preview of an incoming email flashed on the screen.

She froze in place. "Oh my God."

The easy grin on Max's face faded. "Is something wrong?"

Molly was vaguely aware of the Turtle Team in her periphery, dancing and swaying to the music. Everything felt like it was moving in slow motion all of a sudden, just like it had when Ursula dug up the sea turtle egg at the dog beach.

"No, nothing's wrong. At least I don't think it is." Molly shook her head. The phone trembled violently in her grasp. She squeezed it so hard that her knuckles turned white. "I just got a message from the grant committee."

She glanced up, fixing her gaze with Max's.

"Already?" He ran a finger lightly along the inside of the collar of his tuxedo shirt, as if he couldn't breathe. Other than that subtle telltale gesture, he seemed completely calm. Confident. Composed.

More composed than Molly felt, that was for sure.

"Go ahead and open the email. Read the good news so we can celebrate." He nodded toward the phone, which suddenly felt less like a communication device and more like a stick of dynamite in her hand.

She wanted to look, but at the same time, she didn't.

"Molly, come on. You've got this." Max winked.

He was right. Why was she panicking like this? They'd done it. All five dogs had shown they had the potential to identify and alert to the scent of sea turtle eggs. With more time and resources, she could recruit a real team. The data supported everything the aquarium wanted to accomplish. Moreover, her project was far more innovative than anything she'd seen in the boring scientific journals that were always lying around Max's office.

I've got this.

Her hand steadied, and she tapped the envelope icon so that the email from the grant committee flooded the screen. Molly's heart rose to her throat as she began reading.

———

Dear Ms. Prince,

Thank you for applying to the North Carolina State Grant for Ecological Protection. While we found your proposal innovative, the committee has unfortunately chosen to deny your request for funding. We wish you the best of luck with your endeavor and thank you for your commitment to preserving the ecology of the Carolina coast.

Molly read it again, just to be sure, as her heart took a serious nosedive. But no matter how many times she went over the words, they never changed.

She'd failed. They weren't getting the grant money. She'd talked Max into putting his faith in her "innovative" idea and now they'd missed out on the chance to do something normal and boring—the sort of thing that grant committees paid millions for.

Her knees were on the verge of buckling. The angelfish and seaweed waving on the walls abruptly went from seeming dreamlike and lovely to being garish and wrong. Molly pressed her hand to her stomach. Bile rose to the back of her throat, and she felt like she might be sick.

Max had tried to tell her, but she hadn't listened. And now she was going to have to look him in the face and tell him that the aquarium's troubles were far from over. Sea turtle release parties on the beach and dances at the senior center couldn't keep them afloat forever.

But when she lifted her gaze to Max's, the look on her face must have spoken for itself. Before she had a chance to say a word, his expression slammed closed like a book.

—*—

Max was shell-shocked.

Was that an official medical term? If not, it should be. Although somewhere in the back of his consciousness he was aware that *real* shell-shock was a battlefield condition, certainly more serious than what he was experiencing. But he couldn't seem to shake the word out of his thoughts.

Shell-shocked. He imagined hundreds of shells, sun-bleached and worn by the tide, salt, and sea. That's how he felt, all right. Battered, bruised, and wholly insignificant in the face of everything he loved most in the world—this place, these people, this *life*.

"We didn't get it," Molly said woodenly.

He nodded. He'd known it was coming, obviously. He'd watched the color drain from her face as she'd read the email. He'd seen a whole array of emotions pass through her lovely emerald eyes, all of them heartbreaking.

Why couldn't he seem to make himself say anything? This wasn't her fault. He was the director of the aquarium—the decision maker, the *savior* his uncle had hand-picked to turn things around. The blame for anything and everything that went wrong rested squarely at his feet, including this.

Especially this.

Max swallowed hard. He could barely look at Molly. The hurt in her expression was just too much, so he pinched the bridge of his nose, closed his eyes, and tried counting to ten like they did sometimes in yoga...until he realized that yoga was one of the reasons he'd gotten himself into this mess. Yoga, Scrabble, passing out cigars. All of it. For the first time in his professional life, he'd dropped the ball. He'd allowed something other than work to come first, and look what had happened.

*Not something, some*one. *There's a difference.*

What difference did semantics make, though, when he'd ended up letting her down like this? And Uncle Henry, too.

"Max, I'm sorry," Molly said. She looked wide-eyed and lost, and Max felt a fresh wave of guilt wash over him for making her feel like there was something wrong with wanting to take Ursula everywhere she went. If he could have produced her puppy out of thin air and placed the sweet little dog into her arms right then, he would have done so in a heartbeat.

"Don't." He shook his head. Held up a hand. "Don't apologize. This is my fault. My mistake. I should have—"

"Insisted that we do something different for the proposal?" she said. Her face was as white as a sand dollar.

Max nodded. "Yes, exactly."

The Charlie's Angels exchanged worried glances, and their dance steps slowed to a stop.

"Is everything okay?" Opal said, resting a tender hand on Molly's forearm. "Sweetheart, you look like you've seen a ghost."

"It's fine." Molly waved a hand. "Don't worry about me. This is such a nice evening, and—"

"Would you stop?" Mavis rolled her eyes. "We know you well enough to notice when you look crushed."

Ethel nodded. "We're old and wise, remember?"

Max felt his jaw clench. He really didn't want to get into this here, not until he'd had a chance to collect his thoughts and come up with a back-up plan for the aquarium's future—something he should have been working on all along.

"We didn't get the grant," Molly said flatly. "I was wrong. We should have done something more conventional, like Max suggested."

"Oh, honey. Don't blame yourself. You worked so hard on that proposal. The aquarium is going to be just fine, no matter what." Opal squeezed Molly's arm and glanced at Max, clearly waiting for him to jump in and say something.

But he couldn't. No more playing Mr. Nice Guy. He never would have let things slip so far out of his control in Baltimore. And he certainly couldn't make empty promises about the aquarium's future.

"Max?" Mavis prompted. "Don't you have something to say to Molly?"

All eyes turned toward him. Color was beginning to flood Molly's face again. Her cheeks were two bright spots of pink.

He cleared his throat. "You're not to blame, Molly. It was me. I let—"

He didn't even know what he was saying. The music, the lights, the sea creatures floating everywhere—it was all such a stark contrast to the worry gnawing at him that he couldn't form the right words.

Molly's eyes narrowed, glistening like emeralds forged by fire. "Are you trying to say that you let charm override your good judgment?"

Why did that sound so familiar? "Yes, I guess I am saying that."

She let out a laugh that didn't sound at all amused. "Wow."

Opal shook her head. "Molly, I'm sure Max doesn't mean that the aquarium would have won the grant if he'd written the proposal himself."

"On the contrary, I think that's exactly what he means." Molly's tone was sharp, but at the same time, her eyes swam with unshed tears. "Isn't it?"

"There's no way of knowing that for certain," Max said, but his words came out sounding stilted, even to his own ears. How was he somehow making this situation worse every time he opened his mouth?

"Max." Opal sent him a look that could kill.

"No, it's fine. I get it. Message received, loud and clear." Molly sniffed. "He's right. I just can't believe that I let myself think you actually agreed with me and thought it was a good idea. You felt this way all along, didn't you?"

Just as the words left Molly's mouth, there was a lull in the music. Couples around them turned to stare, and a few feet away, one face in particular came into sharp focus.

Max's stomach hardened. Uncle Henry had just witnessed their entire exchange.

Opal fanned herself with a shaky hand. "I think everyone just needs to take a deep breath and—"

"You were right a few weeks ago," Molly cut in, gaze trained on Max as her tears spilled over. "Working together really has been a mistake. But not as big a mistake as thinking we could actually have a future together."

He opened his mouth to contradict her, but he was struck dumb by the sight of her tears sliding slowly, excruciatingly, down her porcelain cheeks. What had he done? He'd made Molly *cry*.

There was an old legend that said mermaids were so powerful that their tears, once shed, turned into pearls. And even though Max knew that Molly wasn't a real mermaid, seeing her cry made him into a believer. He sensed her power deep down in his core, like a blow to the chest, and it felt strangely like something he knew for a fact was real—it felt like love.

But her tears kept falling, like pearls slipping from a string.

"I quit," she said, and then she turned to leave.

"Wait, Molly." Panic propelled Max forward. He couldn't lose her. He wasn't so much concerned about their jobs as he was the rest of their lives. *For as long as we both shall live.* "Don't go. Please."

But Molly didn't hear him. No one did, because Opal Lewinsky had just clutched her chest and sank lifelessly to the ballroom floor.

Chapter 20

AN HOUR AND A half later, Molly sat beside Max on a stiff vinyl sofa in an emergency waiting room at the hospital in Wilmington.

She couldn't seem to figure out what to do with her hands. They felt absurdly useless and empty in the absence of Ursula's warm, soft form. Yesterday...the day before...a week before, she would have reached for Max and woven her fingers through his. But she couldn't do that now, not after everything that had just transpired at the ball. After every terrible thing they'd said to each other.

It was surreal how quickly the magical environment in the ballroom fell away after Opal collapsed. The music stopped, replaced by the piercing, shrill sound of an emergency alarm. Before Molly could make sense of what was happening, Griff was telling everyone to stand back in his most somber firefighter voice while Sam bent over Opal with his fingertips pressed to the inside of her wrist, checking for a pulse.

Molly had never felt so helpless in her life—nor had she ever felt more alone. The inches between her and Max may as well have been a chasm. The only thing worse had been sitting silently beside him in the Jeep as they followed the ambulance across the bridge, all the way to Wilmington. And now this...here, sharing a couch so tiny that Max's leg brushed against hers every time he moved, sending jolts of awareness zinging through her despite about a dozen layers of floaty princess tulle.

"Here, sweetheart." Larry Sims loomed over her, holding a steaming cup of hospital coffee toward her. "It's no fancy latte from Turtle Books, but you look like you could use a little boost."

"Thank you." Molly took the paper cup and let it warm her hands. She couldn't seem to stop shivering. Why were hospitals always so unbearably cold?

Max unfolded himself from the couch, shrugged out of his tuxedo jacket and bent to wrap it around Molly's shoulders. She took a sharp inhale. Having his face so close to hers was just too much to bear. She started to tell him she was fine, but when his eyes fixed with hers the look on his face told her not to argue.

The warmth of his body clung to the silk lining of his jacket, and she had to stop herself from closing her eyes and burrowing inside it as if it was a blanket fort. Instead, she let herself breathe in his familiar, beachy scent—sea-salt breeze and sun-kissed musk. It made her think of stars glittering above the surf, tiny sea turtles making their way to water, and being kissed under a midnight sky. Memories that had seeped into her mind, her bones, her heart.

She couldn't do this. She moved to shrug out of the jacket, but before she could get it off, a man in scrubs and a white coat started walking toward them. A stethoscope was draped over his neck and Dr. Troy Reese was stitched onto his coat in neat blue lettering.

He stopped when he got to the section of the waiting room

that had been overtaken by Opal's nearest and dearest. Mavis and Ethel sat on the sofa opposite Molly and Max, still wearing their prim white gloves from the ball. Larry hovered nearby, ready to bolt for tissues or coffee or whatever anyone needed.

The doctor looked down at the chart in his hands. "Hello, I'm looking for some friends of Opal Lewinsky's. Are any of you Molly Prince and Max Miller?"

Molly went still. Was this good news or bad? Did he want to talk to her and Max because he thought Mavis and Ethel were too old and fragile to handle whatever he needed to say?

Max held up a finger. "That's us."

Us.

Molly's throat squeezed shut.

"Great. If you'll follow me, Opal would like to speak to you both."

That sounded promising, at least. Clearly Opal was alive and conscious. Molly flew to her feet. Max's tuxedo jacket fell from her shoulders and landed on the sofa in a whisper of fine Armani wool.

They followed the doctor down a long sterile hall, toward the bustling ER, divided into makeshift rooms with curtain dividers. Max started to place his hand on the small of her back like he'd done in the ballroom, but stopped short of actually touching her. The sliver of space between his palm and the delicate mesh bodice of her ball gown hummed with electricity.

"Here we are." Dr. Reese pulled one of the curtains open to reveal Opal sitting up in bed against three pillows.

Her ruffled gown was spread neatly over her legs and her white gloves were folded into a perfect square on her lap. She didn't appear to have encountered a recent medical emergency at all. In fact, Molly was pretty certain she was rocking a fresh coat of lipstick.

"Opal." Max smiled and the corners of his eyes crinkled in that way Molly loved so much, and she had to look away. "It's great to see you looking so well."

"Definitely." Molly took what felt like her first full breath since Opal had passed out. "But I don't understand. What happened? Are you okay?"

"I had a heart attack," Opal said.

At the same time, Dr. Reese looked up from his chart and shrugged. "There's nothing whatsoever wrong with Ms. Lewinsky."

Molly glanced back and forth between doctor and patient. Dr. Reese shot a pointed look in Opal's direction.

"Fine." She rolled her eyes. "It was a really minor heart attack. *Super* minor."

Dr. Reese cleared his throat.

Opal sighed. "Perhaps so minor that it was technically nonexistent."

Molly gasped. "Oh, my gosh. You *faked* a heart attack?"

"And there we have it." Dr. Reese swiveled his gaze toward Molly and Max. "She asked to see you two, and I wanted to make sure you heard the truth first. I'm processing her discharge paperwork right now, so she'll be ready to go in just a few minutes."

"Thank you." Molly nodded. She felt wobbly on her feet from sheer relief. "Thank you so much."

"Yes, thank you. We'll make sure she gets back to the island safely," Max said.

The doctor narrowed his gaze at Opal one last time. "Try to make sure this doesn't happen again, would you?"

She smiled sweetly at him without making any promises.

The doctor shook his head and closed the curtain around her bed with an aggressive swish.

"Well, that was certainly enlightening," Molly said, stepping closer to Opal's bed. "Do you want to explain why you'd do something like that?"

Max's gaze slid toward Molly. "Really? Isn't it obvious? You and I were arguing and she wanted us to stop."

Molly gaped at her friend, looking awfully smug and pleased with herself for someone who'd recently entered the building on a gurney. But that had been her plan all along, hadn't it?

"Guilty as charged," Opal said. "I have no regrets."

"You scared us all half to death." Molly crossed her arms. "This was *not* okay."

Opal's eyes twinkled. "It got the two of you back together, didn't it?"

"Yes," Max said.

Simultaneously, Molly blurted, "No."

Max's jaw visibly clenched. "Not *together* together. But we're both here, aren't we?"

"Would you two stop, or am I going to have to pretend to have another medical crisis? Go ahead and try me. I can fake a mean aneurysm." Opal let out a mighty sigh. "You two are clearly crazy about each other. Take it from an old lady who has the benefit of hindsight on her side—you're both acting like children. I don't understand why you insist on arguing over something of so little importance."

Max frowned. "With all due respect—"

Molly finished for him. "—the grant was vitally important. Without it the aquarium might have to close its doors in just a few months."

Opal narrowed her gaze at Max. "What's she talking about? I told you the aquarium would be just fine. Numerous times."

"Yes, you did." Max nodded. "And I want to believe that, too. But we need to consider the facts."

"I *am* considering the facts. I'm considering my bank account, which has more than enough zeros to keep the aquarium going for years. Maybe even decades." Opal shrugged, the perfect picture of nonchalance.

A cold chill skittered through Molly. She wished she'd hung onto Max's tuxedo jacket. "What are you talking about, Opal?"

"I'm rich, but I try not to tell anyone. I like to keep it a secret." Opal pressed a finger to her lips.

"Mission accomplished," Max muttered.

"You can't donate all your money to the aquarium," Molly said. Even if it was true, didn't Opal need that money to live on? Where did it all come from, anyway? Opal was a retired school teacher.

"It's a done deal. I've already talked to my lawyer and we've scheduled the wire transfer. Four million dollars will land in the aquarium's bank account first thing tomorrow." Opal shrugged. "I was planning on telling both of you tonight at the end of the Under the Sea Ball, but…"

Max glanced at Molly, and the sadness in his eyes was palpable. "But we got bad news and let it ruin the entire evening."

An oversimplified version of the events, but true nonetheless.

"Bingo," Opal said. Turtle Beach's favorite word.

Max moved closer and sat on the edge of the hospital bed. "Are you absolutely sure about this, Opal? I don't want you to feel at all pressured to fund the aquarium. I'll figure things out."

Molly tried to not dwell on the fact that he'd just said *I* instead of *we*. After all, she'd tendered her resignation. She was, once again, an unemployed mermaid. At least it had been by choice this time.

Then why do you feel even more crushed than you did when you got fired?

"I'm totally sure. Four million isn't even half the money in my bank account. It belonged to my mother, who inherited it from her mother, who inherited it from *her* mother. My great-great-grandmother was minor royalty." Opal shrugged. "Same old story."

Max's lips twitched into a grin as he snuck a look at Molly. Molly made a mental note to get Opal a tiara for her next birthday.

"Anyway, the money just keeps getting passed around from generation to generation. No one ever spends it. Who am I supposed to leave it to? I don't have children, and if I did, I'd still want to give it to the aquarium. My goal is to die a broke woman. It's going to take some work." She sighed. "Max, if I fail and I'm still a millionaire when I kick the bucket, the aquarium and sea turtle hospital are welcome to whatever is left after I'm gone. It's already all written up in my last will and testament."

"Noted." Max winked at her as he stood up. "But let's not worry about that for a long, long time, okay?"

"No more heart attacks," Molly said. "Real, fake, or any other variety."

"You two are really bossy, you know that? Sheesh." Opal swung her legs over the side of the bed, prepared to head back to the island now that she'd said her piece. "This whole episode could have been avoided if either of you had paid attention to me all those times I said the aquarium and sea turtle hospital would be okay. You have only yourselves to blame."

Max's gaze locked with Molly's again. And this time, the loss she felt when she looked at him seemed like it might swallow her whole.

What had she done? How had she allowed things to spiral so quickly out of control?

Opal was right. Whether Molly wanted to admit it or not, there was plenty of blame to go around.

Chapter 21

IT TOOK MOLLY TWO days to muster up the courage to call her parents and tell them everything that happened—two full days of alternating between wallowing on the sofa in front of an entire season of her baking show and trying to keep Ursula from sneaking out onto the deck so she could spy on Max's house next door.

Molly wasn't even sure if Max had been out there all those times Ursula had shoved her tiny face into the narrow spaces between the wooden slats of the railing, angling for the best view of her favorite hot professor. She wasn't about to take any chances, though.

Their discussion with Opal in the emergency room had been the last time Molly had seen him. Max had promised the doctor he'd give Opal a ride back to the island, and once he'd loaded the patient into his Jeep, Molly announced she'd be riding home with Violet, who'd made a beeline up to Wilmington to pick up the other senior citizens and their accompanying mobility devices in her cupcake truck.

Max had clearly been expecting Molly to climb right into the Jeep, even though it would have been a rather tight squeeze. He might have even hoped that Molly would reconsider her resignation and show up for work the next day in her clamshell bustier and fish tail. He'd looked at her as if he'd just lost his best friend when she told him she was staying back to wait for Violet and her Airstream with the pink spinning cupcake on top.

That couldn't have been right, though. Molly was *not* Max's best friend, and she definitely wasn't his girlfriend or whatever she'd thought she might have been on the night of the Under the Sea Ball. Relationships—*real* relationships—were built on mutual respect and honesty. Max had all but admitted that encouraging her to start the dog-training program and write the grant proposal herself had been a mistake. He'd never truly believed in her or taken her seriously.

Just like The Tourist, who'd lied to her face for an entire year.

Just like her mom and dad, who couldn't stop dropping hints for her to go to grad school.

Just like Molly herself, every time she looked in the mirror lately.

The worst part about wallowing was that she couldn't seem to stop replaying the most painful parts of her confrontation with Max at the Under the Sea Ball in her head. The memories would hit her out of the blue. One minute Molly would be watching a young British college student assemble a Battenberg cake, and the next she'd hear her own voice echoing in her head.

Are you trying to say that you let charm override your good judgment?

The question hadn't been remotely fair. Max had been joking around about his uncle manipulating him into all those nutty activities at the senior center the first time he'd used that phrase. And then, in the heat of the moment, she'd turned those same words back on him. In a moment of hurt and shame, she'd twisted his silly little comment and tried to make it into something unkind.

But Max had taken that ball and run with it, hadn't he?

Yes, I guess I am saying that.

"Ugh, no." Molly clamped her hands over her ears. She couldn't stand thinking about it for one more minute. She'd rather face the music and fill her parents in on the mess she'd made of her life than keep dwelling on exactly how she'd done it.

Ursula blinked her big eyes at the sound of the word *no*, and Molly felt infinitely worse.

She gathered the puppy into her arms and whispered into her fur, "That wasn't directed at you, I swear."

Ursula licked the tip of Molly's nose, all forgiven.

Molly was officially out of excuses. She grabbed her cell phone and tapped the contact information for her parents' landline before she could chicken out.

Her dad answered on the first ring. "Hello?"

"Hi, Dad. It's me."

"Hi, honey. It's great to hear from you. Your mother will be sorry she missed you. She's out getting her hair done."

That explained why he'd answered the phone. Molly's mother usually answered on the first ring. "That's okay. I actually kind of wanted to talk to you, Dad."

"What a nice surprise. Might this be about your grant proposal?"

Here we go.

"Actually, yes." Molly bit down hard on the inside of her cheek. Why was this so difficult? "I messed up. We didn't get it."

"I don't understand. How did you mess up?" he asked.

Had he missed the part about not getting the grant? "We didn't win the grant. I failed."

She held her breath and waited for him to tell her that she should have deferred to Max and his PhD.

To her complete and utter shock, he didn't. "Honey, just because you didn't win the grant doesn't mean you failed. Quite the opposite."

"How so?"

"You put yourself out there. You had a vision and you worked hard to make it happen. Just because the grant committee didn't choose you as the winner doesn't mean you failed."

Who was this man, and what had he done with her father? "You remember my vision included dogs, right?"

"I do, but dogs obviously make you happy." He laughed under his breath. "And I'll admit your little Ursula isn't so bad."

Molly wasn't sure why this surprised her so much. Ursula was an excellent canine ambassador. "On our last night of training, all five of the dogs alerted to the sea turtle scent. It *was* kind of amazing."

Funny how she'd forgotten how wonderful that night had been. Or maybe she just hadn't let herself remember.

"Let me ask you a question, honey—do you have any idea why I'm always encouraging you to consider graduate school?"

Molly rattled off several answers, mostly related to salary, tenure, and job security, but one by one, he shot them down.

"I give up. Why?" she finally said.

"Because for a long time now, it's like you've just been going through the motions. I know you've been hurt, honey. But since your breakup last year, you just haven't been yourself." Her dad's voice went soft—softer than she'd heard it in years. "These past few weeks, you've seemed more alive than I've seen you in a long, long time. You did a good thing."

Molly's throat closed. He was right, and now here she was, hiding in her beach cottage again…alone. And she was more miserable than ever.

"You put yourself out there, kiddo. You got out of your comfort zone, and that's the most important thing. I wish you would have gotten your grant, but the fact that you didn't doesn't mean the process was a waste of time. And it certainly doesn't mean that you failed. Your mother and I just want you to have a full life, and it doesn't have to be on our terms." He sighed. "I'm sorry if I made it sound otherwise."

Molly sniffed. She *really* didn't want to cry again. She'd practically sobbed herself dehydrated in recent days. "You don't need to apologize."

"I think I do," he said, and the tenderness in his tone almost broke her.

But maybe that was a good thing. Maybe the tear in her heart needed to be fully ripped apart before she could put herself back together.

"Oh, Dad. There's so much I need to tell you." Molly tucked her legs up under her, and Ursula stretched out beside her with her little head on her paws, settling in for the long haul.

On the other end of the line, her father's favorite La-Z-Boy groaned into recline position. "I'm all ears."

—⁓—

"King me." Uncle Henry aimed a triumphant grin at Max as he slid one of his red checkers into place on the game board that lay between them on a table in the senior center's lobby.

Max had exactly one black checker left on the board, as opposed to Henry's half a dozen double-stacked kings. Henry could have put the entire game to bed six moves ago, but he kept pushing his game pieces around in seemingly random moves.

Max inched his lone checker forward to a spot where Henry could jump him from three different directions. His uncle's fingertips lingered in the vicinity and then veered to the other end of the checkerboard where he moved one of his kings to a lonely, insignificant corner.

Max narrowed his gaze at Henry, but his uncle didn't look up. He just picked at a piece of nonexistent lint on his cardigan.

For the first time in the two days that had passed since the Under the Sea Ball, Max consciously let himself think about the moments at the dance before everything had gone so horribly wrong—the laughter in Molly's eyes, the way her dress shimmered like starlight, the tantalizing curve of her neck beneath her upswept hair…the things she'd said.

Since that utterly disastrous night, Max had done what he always did when life got messy—he'd thrown himself into his work. With Opal's donation in the bank, he had more than enough to keep him busy. It was a win–win situation—great for the aquarium and great for Max.

Or it should have been. But somehow, the more he tried not

to think about Molly, the more the memories kept tormenting him. And they were never the good memories—never thoughts of her sunshine scent or her candy-floss hair or the way her smile alone could save a man from drowning...never the sublime warmth of her kiss.

Instead, all Max saw when he closed his eyes were the tears that had streamed down her face. He'd made the woman he loved cry.

And he definitely loved her. He'd fallen for Molly, head over heels. But he'd realized it just a beat too late.

His chest burned with the hot sting of regret. He needed to get back to the aquarium, back to his office where things were clear and logical and less likely to leave him feeling like he had an aching, gaping wound in the place where his heart used to be.

Max sat back in his chair and crossed his arms. "Uncle Henry, are you losing this game on purpose so I'll stick around and spend more time with you?"

Henry froze.

Well, look at that. Max came closer to smiling than he had in days. *Molly was right.*

"You could have simply asked, you know," Max said.

"Really?" Henry snorted even louder than Bingo the pug did whenever his flat snout got within sneezing distance of the sand. "Kind of like all the times I invited you to come to the island for holidays or vacations?"

The hole in Max's chest felt like it was caving it on itself. "That was completely different."

"How so? You were too busy working to make the trip back

then, and since the day you arrived in Turtle Beach, all you want to talk about is the aquarium. Seems about the same to me." Uncle Henry reached out, grabbed one of his kings and jumped over Max's last checker.

Boom. Game over.

"But you brought me here to save it," Max countered.

Henry let out a laugh. "Is that what you think?"

Of course he did. Henry had told him that very thing at their first yoga class. Hadn't he?

"Son, the aquarium has been running on a shoestring for years. Did I think you'd be able to turn things around? Of course I did. But that's not why I asked you to take over as director," Henry said.

Max was at a loss. Before he realized what he was doing, he'd started resetting the checkerboard for another game.

"You know how proud of you I am, Max. I love you, son, but you've turned into a total workaholic. I'm guessing it has something to do with your parents and how hard things were for you after they divorced, but take it from an old man. It's no way to live." Henry pushed a red checker from one square to the next, making the first move. "When you got passed over for the director position in Baltimore, I knew it was time to make my move. I didn't ask you to come to Turtle Beach so you could save the aquarium. I asked you to come back here so the aquarium could save *you*."

Max went very still.

Uncle Henry cocked an eyebrow. "It was working, wasn't it?"

Yes…yes, it was.

Max thought about the turtles recuperating in the tanks at the sea turtle hospital, Silver's baby seahorses, and gently lowering Crush back into the ocean while the entire town clapped and cheered. He thought about newborn turtle hatchlings crawling their way to the water, and the look on Molly's face when the last dog at her training class finally alerted to the scent of sea turtle eggs. Max couldn't remember the last time he'd done anything so hands-on back in Baltimore. But in Turtle Beach, Max got his hands sandy on a regular basis. He didn't have to wonder if the aquarium was making a difference in the community and the ecology of the island. He could *see* it…every single day.

But most of all, he'd felt it. Max had opened up and allowed himself to feel more in the past month than he had for the rest of his adult life.

"Yes," Max said quietly. "Yes, it was."

"And sure, maybe I did force you into trying some new things. But I had to. How else were you going to learn how to have fun again?" Uncle Henry waved a hand at the checkerboard.

"Point taken. And yes, I like the volleyball league and the Scrabble tournaments. The pancake breakfast was great. I've even gotten pretty into yoga." Max glanced down at the checkers. "But I'm not enjoying this checkers bloodbath in the slightest."

"That's because ever since Molly broke your heart, you're falling back into your same old routine." Henry sighed. "You're sitting right here in front of me, and I'm missing you like you still live over four hundred miles away."

Ouch. It was a painful assessment, but his uncle wasn't wrong… Except for one important detail.

"Molly didn't break my heart." Max looked at Uncle Henry— *really* looked—taking in the lines in his face that hadn't been there the last time Max had been on the island, the whiter shade of his hair. Henry wouldn't be around forever, but Max was here now. He was home. It wasn't too late to really live...to really *love*. "I broke Molly's."

He'd let her believe that he thought she wasn't good enough for the grant committee, for the aquarium, or for him. And when he'd realized he loved her, he'd make his biggest mistake of all— he'd let her walk away instead of telling her how he felt.

It wasn't the aquarium that had saved Max. And it wasn't Turtle Beach. It was Molly. She'd pulled him out of the ocean when he'd been drowning, and bit by bit, smile by smile, kiss by perfect kiss, she'd kept on saving him. As powerful and constant as the tide.

He should have fought for her. He should have kicked and thrashed and fought like he'd been drowning.

Henry's mouth curved into a knowing grin. He swept the checkers away and folded the game board in half. "What are you waiting for, son?"

———

"I can't *believe* I let you guys talk me into coming here tonight." Molly stood near the entrance of the senior center and did her best to blend into the woodwork—not such an easy task when Ursula was wagging her tail and straining at the end of her leash in an effort to greet every person who walked through the automatic sliding glass doors.

"It's Tuesday." Ethel tipped her head toward the table beside them, covered with bingo sheets and colorful ink daubers. "Where else would you be?"

Wallowing, perhaps?

Molly wasn't doing that anymore, though. She'd spent enough time feeling sorry for herself the past few days. It was time to hang up her mermaid costume and forget about Max and move on.

She had no idea how to do that, exactly. Molly still had no desire to enroll in graduate school and, for now at least, her dad had promised to drop it. But after spending over an hour on the phone with her parents earlier today, she'd decided they were right—she couldn't start hiding again. Molly had been happier during the past month than she'd been in as long as she could remember. She couldn't fully retreat to her comfort zone again.

But bingo night?

It was…a lot. She'd been hoping for a softer reentry, or at least one where she'd be less likely to run into Dr. Max Miller.

"Oh, look. Henry Miller is saving a seat for someone," Opal said, gaze flicking from Molly to the empty chair beside Max's uncle and back again. "I wonder who it could be."

Molly held up a hand. "Stop. *Please.* I know what the three of you are doing, and it's not going to work."

The Charlie's Angels blinked at her from behind their walkers.

"Whatever do you mean, dear?" Mavis said.

"I'm not here for Max. Or romance…with anyone. I'm here for bingo and cupcakes." Molly had her eye on Violet's special of the night, Lucky Lemon Lavender. She was just waiting for the line at the cupcake truck to thin out a little.

"Oh, geez. You're not going to adopt another dog, are you?" Ethel arched an eyebrow and aimed a meaningful glance at Ursula. "Because I know a Cavalier King Charles spaniel who might have some thoughts about that."

"Don't be silly. I would never. Ursula is my significant other," Molly said, bending to pick the puppy up. Ursula melted into her arms.

"Here we go again." Ethel rolled her eyes.

"Molly, dear, you know how much we love Ursula. She's the sweetest, most talented dog on the entire island," Opal said.

Mavis leaned over to cover Nibbles's tiny ears. "How dare you."

"Oh come on, it's true and you know it." Opal sighed. "But it's possible to have a precious dog that you're crazy about *and* have a boyfriend at the same time. You and Max are perfect for each other. What am I going to have to do to make you see that— fake another heart attack?"

"Please don't." Molly shook her head. Opal's last fake cardiac event had shaved at least a year off of her life. "It all worked out for the best. I thought Max had changed, but clearly I was wrong. All he sees when he looks at me is a silly girl in a mermaid costume. I should have gotten the hint when he called me and my dog scientifically insignificant and fired us."

"That was weeks ago. Max has definitely changed. *Everything* has. The aquarium is fully funded. There's no reason at all that you can't go back to being a mermaid. He didn't fire you this time." Opal wagged a finger at Molly. "You fired yourself."

True, sort of. And Molly would have been lying if she said she didn't miss it. Maybe one day she'd be able to slip back into her fish tail, swallow her pride, and ask for her job back, but today was *not* that day. Seeing Max again would have killed her.

"Opal, I have to ask—why have you been trying so hard to push Max and me together?" Molly asked. The Charlie's Angels had been known to dabble in a little matchmaking in the past, but Opal had really seemed to go the extra mile this time.

Opal shrugged. "I don't know what you mean."

"Just tell her," Ethel said.

Mavis nodded. "You're not fooling anyone, Opal. She knows something is up."

"Honestly, you design one half-naked sea god sand sculpture and fake one heart attack and people think you have an agenda." Opal huffed, but when Molly didn't say anything and just kept waiting for an answer, she finally relented. "Fine. I felt really bad about what happened with The Tourist. I'm the one who showed you that engagement announcement in the paper. You were so crushed, and I guess I sort of felt responsible."

"Opal, don't tell me you've been feeling bad about that for a full year? Nothing about my train wreck of a relationship was your fault. In fact, I'm grateful that you uncovered the truth."

"Are you sure?" Opal said.

Molly nodded. "Absolutely."

"I'm glad." Opal blew out a relieved breath. "But that was only part of the reason—the main reason I tried to push you and Max together is because you're perfect together. You still have feelings for him. I *know* you do."

The best thing to do would be to deny it. If she didn't, the Charlie's Angels would never give up their shenanigans. But try as she might, Molly couldn't tell them she didn't have feelings for Max. The words simply wouldn't come out of her mouth.

No, no, no. Her heart pounded so hard that she could feel it in her throat. *I'm not in* love *with him, am I?*

She couldn't be. She didn't *want* to be. But if she wasn't, then why had she given up everything she cared about most in her life in order to avoid being forced to see him on a daily basis?

"Oh. My. Gosh." Mavis's jaw dropped open as she looked at something over Molly's right shoulder.

Ethel's eyes went wide. "Well, would you look at that? Speaking of half-naked sea gods…"

Opal's face lit up like the fireworks that the town always shot off over the boardwalk on the Fourth of July. Her eyes flashed over to Molly. "I think you should turn around, dear."

Molly's heart leapt straight to her throat. She wanted to know what all the hubbub was about, but at the same time she was afraid.

It's Max. She just knew it. Was she ready to see him again, so soon? No…but the rebellious flutter deep in her belly felt an awful lot like hope.

She spun around to face her future. The doors to the senior center swished open, and in walked Max—but not like Molly had ever seen Max before. Not in the flesh, anyway.

He was the real, human Max. The same Max who'd held her hand while they'd watched baby seahorses, who'd dipped her on the dance floor, who'd kissed her silly while her toes sank into the sand and her heart soared to the moon and back. But he didn't look like that version of Max at all. Gone were the glasses and the buttoned-up oxford. In fact, this Max wasn't wearing any kind of shirt. His chest was bare, and he had a shiny gold crown on his head decorated with shells and bits of beach glass. There was a trident in one of his hands, and he held a plush baby sea turtle aloft in the other. He was the real Max, dressed as the wild, untamed sand version of himself.

Molly blinked. She might have thought she was experiencing some bizarre lovesickness-induced hallucination if not for the fact that bingo night came to a complete and total standstill when he walked through the door.

Tourists stared. Bingo daubers froze midair. People started snapping photos with their smartphones. Ursula took a flying leap out of Molly's arms and scrambled toward Max as fast as she could.

Molly's heart felt like it just might follow.

She tried to keep her composure, but despite her best efforts, she felt her mouth curve into a ridiculous smile as he walked toward her.

"What are you *doing?*" she said as he came to a stop right in front of her. The stuffed turtle in his hand had googly eyes glued onto its head. *Googly eyes!*

Max winked. "It's Tuesday night. Where else would I be?"

She looked him up and down, cheeks blazing with heat as her attention lingered on his bare chest. "And you typically dress like Neptune for bingo?"

"When I'm trying to make a grand gesture, I do," he said, and his expression turned bittersweet.

She took a ragged inhale. Ursula peered up at her, wiggling

with ecstasy. The puppy had clearly made up her mind to forgive and forget. Molly envied her ability to love with such an open, vulnerable heart.

She wanted to be like that. She wanted to live and laugh and love without regret. She wanted to see the world like her little dog did—beautiful and brand new every morning, even with its flaws. Maybe even because of them. She wanted it so bad that she took a step closer to Max, reached for his hand and squeezed it tight.

"I'm so sorry." He pressed his forehead to hers, eyes shining as bright as the sea in high summer. "You, Molly Prince, are definitely not insignificant, scientifically or otherwise. The truth is that I've never met anyone as significant as you are. I'm in love with you."

He lifted his fingertips toward her face. She thought it was to move a lock of hair from her eyes, but when the pad of his thumb grazed her cheek, she realized he was tenderly brushing away a tear. She was crying again—but this time they were happy tears, pearls of a different color.

"Someone call 911. I might be having a heart attack for real." Opal let out a dreamy sigh. "This is the most romantic thing I've ever seen."

"More romantic than when she saved him from drowning?" Mavis said.

Yes, Molly thought. *More romantic than that, because this time, we're saving each other.*

"Oh, Wilson," she whispered. "I love you too."

Then she kissed him, and at long last, with her heart open wide, Molly the mermaid finally found her sea legs.

Get ready to laugh out loud with this hilarious romantic comedy!

Featuring:

- A grumpy firefighter who thinks his way is the only way

- A bubbly cupcake vendor who thinks her pup can do no wrong

- Adorable Dalmatians who swap places—and the chaos that ensues

- An opposites-attract romance that'll warm your heart

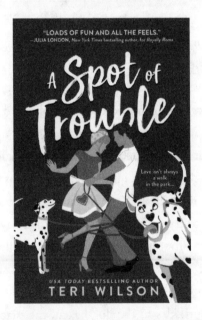

Named by *Reader's Digest* as one of the Best Romances of ALL TIME

Chapter 1

FOR AS LONG AS Violet March could remember, Turtle Beach, North Carolina, had been a one-Dalmatian town.

Not entirely true, because until the day Violet found Sprinkles at a pet rescue fair in nearby Wilmington and adopted her on the spot—pun intended—there had been zero Dalmatians in her hometown. None whatsoever. A Dalmatian drought, so to speak.

But now Violet had Sprinkles, Turtle Beach's total Dalmatian population. Everyone in the seaside town knew the spirited black-and-white dog belonged to her. Violet and Sprinkles were inseparable. If Sprinkles had been a person, they might have been soul mates. But alas, Sprinkles was a dog. An adorable, spotted sweetheart of a dog with an unfortunate penchant for getting into trouble, which made it all the more baffling that someone would have the nerve to try and dognap her in broad daylight.

"Hey! Hey, you, stop it right now!" Violet flailed her arms and screamed. Sea foam swirled around her ankles as she jogged from the shallows onto the warm, dry sand.

Bringing Sprinkles to the dog beach, the island's small dedicated stretch of shoreline for dogs to romp and play, had become something of a ritual on the mornings Violet taught yoga. After an hour or so of chasing a tennis ball and barking and jumping at the waves, Sprinkles could almost sit still until final relaxation pose. Of course, Violet never imagined the dog beach could be a hotbed of canine crime.

Violet called out again, but the dognapper didn't even flinch. He just kept walking in the opposite direction with Sprinkles tethered to his wrist by a long red leash. She glanced around, half-expecting her dad or one of her brothers to jump out from behind a clump of seagrass and come to her rescue. They had a tendency to hover. A lot.

But for once in her life, her personal protection squad was nowhere to be seen. She was on her own, not a blue police uniform in sight. On any ordinary day, this would have thrilled Violet to pieces. Now, not so much.

"Let go of my dog!" she yelled, sprinting and kicking up sand in her yoga clothes.

A few heads turned her way, but the early morning crowd at the dog beach skewed older. Geriatric, mostly. The senior citizens of Turtle Beach were well-acquainted with Violet and therefore accustomed to the chaos that surrounded her on any given day. Naturally, they seemed more amused than alarmed when she darted past.

Their dogs, on the other hand, sprang into action, quickly giving chase. Within seconds, there were half a dozen dogs nipping at Violet's heels. By the time she made it to the far end of the dog beach, someone had taken a bite out of the hem of her lululemons. Mrs. Banks's corgi, most likely.

Perfect. Just perfect.

"Hey," she yelled again. "What do you think you're doing?"

This time, the criminal stopped. He turned around and arched an amused brow as he took in the sight of her bent over, breathing hard, with a random collection of dogs milling about her feet.

So he thought dognapping was funny, did he?

She glared at him, and that's when she noticed the letters stitched onto the pocket of his charcoal gray T-shirt—TBFD. Turtle Beach Fire Department. Violet felt her eyes widen in horror.

The dognapper was a fireman, because of course he was.

Not that Violet had anything against firefighters and their kitten-saving skill set *per se*. It was complicated, that's all.

The fireman's brow furrowed. "I'm, ah, walking my dog. This is the dog beach, is it not?"

"Walking your dog? Very funny." Sprinkles was the only Dalmatian in town. Again, *everyone* knew that.

She punched three numbers into her phone.

"Did you just dial 911?" The fireman cocked his head, and Sprinkles instantly mirrored his movement. They looked rather adorable together—the dognapper and the traitor.

"Of course I did."

"You really don't need to do that." He pointed at the silver badge sitting right below the letters stitched onto his shirt pocket. "I'm one of the guys who comes when you make that call. Is there something you need help with?"

Violet ignored him—manly wide shoulders and all—and gave the details of her whereabouts to the 911 dispatcher. The operator, Patty Jenkins, knew Violet by name. It was a small town, and Mrs. Jenkins sat at a desk approximately ten feet away from her father's office.

"Send my dad…or Joe, or Josh. Send anyone, but please tell them to get here quickly. Someone is trying to kidnap Sprinkles." Violet's gaze flitted from the top of the fireman's head to the tips of his polished black boots. "A *firefighter*."

"Oh, dear," the operator said.

"Exactly." Violet would have identified which fireman in particular was trying to abscond with her four-legged best friend, but she didn't recognize him. So she ended the call, crossed her arms, and pinned the offending man with a glare. "The police are on the way. Don't even think about running."

"I wouldn't dare," he said drolly.

His utter shamelessness after being caught redhanded was really beginning to get on her nerves. As was Sprinkles's nonchalance. Didn't she realize she was in danger?

The dog let out a squeaky yawn and plopped into a down position at the fireman's feet. Violet sighed as Sprinkles closed her eyes and rested her chin on the toe of his boot.

Seriously?

Sprinkles had developed Stockholm syndrome in a matter of minutes. Maybe it was a Dalmatian–fireman thing. Or maybe it had something to do with her kidnapper's charmingly mussed dark hair and his startling green eyes. Bottle-green, like corked glass floating in the ocean with a secret love note hidden inside.

Not that Violet had noticed those things.

Much.

The dogs that had joined her on the chase down the shore definitely seemed to notice. They sniffed at the fireman's feet, wagged their tails, and in general fawned all over him. When he crouched down to pet the corgi, the collective tail-wagging went into overdrive.

Honestly, the whole tableau was beginning to look like a page from one of those sexy firefighter calendars. Violet was aggressively annoyed.

"Just give me my dog, okay?" She sighed, hating the tiny hint of desperation in her voice. Clearly this man had no idea how much she loved her pup. "If you do the right thing now, maybe you won't get arrested."

"*Arrested?*" He stood, much to his canine fan club's disappointment. Tails drooped. A poodle mix sporting pink bows on its ears let out a mournful whine. "Yeah, that's not going to happen."

Good grief, he was smug. She couldn't wait for her dad or one of her brothers to show up and slap a pair of handcuffs on him. His perp walk was going to be a thing of beauty. Maybe she'd video it and put it on YouTube. Or TikTok, or Instagram stories, or whatever social media site the kids were using these days.

Violet herself wasn't ancient. At twenty-eight, she was technically a millennial. But she taught gentle yoga at the senior center, which meant most of her closest friends used walkers. Naturally, she'd developed something of an old soul herself.

She glared at the firefighter, who looked light years from needing a walker. He could probably downward dog all day long without tipping over once. They held each other's gazes for a beat or two—just long enough for Violet's cheeks to go warm. Her insides were suddenly full of butterflies, which she attributed to the fact that she was currently the victim of a crime. Then the wail of a police siren pierced the loaded silence.

Violet shot the fireman a triumphant smile. "Not going to happen, huh? Keep telling yourself that, Cruella."

———

Never in his life had Sam Nash been likened to a Disney villain.

On the contrary, people typically slotted him nicely into the Prince Charming camp. Sam wasn't particularly fond of that label either, but he had to admit that it was preferable to being compared to a sinister diva with a fondness for Dalmatian fur and an unfortunate two-tone wig.

"Look," he said to the obstinate woman who seemed intent on having him thrown in jail, "this is all nothing but a misunderstanding."

But she didn't appear to hear him because she was too busy waving wildly at the two uniformed police officers who'd just crested the dune and were headed in his direction.

Common sense told Sam he should be relieved at their presence. Maybe now he'd have an opportunity to explain himself. Between the three of them, maybe they could talk some sense into his accuser. But some strange instinct made him feel like his trouble was just getting started.

Sure enough, as the officers drew closer, Sam could see the scowls aimed squarely in his direction. The two cops had apparently already chosen a side in the Dalmatian war and it wasn't his. His only supporters appeared to be the lingering dogs. A Lab mix nudged its head beneath his hand, angling for a scratch.

With a sigh, Sam acquiesced.

He'd thought long and hard before picking up his life and moving to Turtle Beach. Everyone at his station back in Chicago thought he'd lost his mind. *You'll die of boredom,* they had said. *The only actual fires you'll see are sparklers on the Fourth of July.*

Sam hoped they were correct. He could use more boredom in his life. He craved it, actually. All he wanted was a quiet little existence in a quiet little seaside town. How had things managed to go so wrong so quickly?

He shifted his focus back to the flailing woman. *She* was the reason. No doubt about it.

His temples throbbed with irritation, and somehow the fact that he found the troublesome woman attractive irritated him even more. Not that he was remotely tempted to do anything about that attraction. Ever. It was just kind of hard not to notice the way the waves lapped at her feet as if she were some kind of furious moon goddess.

"Joe! Josh!" She let out a high-pitched squeal and threw her arms around the nearest cop. Sam had a sudden vision of himself behind bars. "Thank goodness you're here."

The officer who wasn't currently being bear-hugged narrowed his gaze at Sam. "What seems to be the problem here?"

The retirees at the other end of the beach were now watching the scene with rapt interest.

"He's got Sprinkles." The woman pointed toward the spotted dog at the end of Sam's leash. "He stole her when I wasn't looking, and now he won't give her back."

"This isn't your dog," Sam said. It seemed important to get that little nugget of information out in the open before the discussion went any further, especially in light of all the police PDA.

The two cops glanced at the Dalmatian, whose name was

Cinder, not Sprinkles. She'd been Cinder since the day Sam adopted her from the city pound.

"She definitely looks like Sprinkles," one of the policemen said.

The other officer nodded. "And Sprinkles *is* the only Dalmatian in Turtle Beach."

"*Exactly.*" The woman glared at Sam and held out her hand. "Give me the leash."

"No," Sam said.

"No?" Officers Joe and Josh echoed simultaneously.

"No," Sam repeated, more firmly this time.

The nearby corgi snorted his displeasure at hearing one of dogdom's least favorite words repeated in such rapid succession. The retirees were now headed their way, a few of them leaving winding trails in the sand from the wheels of their aluminum walkers.

"Sprinkles, wherever she is, isn't the only Dalmatian in town. Not anymore." Sam nodded toward his dog, still maintaining a perfect down position beside him despite the epic level of the surrounding chaos. "This is Cinder. She belongs to me, and my name is Sam Nash. We're new to Turtle Beach."

"And you're a..." Officer Joe looked him up and down. "A fireman?"

One of the senior citizens—an old man wearing suspenders and a newsboy cap—shook his head in apparent disgust.

Sam had no clue why *fireman* seemed to be a dirty word all of a sudden, but he had no intention of sticking around to chat about it. He didn't want to be late for his first day on the job, plus he had a beach house full of moving boxes that needed unpacking.

He nodded. "I'm the new fire marshal. Cinder is my partner. Check the name on her tag."

The policemen peered at Cinder and then back toward Sam's nemesis, which was somewhat of a foreign concept for Sam since he'd never had a nemesis before. But if he had to have one, at least his nemesis was nice to look at, with waves of tumbling strawberry-blonde mermaid hair and eyes the color of sea glass.

She was a mess, though. *Clearly*. A brazen, beautiful mess.

"Please." She rolled those lovely blue-green eyes so hard they practically rolled right out of her head. "Are you saying I can't recognize my own dog?"

Sam shrugged one shoulder. "That's exactly what I'm saying."

"Impossible." She tucked a lock of hair behind her ear.

One of the cops cleared his throat. The other one's lips pressed together in a slight grimace. The retirees glanced back and forth between them. Officers Joe and Josh seemed conflicted, which made Sam feel like he might just walk away from the dog beach a free man.

"Violet," Officer Joe said in a measured tone, "do you think maybe…"

Before he could finish his thought, a blur of black-and-white spots leapt into their midst and shook itself, spraying all those assembled—human and dog alike—with seawater.

Correction: not just seawater, but some horrible combination of seawater and whatever fishy substance the spotted trouble-maker had recently rolled in.

Senior citizens fled as quickly as they could in all directions while dogs barked at the ensuing panic.

"Oh my God." Officer Joe covered his mouth and nose with the crook of his elbow.

Officer Josh choked out a gagging sound.

Violet's cheeks went as red as a fire hydrant. She shot a sheepish glance at Sam and then quickly looked away.

"Sprinkles, I presume?" Sam arched a brow while the newest Dalmatian on the scene writhed around on its back in the sand, pleased as punch to be the center of attention.

"Yep." Officer Josh nodded and stepped out of range of the flying sand. "That's definitely her."

The dog was an even bigger mess than her owner. Why was Sam not surprised?

"Sprinkles, stop. Stop it right now," Violet said.

Sam had zero faith that the dog would obey, but miraculously, he was wrong. At the sound of Violet's voice, Sprinkles hopped into a sit position and stared up at her, wild-eyed, pink tongue lolling out of the side of her doggy mouth.

It might have been cute if the animal hadn't smelled like she'd just crawled out of a whale carcass.

The stench was beyond horrendous. Sam's eyes watered. "I take it I'm free to go now?"

The officers nodded, again in unison. "Yes."

Now that Sam was no longer bracing himself for life in prison, he took a closer look at the silver bars pinned to their uniforms. The same last name—*March*—was engraved on both of them.

Interesting.

He wondered if Violet's last name was March as well. That would explain the bear hugs. But Sam didn't have time to stick around and ask questions. Besides, he wanted to get as far away from Sprinkles as he possibly could.

Violet too, for that matter. She wasn't as stinky as her dog—far from it, actually. At some point during their confrontation, he'd caught a hint of sugared vanilla from her wind-tossed hair. The woman was trouble, though. And she seemed to have no intention of apologizing for making a spectacle out of him. Or for calling the police. Or for her dog's vile smell.

"Cinder," he said, and his dog hopped to her feet, the perfect picture of canine obedience.

Sprinkles's head swiveled in their direction. She wagged her tail and came closer as Cinder's nose twitched. Sam remembered reading an article in *National Geographic* a while back that said a dog's sense of smell was approximately one hundred thousand times stronger than a human's. Poor Cinder.

"They really do look a lot alike." Violet's bow-shaped lips curved into a contrite smile.

She was right. Nose-to-nose, the two dogs looked like mirror images of one another. With their glossy black-and-white coats, they matched each other spot for spot, from the tips of their tails to their identical black heart-shaped noses.

But it still wasn't an apology, and Sam was in no mood for niceties.

He gave Cinder's leash a gentle tug and brushed past Violet without a word. She huffed out a breath, and just before Sam got out of earshot, he heard one of the elderly bystanders mutter an undeniable truth.

"This town might not be big enough for two Dalmatians."

Chapter 2

WHAT HAVE I DONE?

Sam stood on the sidewalk at the intersection of Seashell Drive and Pelican Street, studying the modest downtown area of Turtle Beach. For starters, "sidewalk" was a bit of a stretch. It was more of a gravelly path, surrounded by overgrown seagrass. Downtown itself appeared to take up no more than six square blocks of the narrow barrier island, stretching from the Salty Dog Pier at one end to the Turtle Beach Senior Living Center at the other. From where his feet were planted, Sam could see the foamy ocean waves of the town's beachfront in one direction and just a glimpse of the smooth glassy surface of the intracoastal waterway in the other. The island, his new home, was *that* narrow.

"Maybe this town *isn't* big enough for two Dalmatians," he muttered.

Cinder's ears swiveled to and fro.

"Just kidding," Sam said, resting a reassuring hand on her head.

Still, picturing an idyllic beach town in your head and seeing it in person were two entirely different things. Sam had never been much of a beach person. Or a small-town person. He was very much a Dalmatian person, though. That point was non-negotiable.

As for the rest, he'd adapt. Turtle Beach was clearly the complete and total opposite of Chicago, but that was the whole point, wasn't it? Sam had upended his entire life, based on nothing but a fifteen-minute Zoom interview and a perfunctory Google search of the North Carolina coastline. Now here he was, living the dream.

Thus far, though, his new life hadn't been nearly as serene and peaceful as the Turtle Beach brochure promised. He wondered when the idyllic part was supposed to kick in. With any luck, soon.

As in immediately.

"Let's do this," he said to Cinder, more out of habit than anything else, as he headed toward the firehouse.

As usual, Cinder walked alongside him in perfect heel position. Sam didn't need to prompt her to stick by his side. Unlike her carbon copy disaster of a Dalmatian—the memorable Sprinkles—Cinder knew how to behave. In fact, before they'd left Illinois, Cinder had been awarded the Chicago Fire Department's esteemed Medal of Honor in recognition of her long and faithful service.

Emphasis on *faithful.* Every black spot on Cinder's body would fall off before she'd embarrass him the way Sprinkles had just humiliated Violet. It just wouldn't happen. Then again, Sam had invested countless hours into training his dog and bonding with her because he was a responsible pet owner. Somehow he doubted Violet fit that particular bill.

But that wasn't Sam's problem—not unless her disorderly Dalmatian had a habit of violating the fire code. From what he'd witnessed thus far, he wouldn't put it past her.

Sam frowned as the firehouse came into view, not because of the matchbox size of it, but because sand had somehow made its way into his shoes already. He was going to have to learn to deal with that oddly specific problem, just as he was going to have to remember to slather sunscreen onto his face every morning and to avoid even the remote possibility of another Dalmatian confrontation at dog beach.

Weirdly, he was also going to have to grow accustomed to the town's apparent animosity toward firefighters. Two police officers caught sight of him as he approached the firehouse, and they openly scowled at him from the paved driveway of the police station, situated directly across the street. Even Cinder noticed. She let out a low rumbling noise and moved closer to Sam until he could feel the growl vibrating through her black-and-white body.

"It's fine, Cinder," he murmured.

It was *not* fine. It was, in fact, the very opposite of fine. Sam smiled and waved at the police officers like any normal person would do, but was met with nothing but confused, albeit slightly less hostile, glances.

"Did you just wave at those cops?"

Sam turned to find a Turtle Beach firefighter, one of his own, polishing the shiny red exterior of the pumper truck sitting just outside the apparatus bay.

"I did," he said.

"Yeah, we don't do that." The other firefighter shook his head. "Especially now."

Sam didn't even know where to start. There was so much to unpack here, he was at a loss. "We don't do what, exactly? Interact with fellow first responders?"

The fireman let out a snort of laughter. "Not when they're cops. Come winter and fall, maybe, but not now."

Sam glanced up and down the quaint street where eager beachcombers loaded down with collapsible chairs, sun umbrellas, and colorful towels were already making the trek from the narrow rows of beach cottages over the dunes toward the sea. "Tourist season?"

"What? No. *Softball* season." The fireman shook his head. "You really *are* new here, aren't you?"

"Sam Nash." Sam held out his hand.

"Griff Martin. Welcome to TBFD." Griff shook Sam's hand and then glanced down at Cinder, sitting in a polite stay position at Sam's feet. Apparently, the sight of a firefighter waving at a pair of police officers had been so much of a novelty that Griff had yet to notice the spotted dog. "Whoa. First day on the job, and you've somehow managed to dognap Violet March's Dalmatian. Maybe you know more about softball season than I realized."

Sam's gut clenched. *Not again.* "This dog doesn't belong to Violet March. She belongs to me."

Griff shot him an exaggerated wink. "Sure she does."

"I'm dead serious."

Griff's face split into a wide grin. "I like you, man. You're funny, but everyone knows Sprinkles is the only Dalmatian in town."

Sam's first day in Turtle Beach was beginning to feel like the movie *Groundhog Day.* And not in a good way. He glanced across the street toward the police headquarters, preparing himself to try and talk his way out of another arrest for canine-related crimes.

Griff shoved his hands in the pockets of his TBFD-issued cargo pants and leaned a little closer—close enough for Sam to catch a whiff of coffee on his breath. "Stealing the police department's unofficial mascot is a baller move, but just so you know, the police chief's daughter is off-limits. You should return Sprinkles to wherever you found her. Chief Murray's orders: we can't mess with Violet—particularly not after what happened last year. Things went a bit too far."

Again, so much to unpack. But against all odds, Sam was suddenly less concerned about Cinder's mistaken identity than he was about Violet March and whatever misfortune she'd encountered last year, seemingly at the hands of a firefighter.

He thought about her tousled mermaid hair and the foamy ocean waves swirling at her feet and, for the first time, wondered if he'd mistaken the look in her luminous blue-green eyes for fury when in fact it had been something else—vulnerability.

Nope, she'd been livid. Just maybe not as unhinged as he'd previously thought.

Don't ask. Do. Not. It's none of your concern.

"What happened to her?" he said.

Damn it, he'd asked.

But before Griff could clue him in, the man who'd conducted Sam's Zoom interview last month came striding toward them. His welcoming smile faded as his gaze trailed from Sam's face all the way down Cinder's leash to the Dalmatian's tail, sweeping the pavement in a happy wag.

Sam knew what was coming, but frustration seethed from his every pore nonetheless.

"What are you doing with Violet March's dog?" Chief Murray crossed his big, beefy arms as he stared down at Cinder.

"This isn't Sprinkles," Sam said wearily. Was it possible to scrub the spots off a Dalmatian? Or maybe connect them like a giant dot-to-dot puzzle? Anything to make Cinder look less like Sprinkles and put an end to the Dalmatian speculation.

"This is Cinder." The dog's ears perked up at the mention of her name. "She's a fire safety dog. She's trained to accompany me on inspections and to demonstrate fire safety techniques during presentations."

A long pause followed. The only sounds Sam heard were Cinder's soft pants and the ocean roaring in the distance. He missed the rattle of the L train, the moaning stops and starts of city buses, and the grind of morning traffic. The constant hum of Chicago's street noises was in his blood, and he felt adrift without it—yet another thing about his move he hadn't anticipated. After all, people paid good money to hear waves crashing against the shore on apps for their phones or sound systems. Not Sam, per se, but people.

Normal people…people who didn't wake up in the middle of the night in a cold sweat, followed by three torturous hours of staring at the ceiling, immune to the calming effects of the sea.

"Huh," both Griff and Chief Murray said after a beat, as if Sam's description of Cinder's duties had been spoken in some kind of foreign language.

Sam's head pounded. He had a sudden craving for deep dish Chicago-style pizza, the world's best migraine cure.

"So this dog is like your partner?" Chief Murray bent to take a closer look at Cinder.

"Yes." They'd covered this already in Sam's interview. He was sure of it. He wouldn't have packed up and moved to North

Carolina without telling his new chief about his dog. Cinder was half the reason Sam had been able to make the change from fighting fires to seeking a job as a fire marshal.

The job offer from TBFD had been a godsend. After Chief Murray's email had arrived, Sam had been too busy counting his lucky stars to wonder why such a small department needed to add a full-time fire marshal to its roster. As crazy as things seemed, they were beginning to make sense.

"Just so we're clear, I'm not really interested in playing softball," Sam said.

He was here to do a job, not to become involved with the community. Besides, it had been a long time since Sam had held a bat in his hands. Nearly a year.

Chief Murray straightened, regarding Sam through narrowed eyes.

"Dude." Griff shook his head. "Participation in the summer softball tournament against the police force is mandatory."

Sam sighed. This place was beyond nuts. He should have turned tail and run back when he'd almost been arrested. "Mandatory? Doesn't that contradict the very nature of extracurricular activities?"

"Griff's right," the chief said. "Not only is it mandatory, but it's also the whole reason you were hired. Guns and Hoses starts Saturday."

Guns and Hoses. Sam's mouth quirked into a half grin, despite himself. The name of the tournament was cute, like everything else in this whimsical beach town.

Except maybe the oddly competitive nature of said softball

tournament. And whatever unfortunate thing had happened to Violet March.

He knew he shouldn't worry about it. In fact, all signs thus far had pointed to the obvious conclusion that if he was going to survive here, he needed to stay as far away from Violet and Sprinkles as possible. Had the ongoing Dalmatian situation taught him nothing?

Chief Murray slapped him hard on the back—hard enough to rattle all thoughts of the police chief's daughter and her trouble-some spotted sidekick right out of his head. "Welcome to Turtle Beach, slugger."

In retrospect, Violet realized she'd been a tad hasty at the dog beach this morning. The firefighter had tried to explain what was going on, and she hadn't let him. As her brothers Josh and Joe had oh-so-helpfully pointed out after the chaos died down and her yoga friends aimed their walkers back toward the Turtle Beach Senior Living Center, she'd treated *a* fireman like he was *the* fireman. The result had been nothing short of a complete and utter Dalmatian humiliation.

The poor man had apparently been a resident of Turtle Beach for a grand total of twelve hours—information which Josh had managed to discern with a single call to the town's one and only Realtor, who'd conveniently been his prom date back in his days at Turtle Beach High. As much as Violet hated to give the new-in-town fireman the benefit of the doubt, she realized he'd probably never heard of Guns and Hoses.

Yet.

That would change, obviously. In the meantime, she might owe him a *teensy* apology for trying to get him arrested. Softball season hadn't even officially started yet. If she was going to get through the annual tournament with a modicum of dignity intact, she needed to try to defuse the situation.

Besides, his dog was awfully cute. Despite the uniform, he clearly possessed one of her favorite qualities in a man—an appreciation for Dalmatians. How terrible could he possibly be?

Careful, there. Remember what happened the last time you let your guard down around a pretty face in a fire helmet.

As if she could forget.

But she didn't want to date the man. Been there, done that, got the T-shirt. Never again. Violet was over romantic relationships. From here on out, all she cared about was Sprinkles and her shiny new cupcake truck.

And her family, obviously. And her friends. And the police department completely annihilating the fire department this Saturday in the opening game.

Okay, fine, she cared about a lot of things, but dating occupied the last spot on the list. Absolute rock bottom. The fact that she was currently standing in front of the fire station with a pink bakery box in her hands and Sprinkles at her feet was a simple matter of self-respect. She hated the weird combination of guilt and sadness she always saw in Chief Murray's eyes when he looked at her, and she knew good and well that every cupcake the TBFD bought and consumed was a pity purchase. Not that her cupcakes weren't good—they were *amazing*, thank you very much. She just wanted to move on and return to despising firemen in a normal, healthy, *sports-related* way.

Violet squared her shoulders and glanced down at Sprinkles. "We can do this. Five quick minutes inside the belly of the beast, and then we're out of here."

But when she took a step toward the bright red door of the firehouse, the Dalmatian didn't budge. Violet gave the leash a gentle tug, and still…nothing.

"Sprinkles, please. Just listen for once. There's a vanilla bacon maple cupcake with your name on it if you'll just follow me into the firehouse and stick by my side for moral support," Violet whispered.

The promise/bribe worked, thank goodness. Sprinkles sprang forward and bobbed happily at the end of her leash as Violet pushed through the red door. She didn't normally feed her dog cupcakes, for the record. Desperate times and all that.

"Violet." Griff Martin blinked hard from his seat in the dispatch area when he caught sight of her. "Um…what are you doing here?"

He looked past her, no doubt expecting her to be accompanied by Joe, Josh, or other various members of the TBPD.

She raised her chin. She was a grown woman, and she could take care of herself and get her life back on track all on her own. "I'm here to see the new fireman. We had a little misunderstanding earlier this morning."

"Look." Griff held up his hands. "I told him to give the dog back and he insisted it wasn't yours."

"Oh, I know." Violet tipped her head toward Sprinkles. "Sprinkles is fine, see?"

Griff's gaze narrowed. "They really do look an awful lot alike, don't they?"

Thank you! She shot him a victorious grin. "Yes, they do."

Sprinkles was cuter, though. Obviously.

"Can you just tell him I'm here?" She glanced down at the pink bakery box in her hands and then back up at Griff's bewildered face. "I have a little peace offering for him. It was the least I could do after his near-arrest. I'll just give it to him, and then we'll be on our way."

"Hoo boy. Near-arrest?" Griff winced. "I'm not even going to ask. Sam's getting set up in his new office. Follow me."

He rose from his creaky office chair and led Violet toward the common area of the firehouse, where her appearance in enemy territory brought everything to an immediate standstill. No one moved. Or breathed. Or uttered a word. A firefighter who Violet recognized as the Hoses' first baseman spilled coffee down the front of his shirt from a ceramic mug that read *WTF Where's the Fire* as he gaped at her. A pair of firemen on opposite sides of a Ping-Pong table froze comically in place while their tiny white ball bounced across the room.

Sprinkles's toenails click-clacked against the tile floor as she scrambled after it, nearly jerking Violet's arm out of the socket in the process. The bakery box came perilously close to slipping from her grasp. She managed to keep hold of it long enough for Sprinkles to trot back to her side with the Ping-Pong ball in her mouth.

"Here you go," Griff said, stopping at a closed door situated behind two neat rows of leather recliners facing an enormous flat-screen television. "This is the new guy."

"Thanks." She pasted on a smile. "I'll take it from here."

"My pleasure." Griff gave Sprinkles a scratch behind her ears and headed back toward the dispatch desk.

Violet pretended not to notice the warning glares he shot at the other firemen as he passed through the common area, but a ribbon of relief wound its way through her as they stopped openly staring at her.

Okay. She took a deep breath and knocked. *Here goes nothing.*

"Come in," someone growled from the other side of the door. She would've recognized that cranky tone anywhere.

Violet wondered why he had an office. From what she knew about firemen—which was more than she cared to admit—they didn't sit at desks all day. In fact, the last time she'd darkened the door of the firehouse, Chief Murray had been the only member of the department who'd had an actual office. His was located just off the galley-style kitchen, and a quick glance confirmed it was still there.

Whatever. She just needed to make nice and hand over the cupcakes so she could go back to the dog beach with her head held high.

She opened the door and stepped inside, where the aforementioned grumpy fireman sat bent over the most meticulously organized desk Violet had ever set eyes on. A desk plate with the words *Sam Nash, Fire Marshal* on it was placed near the edge of the smooth wooden surface. Oh right, he was a fire marshal, not a regular fireman. That explained the office. Four fountain pens were lined up neatly beside his name plate, spaced apart at perfectly equal distances. The file in front of Sam contained a stack of paper so pristine that it looked like he'd just taken it off the printer. Not a crease in sight.

Sprinkles's identical twin rested on a fire engine–red dog bed in the corner of the room, regarding Violet with soft brown eyes.

"Hi," Violet said.

Sam finally looked up.

"Oh. Hi." He pushed back his chair and stood. Why did it suddenly feel like there wasn't nearly enough air in his tiny office? "It's you."

Sprinkles scurried toward him and spat the Ping-Pong ball out of her mouth, where it bounced at Sam's feet. Miraculously, the other Dalmatian completely ignored it.

Sam's gaze shifted toward Sprinkles. "And you too."

Sprinkles wagged her tail and nudged Sam's hand until he patted her. Violet's heart gave a rebellious little tug. Did he have to look so good petting her dog? There was a gentleness in the way his fingertips ran over her smooth, black-and-white coat—a tender reverence that put a wholly inappropriate lump in Violet's throat.

"Don't worry. She's had a bath since you last saw her," Violet said, trying her best to focus on something less dangerous, like Sam's insanely organized office supplies.

"Yeah, I can smell that." Sam wiggled his nose. "Am I imagining things, or does she smell like cake now?"

"Oh, that's not her. I brought you cupcakes." She thrust the pink box toward him.

His gaze remained impassive. "You did?"

"As a peace offering." Her face went hot. "It's what I do—I'm a baker."

She added that last bit because it seemed crucial to point out that she hadn't gone to any extraordinary lengths to cook something for him. She was a career woman, not Betty Draper.

Granted, she was a career woman who spent most of her time in a frilly pink polka dot apron and still lived in the rambling March family beach house with her father and two older brothers. Plus she'd owned her cupcake truck for less than a week, but those things didn't make her any less of a professional.

"I see." Sam glanced down at her whimsical logo: a Dalmatian behind the wheel of a food truck topped with a giant spinning cupcake. "Sweetness on Wheels, that's you?"

"Sure is. Like I said, I just wanted to come by and apologize. Things are kind of nuts here when it comes to softball, and for a minute, I thought you were trying to steal Sprinkles as some sort of prank. But I realize now that you're new in town. Cinder clearly belongs to you, and you obviously don't know a thing about our feud."

Sam's gaze met hers, and then that stern mouth of his curved into a lopsided smile that made her go all gooey inside, like one of her molten hot chocolate cupcakes. Ugh, what was wrong with her?

She plunked the bakery box down on his desk with shaky hands, and when she looked back up at him, her gaze snagged on something over his left shoulder—something that snapped her immediately back to reality.

Sam raked a hand through his perfect hair. "Actually, I—"

Violet cut him off before he could continue. "What is that?"

Her tone went razor sharp, prompting Sam's smile to vanish as quickly as it had appeared.

His gaze narrowed. "What's what?"

Violet wasn't about to spell things out for him. She didn't have to. The damning evidence was hanging right there on the back wall of his office in the form of a framed newspaper article with a huge headline that read *Local College Hall of Famer Sam Nash Turns Down MLB Contract to Join Chicago Fire Department.*

Sam was practically a Major League Baseball player? This could only mean one thing. He was a ringer!

The fire department had brought him to Turtle Beach and installed him in a fancy office for the sole purpose of snagging the Guns and Hoses championship trophy this season. What's more, he didn't even have the common decency to try and hide it.

How low could a person get? How dare he come marching into town with his athletic build, his Hall of Fame muscles, and his despicably handsome face and think he could just hand the TBFD a victory. It was basically stealing. He deserved to rot in her father's single-cell jail across the street. Maybe she should call 911 again.

"Violet?" Sam's brow furrowed, as if he hadn't a clue what she was suddenly so upset about.

Sprinkles and Cinder touched noses, tails wagging, and the adorable sight of the dogs together nearly broke Violet's heart. Somehow the fact that Sam had a Dalmatian made his betrayal so much worse. He didn't deserve such a spotted sweetheart of a dog. Violet couldn't *believe* she'd wasted a single second feeling bad about falsely accusing him of dognapping. She'd swallowed her pride and baked him cupcakes, and the man was nothing but a Dalmatian abomination.

Sam held up his hands. "I'm not sure what's going on here, but—"

Finally, he followed her gaze and turned to glance over his shoulder. He muttered an expletive and ground his teeth so hard that an ultra-manly knot flexed to life in his jawline. Violet averted her gaze before she accidentally went all swoony again.

"Look, I can explain," he said.

Why did that seem to be the one thing men always said when they'd done something atrocious?

"Don't bother. I've heard that line before." Most recently, from another fireman who'd worked at this exact station—a fireman who hadn't been able to explain a thing, except that he'd used her.

Everything always came down to softball in Turtle Beach. When was she going to learn to steer completely clear of anyone with a badge?

She snatched the pink bakery box off of Sam's desk. "Come on, Sprinkles. We're leaving."

"Seriously, you're taking my cupcakes back?" Sam planted his hands on his hips and actually had the nerve to look incredulous.

"I certainly am," Violet said.

No more playing nice. She was finished with giving him the benefit of the doubt. Her initial instincts about Sam had been right all along. She should never have let herself be swayed by his charming doggy dad routine or his devoted Dalmatian.

From now on, when it came to firemen, Violet March had finally learned to see things in black-and-white.

If you love bright, sparkling love stories and heartfelt romance, read on for a look at this uplifting, feel-good fiction from Tracy Goodwin:

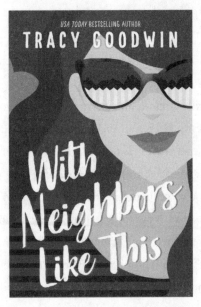

Chapter 1

AMELIA MARSH HALTS MIDSTEP, stricken by the laughter and squeals of a half-dozen children racing towards her.

"Incoming!" Grabbing her daughter and son, she wraps them in her arms, turning just in time to avoid the melee. One for the win column! Sure, those children appear to be sweet and innocent clad in their frilly dresses and formal ties, but she knows better. Amelia is a mom after all, and this is war—playground style. She's got the superpower of keeping her children in check. Like the Hulk/Bruce Banner, those powers come and go. Some days, Amelia is a master, while other days…well, not so much.

The playground is surrounded by trees and lush green grass; however, its pretty setting is *this* parent's nightmare. Kids of all ages shout, wrestle, and run like they're all on one heck of a sugar high. While she's scoping a group of younger boys wrestling in the kiddie play mulch underneath the jungle gym, Amelia's eldest tugs at her arm.

"Mom, can we play?" Her son, Jacob, asks, looking up at his mom with his signature bright smile. At ten years old, he is a charmer. What's worse? He knows it. One flash of his megawatt smile and he receives free cookies at his favorite bakery, or snags extra stickers at their local supermarket.

A little girl rushes past them, dressed in a pink tutu with a bunny tail that hangs haphazardly in the back. The child's faux tail bounces with every step she takes, and her bunny ears remind Amelia of their mission: today, they are attending their community Easter egg hunt and taking pictures with the Easter Bunny.

This is their first major outing since the big move back to Amelia's hometown of Houston, since her divorce, since their lives drastically changed. The last thing she wants is her children running around in the sweltering Texas sun, then taking pictures with some costumed cottontail while they sweat profusely with tangled hair or—worse yet—covered in mulch. She glances again at that same group of boys, who now have pieces of mulch stuck to their clothes and in their hair. The chances of more than one shower needed: likely. Drain-clogging potential: high. Just what Amelia's trying to avoid.

Crouching in front of her son, she ensures that her long skirt is covering her legs, then reaches for the hands of Jacob and his sister, Chloe. They're twenty-two months apart, the best of friends on most days, and bicker like nobody's business the rest of the time. "Why don't we take pictures with the Easter Bunny first, then you can run around. Deal?"

Jacob wrinkles his brow, considering his mom's offer. He's not buying what she's selling, and Amelia's glad that she didn't go all out like some other parents. Contrasting the once-pristine girls and boys wearing their best attire and ruining their special outfits, her kids are wearing clothes of their own choosing—cargo shorts and a polo shirt for Jacob, while Chloe wears leggings and her favorite ruffled shirt with a pink flamingo on it. No fancy shoes, either. Just socks and sneakers.

Picture-taking Marsh style is practical by necessity, because their family is cursed when it comes to family photos. Without fail, the better dressed her children are, the worse the picture. There could be fifty photos taken, and not one would include both of the kids smiling or looking at the camera at the same time. But, when they wear comfortable clothes—their favorite clothes—voilà! It's like a Harry Potter moment with magical smiles and happy memories.

At this community event, she seems to be the only parent with this mindset, seeing the abundance of children once dressed to impress now getting dirty, sweaty, and screaming louder than the audience at a Metallica concert.

"I promise you can play after—"

"They have cookies! Can we have cookies, Mom?" Chloe, her eight-year-old spitfire tomboy, points to a little boy eating a large cookie, then sprints toward the clubhouse, followed close behind by Jacob. When all else fails, cookies will do the trick and, thanks to a little boy covered in grass stains, a trail of cookie crumbs is leading Amelia's children away from the lure of a crowded playground.

"Save some for me!" she calls to them, walking close behind until they reach the pool clubhouse, also known as their community's "aquatic center." It's a fancy name for a small in-ground pool and a building with bathrooms.

Their subdivision of Castle Rock is a newer one, situated in the northern suburbs of Houston in a town named Timberland, Texas. Here, in what is known as the *Lush and Livable Timberland,* where natural pine trees that were once in abundance are rare thanks to the building boom, residents pride themselves on their thick green lawns and blooming flower beds.

Under the shade of the clubhouse and its covered patio, Amelia spies tables accentuated with spring-themed tablecloths whipping in the warm breeze, upon which plates of cookies with colored icing and cups of lemonade are arranged around stuffed-animal bunnies and Easter decorations.

She's traded sweat and dirt for icing and lemonade. Given the fact that her kids used to hate any and all imaginary figures in costumes, from Santa to the Easter Bunny to their school mascot, Amelia will take whatever photos she can get. Cargo shorts? Sure. Flamingo shirt? Done. Icing turning their tongues blue like Smurfs? She'll deal.

Such is the single mom in her. Always trying to please, to make the kids happy, and to find her own sense of satisfaction. Without her ex-husband, Daniel. It was his choice to start a new life with his mistress. Did it hurt? Yes. Because he walked out on their children and because he caused them pain. Though Daniel may have wanted out, he also wanted everything that he valued— their house, their money, their investments. What he didn't value are Amelia's biggest blessings: Jacob and Chloe.

Granted, she's no pushover. With the help of a brilliant attorney, Amelia fought for what her children and she deserved. When the divorce was finalized, it was time to remove her children from the situation and give them a chance to heal—near some of Amelia's best friends.

Today, she's on her own, with her children—who are scarfing down cookies like they haven't eaten in days. "Slow down, sweeties. Let's take a break from the cookies."

Mom rule number one: never let your kids overeat and throw up. As a matter of fact, avoid vomit at all costs. Gross, but true.

"Hello there." A saccharine-sweet voice and a terse tap on Amelia's shoulder grabs her attention. "I'm Carla, from the community's management company. I don't believe we've met."

"Nope, not yet." Amelia would remember Carla, who is a sight to behold with teased red hair, full makeup, and a pristine pantsuit. How is this woman not melting in today's heat? In her light maxi dress and messy bun, Amelia is already perspiring, but Carla's heavy makeup remains flawless. Is she human or is heat endurance *her* superpower?

"Hi, Carla. I'm Amelia Marsh. These are my children, Jacob and Chloe." Her daughter waves while her son gulps more lemonade before flashing his signature grin.

Carla narrows her eyes, staring at Amelia's children, seemingly immune to Jacob's charms. In turn, Jacob smiles wider, arching his brow. With still no response from Carla, Jacob gives up and studies his feet, while Amelia gives him a reassuring pat on his back.

"Where's the Bunny?" Chloe asks.

"He's coming. How about you line up over there?" Carla points at the seating area where four carefully arranged lawn chairs remain empty, and a line has already formed, full of flushed and disheveled children. Parents are doing their best to right the damage done by playtime. *Good luck with that.*

Amelia's children look to her for approval, and she nods. Jacob smiles, his teeth blue from the icing. "That's my boy!" Amelia encourages him with a thumbs-up.

Mom rule number…who knows, since there are so many mom rules that she's lost count, but this is one of the most important rules of all: you can only control so much. Amelia has traded the messy, sweaty, grass-stained debacle for blue teeth. The glass half full theory is that the blue might not show up in the picture.

"Keep drinking, buddy." She smiles as Jacob takes another sip of his lemonade, then she turns to Carla. "What's the difference between the HOA and the management company?"

"The Homeowners Association consists of Castle Rock residents, some of whom preside on its board of directors. The management company, for which I work, handles the logistics, enforcing the bylaws—in other words, the community rules, and—"

"Collecting the annual dues," Amelia adds with a smile. Now she understands. "I know my dues are paid for the year. I took care of that at closing."

Studying Carla, Amelia notes that the woman has a half smirk/half grin plastered on her face. Just like her makeup, it isn't moving.

"I'm sorry about the letter arriving so soon after you moved in. But rules are rules, you know."

Amelia's catches the woman's exaggerated grimace. "Letter? I'm lost. Why would I receive a letter when I paid my dues?"

"Oh, no. You haven't read it yet." Carla gasps, her hot pink nails matching her lipstick as she covers her mouth with her hands.

"Nope, I haven't received it yet. What's in this letter? It sounds ominous." Amelia's humor falls flat on the stoic-faced Carla.

"There are rules."

"Right. You've repeated that. Three times, I believe. Possibly four." Shoving her sunglasses on top of her head, Amelia refuses to break eye contact with Carla, whose expression remains serious. "Rules like what, exactly?"

Carla shifts, then whispers, "Your gnome."

"My what?" Is *gnome* some sort of code word for one of her children? Amelia's head snaps immediately to her kids. Jacob laughs while Chloe chats with him, probably reciting one of her famous knock-knock jokes. The kids are safe, so her attention returns to Carla. "Did you say my 'gnome'?"

"Your garden gnome. The one in your front yard," Carla counters.

Amelia laughs. She can't help it. Carla's mock horror that this new resident finds her comment amusing quickly fades into impatience, her eyes emanating frustration and disapproval, the lines around them deepening.

Clearing her throat allows Amelia time to keep her expression neutral, her tone calm, and her snark to a minimum. "Do you mean my tiny, hand-painted garden gnome hidden within the bushes, flowers, and mulch that comprise a small portion of my front yard? You can barely see it."

Carla scoffs. "I see everything. It's my job to inspect the front yards. I drive by intermittently, so I can ensure our community remains up to the standards set in the bylaws."

Of course she does. The fact that Carla *sees everything* is a bit alarming.

Sticking to the topic at hand, Amelia explains, "My children made me that gnome for Mother's Day last year." Before the divorce. Before their move. It was displayed prominently in the front yard of their old home. That gnome represents her children's only request when moving to Houston: that she'd place it in their new front yard. It helps them feel at home.

"You must remove it, I'm afraid. Rules are rules, and some people's trash is others' treasure, so to speak." Carla grins, seemingly oblivious to the fact that she just insulted Amelia and her beloved gnome.

"Trash?" *Carla. Did. Not. Just. Say. That.*

Carla nods. "Not that I find your troll trashy, of course. Playing devil's advocate, the truth is that you may like it, but your neighbors may find it tacky. Besides, the ban is in the bylaws."

So, this woman has called her kids' gnome *trash*, *tacky*, and a *troll*. For any mom, especially Amelia, those are fighting words. "Who bans garden gnomes that you can barely see in their bylaws?"

"Your HOA. If you don't like it, I invite you to attend your next quarterly Homeowners' Association meeting. You just missed the last one, but I'll send out an email blast to all residents, signs will be posted at the entrances to the neighborhood, and an announcement will go up on the community website approximately ten days in advance of the next meeting." Applause drowns out Carla, and Amelia turns to see the Easter Bunny waving at the kids.

"Time for pictures! Have a good day." And just like that, Carla dismisses Amelia, sauntering away to schmooze with other residents.

Amelia blinks. *What the heck?* Gnomes are off limits, but bunnies are okay? She scans her surroundings which, like most front yards in her subdivision, are decorated with colored ribbons, bunny cut-outs, and enlarged egg décor. Yeah, bunnies on full display are fine, yet one tiny, beautiful gnome—the gnome that her kids made for her—must go? The same gnome that makes their new house a *home*.

The Easter Bunny high fives Jacob and Chloe, and Amelia makes a beeline to them, just as her daughter begins hiding behind her brother. Apparently, Chloe hasn't gotten over her fear of fake bunnies after all. This one is cute, sporting a purple suit jacket, a yellow vest, and a rainbow-colored bow tie. Though this event is held weeks before Easter, beads of perspiration trickle down Amelia's spine, causing her to pity the poor soul who drew the short straw and must wear a furry costume in this heat and sticky humidity. Hopefully, his or her costume has a fan.

"Hi, Bunny!" She smiles and high fives the faux fur paw of whoever is in the costume.

Nodding and swaying to the beat of Taylor Swift's "Shake It Off", which is blasting through the pool speakers, this rabbit is in character. Amelia needs to shake Carla off, since her blood pressure is still high from the woman's lack of tact and the accompanying ban notice. Over a gnome? Really? So, Amelia takes Taylor's advice, singing and dancing with her children in line. The Easter Bunny must be a Swiftie, too, because the person in the costume dances over to the chairs before taking a seat.

When it's their turn for picture time, Amelia hands her cell to a man standing next to Carla, who will take the picture for them. Carla...ugh. The sight of her after that catty "tacky" comment makes Amelia's heartbeat pound like an anvil.

Normally, Amelia would have let Carla's comments about the letter go. Who knows? She might have even removed her gnome.

But Carla insulted Jacob and Chloe's art, even after Amelia explained the importance of it.

One simple, passive-aggressive comment is all it takes for her to decide that she can't let it go. Instead, Amelia may drive the kids to Target, Walmart, or both after they spend time at the playground and buy out their entire garden gnome department. If she's lucky, maybe they'll be on sale, and she'll display an extended gnome family on her front lawn. If the HOA wants to send her a letter, she might as well earn it.

As they approach the Bunny for their picture, Chloe hides behind Amelia's skirt while Jacob charms the fluffy cottontail immediately with a knock-knock joke. No matter which way Amelia turns, her daughter won't come out from hiding. Amelia half expects Chloe to hide *under* her skirt any minute. Every time Amelia moves, so does Chloe, taking her mom's dress with her. "Sit on my lap, Chloe. Let's take the picture together."

With Jacob on one side, and Amelia and Chloe on the other, they pose with the Bunny.

When the man holding her cell prompts them to smile, Amelia instructs her kiddos to smile, adding, "Say 'garden gnome!'"

"Garden gnome!"

It's official. The Bunny must think I've completely lost my mind.

On the bright side, the kids smiled, laughed, and took a great picture. Add to that the fact that Amelia's got a plan.

The HOA better look out, because this mom protects her gnomes at all costs.

Chapter 2

THANKS TO A BROKEN fan in Kyle Sanders's costume, he's about to suffer heat stroke by rodent impersonation. It's not exactly the way he expected to go, but hey, if you're going to sweat to death, why not do so wearing a goofy Easter Bunny costume? Go big or go home, right? Sure, it'll be humiliating, especially when it hits the local news. And it would traumatize a lot of children.

Oh man! The kids...

In an effort to hide his demise from the neighborhood children, Kyle darts into the cleaning closet of the Castle Rock community's pool house, desperate to cool off. Struggling with the top of the costume, a muffled curse word escapes his lips as one of his pawed feet lands beside a bucket and a mop slams against his bunny forehead.

Why did I ever volunteer for this?

Taking a step to the side, his oversized furry foot lands in the empty bucket. Still, Kyle manages to use his floppy tail to leverage himself against a wall. "The things I do for this community. Come on!"

Managing to free his face from the bunny head, Kyle tosses the thing onto a small table taking up too much space. He then rips the Velcro at his back and frees both arms, sliding the costume down to his waist. Drenched with sweat, he grabs his sports drink and takes several desperate gulps from the large bottle.

Though his foot may remain stuck, at least he won't die of dehydration. Limping over to the small table with the decapitated rabbit head, Kyle narrows his eyes, staring at the bunny's face which remains frozen in place, that wide, toothy grin taunting him along with its glossy eyes and fake wire-rimmed glasses.

Blood-curdling, high-pitched screams cause him to jump, as his eyes dart to the closet door, which is now open. Standing in the doorway is the cute mom wearing the casual dress who has covered her daughter's eyes, gaping at Kyle as her son yells, "The Easter Bunny isn't real! He isn't real!"

"I'm sorry!" It's all Kyle can manage. Repeating it louder, over the screams, doesn't do much.

I've traumatized this woman's children! I've destroyed their innocence. It's all he can think as his neighbor—Kyle doesn't know her name because they've never met—leads her kids into the closet and slams the door shut in an attempt not to traumatize anyone else's children, he supposes.

"Jacob, Chloe, it's okay," she says in a soothing voice, caressing her kids' shoulders. "This is the Easter Bunny's helper. Think about it. EB can't be everywhere at once, right?"

She wipes her little girl's tears as her son surveys Kyle with a skeptical expression. "You're the Bunny's helper?"

Sure, why not? Right now, Kyle would agree to anything that will calm the kids. "Yes, I am." He glances to their mom, who nods at him, as if encouraging Kyle to elaborate. "Your mom is right. The Bunny is busy painting eggs, making baskets, buying candy—"

"He buys candy? From where?" This little boy asks a lot of questions.

Kyle shrugs. "A candy store."

"What does he pay you?" the kid asks him.

"Not enough." It's the first thing that comes to mind. In truth, Kyle doesn't make a dime for this. He's a volunteer, donating his time so the community can save money. He's also the community's Santa. Multitasking is his thing. Along with running his own business, he is the acting HOA board president, which means residents yell at him about the cost of their annual dues (in spite of the fact that the cost of dues hasn't risen once in Kyle's four years as president), letters they receive from the management company prohibiting decorations in their front yards and criticizing the height of their lawns, and all other concerns. Meanwhile, he sweats in a rodent costume on an eighty-plus-degree day for kids who don't belong to him. It's a thankless task.

"What's your name?" the boy asks Kyle, jerking him from his concerns regarding the heavy costume still covering the lower half of his body.

"My name?" That's an easy one. "Kyle Sanders. What's yours?"

"I'm Jacob Marsh, and this is my mom, Amelia Marsh. My sister, Chloe Marsh, is there," he points at the little girl, whose red cheeks are tear-streaked.

"Got it." Chloe, Jacob, and Amelia. *Amelia Marsh.* A brunette with a killer smile, Amelia is luminescent, wearing minimal makeup and exuding a natural glow. Her dress is sleeveless and floor length, but when the breeze blows in the right direction, sandals that lace around her ankles attract Kyle's attention. She's left him breathless, or maybe it's the lack of oxygen in the cramped closet.

"Mom, I've still gotta pee." Jacob doesn't hold anything back.

Amelia steps forward. "We were looking for the restrooms. I'm sorry—um…"

"Kyle," he reminds her. "The men's room is one door down; the ladies' room is two doors down that way." Pointing to his left, Kyle stands stock still. With his annoying costume foot still stuck in the bucket, he isn't going anywhere.

"Right. Let's go, you two." Amelia opens the door a crack and ushers her kids out, before adding, "I'll be right back."

As she closes the door behind her, Kyle is left to stand in silence for what feels like forever. Just when he begins to think she's abandoned him, Amelia returns wearing a sweet grin. "Sorry, I had to make sure the bathrooms were single stalls, and that my children were safe behind locked doors. You look like you could use some help."

"Nope. Just chilling." Kyle places his hands casually on his hips. "This is how the Bunny's helper rolls."

Shaking her head, she laughs. "You're not rolling. You're trapped, from the looks of it. Here I thought rabbit's feet were good luck."

Kyle shifts his weight to his free foot. "I know! That's what I've been told."

"They lied to us. Unless…" Amelia smirks, tilting her head to the side. "The truth is that messing with a rabbit's foot *is* bad luck. I don't need any more of that. Perhaps I should pass?"

"No, please!" Kyle's plea is urgent. "It's not bad luck if the rabbit's foot is stuck in a snare and still attached to the rabbit. Besides, I didn't break a mirror."

"Duly noted." Amelia bends down, shoving a stray lock of hair from her face as she studies the bucket. "I was kidding, you know. I wouldn't leave you here, stuck like this."

"Good to know." Kyle exhales, watching her lips upturn into a wry grin. "You've got a sense of humor."

"So I've been told." Amelia reaches for the bucket and struggles to free Kyle's foot. "I've almost got it." She gives it another hard yank and Kyle's foot is free, though Amelia lands with a hard thump beside him.

Kyle offers his hand and helps her to her feet. Face-to-face, their eyes lock and he notices the gold flecks in her deep brown eyes. They're mesmerizing. He inhales, overcome by her intoxicating scent—a floral perfume with hints of musk.

"Thanks for coming to my rescue. Freeing me from a pail and convincing two traumatized children that I'm the Easter Bunny's helper takes skill."

She averts her gaze from Kyle's. "I did what anyone would have. Except a lot less gracefully."

"You're speaking to the guy who got his foot stuck in a mop bucket." Kyle raises his brow.

"I'm not one to judge." Her eyes shine with amusement and something more. *Is she flirting with me?* Before Kyle can fully ponder that thought, Amelia turns towards the closed door.

"In spite of your humility, I do owe you a debt of thanks." He offers her his hand, and she shakes it. Her skin is soft.

"Anything for the Easter Bunny's helper."

Acknowledgments

I owe a gigantic hug and a thank-you to everyone who made this book possible—my wonderful agent Elizabeth Winick Rubinstein and everyone at McIntosh & Otis, Deb Werksman, and the entire team at Sourcebooks Casablanca.

A Line in the Sand was an utter joy to write. Would you believe that Ursula was originally supposed to be a poodle? I love poodles. My first dog was an apricot toy poodle who I named Sir Lancelot of Wilson. Full disclosure: I was twelve years old at the time and had just seen the movie *Excalibur*. Lance was a wonderful dog who always sported a pink rhinestone collar and matching leash. Thus my lifelong affection for dogs was born.

Poodle love aside, right before I started writing this book, I got a new Cavalier King Charles spaniel puppy named Charm. Charm is my third Cavalier, and she's a little handful, y'all. I love her to pieces. Of course, I immediately decided Ursula needed to be a Cavalier. As she's written, Ursula is exactly like Charm, if only Charm owned a lobster costume. Maybe I need to remedy that. *wink*

Thank you so much for reading and spending a little time with "Ursula" and me in the whimsical world of Turtle Beach.

xoxo Teri

About the Author

Teri Wilson is a *USA Today* bestselling author of heartwarming, whimsical romantic comedy and contemporary romance. Three of Teri's books have been adapted into Hallmark Channel Original Movies by Crown Media, including *Unleashing Mr. Darcy* (plus its sequel *Marrying Mr. Darcy*), *The Art of Us*, and *Northern Lights of Christmas*, based on her book *Sleigh Bell Sweethearts*. She is also a recipient of the prestigious RITA Award for excellence in romantic fiction for her novel *The Bachelor's Baby Surprise* and a new inductee to the San Antonio Women's Hall of Fame.

Teri has a major weakness for cute animals, pretty dresses, and Audrey Hepburn films, and she loves following the British royal family. Feel free to visit her at teriwilson.net and connect with her on social media! You can also add and share her books on BookBub and Goodreads.